THE HERO + VEGAS = NO REGRETS

LOUISE BAY

Published by Louise Bay 2025

ISBN – 978-1-80456-041-9

BOOKS BY LOUISE BAY

All Louise Bay Books are available for free in Kindle Unlimited or on Amazon to buy.

Each book is a stand alone

The Colorado Club Billionaires

Love Fast

Love Deep

Love More

The New York City Billionaires

The Boss + The Maid = Chemistry

The Play + The Pact = I Do

The Hero + Vegas = No Regrets

The Doctors Series

Dr. Off Limits

Dr. Perfect

Dr. CEO

Dr. Fake Fiancé

Dr. Single Dad

The Mister Series

Mr. Mayfair

Mr. Knightsbridge

Mr. Smithfield

Mr. Park Lane

Mr. Bloomsbury

Mr. Notting Hill

The Player Series

International Player

Private Player

The Gentleman Series

The Ruthless Gentleman

The Wrong Gentleman

The Royals Series

King of Wall Street

Park Avenue Prince

Duke of Manhattan

The British Knight

The Earl of London

The Nights Series

Indigo Nights

Promised Nights

Parisian Nights

Standalones

An American in London

14 Days of Christmas

Hollywood Scandal

Love Unexpected

Hopeful

The Empire State Series

Sign up to the Louise Bay mailing list at www.louisebay.com

ONE

Worth

A New York brunch can be just brunch—a get-together with friends to carb off a hangover or go through the Sunday papers. But today isn't just brunch. I can tell by the way Leo—one of my five best friends—is nervously fingering his collar. And by the way his new fiancée, Jules, is shifting her weight from hip to hip.

In fairness, the stakes are high today. We—Leo's friends-slash-brothers in all but blood—will be meeting Jules' best friend for the first time. It's going to be fine. I'm sure of it. But the happy couple wants it to be more than fine.

"What do you think, Worth?" Jules asks. "Is it too obvious to put Fisher next to Sophia?"

I glance between Jules and Efa, the only two women in the room. "Obvious how?" I ask, picking my words carefully. I'm not sure exactly what *should* be obvious.

"That we're setting them up," Efa says, thwacking me on the arm as she leans forward on the table.

"I think it's fine with Worth on the other side of her," Jules says, answering her own question. "Like, she's not going to think we're setting her up with Worth *and* Fisher."

I push my hands through my hair, trying to think what to make of that statement, when there's a rush of noise by the door.

I glance around to see... the top of a woman's head. She has long blonde hair that reaches the floor as she bends over to pull off a heel and toss it on the ground.

"I have to take these shoes off. They're not made for walking. I was trying to be ladylike and refined, but you can take the girl out of Cincinnati—"

She straightens and we lock eyes. She's beautiful. Her blonde hair is lighter at the front, like she's spent the entire summer outside. And I can't tear my gaze from her mouth—dusky-pink lips that form an almost-perfect circle as she stares back at me. I trace a line around the edge of her lips in my mind. A smattering of freckles kiss the bridge of her nose, and her hair is long and loose. I have to fight a full-body shudder at the thought of how it would feel against my skin.

Jesus, I want to stalk right over to her, back her up against the wall, and kiss her into Wednesday of next week. I'm not sure I've ever felt such a visceral, primal urge to be close to a woman in my life.

In fact, visceral, primal urges aren't the norm for me at all. That's exactly what makes me good in a crisis. I'm a cool head. A logical thinker. I don't make rash decisions.

I don't get the sudden urge to *possess* a woman. Not until today.

I'm vaguely aware of chatter behind me as the woman and I stare at each other like we're sharing the exact same thoughts. All of a sudden, Efa pulls the beauty into a hug, effectively breaking our eye contact and bringing me back to the moment.

"Worth!" Jules practically bellows. "Meet my best friend in the entire world, Sophia." She turns to Sophia. "I'm sitting you next to Worth, because honestly, he's the best man in the world after Leo—"

"Hey," Efa calls from across the room. "What about Bennett?"

"You didn't let me finish my sentence. Whoever said the British are polite never met you!"

Efa and Jules dissolve into laughter, and Sophia's eyes grow wide. She glances over at me, confused. I want to go to her, assure her that Efa and Jules are joking and there's nothing to be concerned about, but before I put one foot in front of the other, she starts toward me.

"Hi," she says, her smile blinding like I'm looking at the sun or something. She seems to be surrounded by lightness, like she's glowing. I hear Bryan Ferry in the background, singing about being a slave to love—or am I imagining it? I need to snap the fuck out of whatever this is or I'm going to start seeing bluebirds lifting her napkin into her lap and squirrels pulling out her chair.

"Hey," I say. Normally I'd hug anyone introduced to me by Efa or Jules, but I can't risk touching Sophia. Instead, I hold out my hand, like I'm in a fucking boardroom.

I'm an idiot.

A fucking idiot.

Surprisingly, her smile widens, like offering to shake her hand is even better than scoring the winning touchdown at the Super Bowl. We stare at each other for a beat, oblivious to what's going on around us. I'm vaguely aware of more people at the door and the clinking of glasses, but I have no desire to move out of the bubble I find myself in —*we've* found ourselves in.

Sophia slides her hand into mine and a small gasp escapes her lips. A growl reverberates in my chest. Her hand feels so soft, so tiny, so... mine, it's difficult to describe.

Jules breaks the moment by shouting, "Turn this music off, Leo. Put on something fun." Then she takes Sophia's free hand and pulls her away from me. Sophia glances back over her shoulder, and I can't do anything but stare at her: the way her hair falls down her back, wavy and loose, like water running over stones; the way her jeans hug her ass in exactly the way I want to; the way I can feel her hand in mine, even now when she's across the room.

"Bryan Ferry is fucking cool," Leo replies.

He's right. Bryan Ferry is fucking cool. Although I never thought so until just now.

Everyone arrives except Byron, who's rarely in New York. He's messaged the group to say he's in Acapulco. I'm probably the only one who knows that actually means he's in Colorado. Long story.

Jules guides us to our seats. We all have place cards. Now, I like the fact that our group of six is expanding to include the women who have fallen for my best friends. Things are bound to shift and change, and I'm okay with that too. I also really like Efa and Jules. But place cards? Next we'll be wearing tuxedos for brunch.

I scan the place settings and find my name next to Sophia's. Okay, so maybe place cards aren't such a bad thing. Fisher sits down on her other side—which is when Jules and Efa's excited chatter about setting up Sophia with Fisher comes back to me.

Sophia is meant for Fisher. Not me.

A dull kernel of disappointment lodges in my gut, and I try to shake it off as everyone takes their seats around the table. How can I be disappointed? Fisher is a great guy. I love him like a brother. He's the life and soul of the party, creative but with a business brain. In personality, he's almost my exact opposite. Jules is Sophia's best friend. If Jules thinks Fisher is a good fit for her, she must be right.

This is fine. This is how it's meant to be. Fisher and Sophia. *Perfect.*

I pull in a breath and sit. I try to tune Sophia out as she sits next to me. I leave her to talk to Fisher and half listen to the chatter around the table. Mostly, I look out across the Manhattan skyline, thinking about the meetings I have coming up this week. There will be a lot of them, because I just found out the property developer who I invested in to convert an old hotel on Ninth Street into an apartment block has disappeared. With a chunk of my money.

Investing in people is my job, and that always comes with a degree of risk. But I'm surprised by this guy. Ninth Street has a lot of potential. In the end, I won't be too much out of pocket—I own the building and he sacrifices his shares in the project because he's disappeared and stolen money. Trouble is, I can't really put a price tag on the time it's going to take to figure out a new plan. I have enough on my plate.

"Worth?" a voice calls, and I'm brought back to the moment.

I turn to find Sophia looking right at me, blue eyes sparkling and impossibly bright, impossibly beguiling. She glances between my eyes and my mouth, then smiles wide when she realizes I don't know what she's asked. "Please could you pass the butter?"

"Butter," is all I can say, but I don't move. I can't help it. It's like her stare has me turned to stone.

She laughs, and it's such a sweet sound, I can't help but smile. "Butter," I say again, and force myself to look away long enough to locate the little dish. I slide it next to her plate, not daring to look at her again.

Fisher and Sophia.

But this time I can't zone out. This time, I'm aware of every movement and sound she makes. It's like I'm tuned into her frequency and can't do anything about it because my dial is broken. I'm completely aware of everything about the woman sitting next to me.

"Are you really going to wait two years for that rooftop to be ready to marry your fiancée?" Sophia asks Leo.

"Good point," I say. "I vote Leo will do anything Jules wants."

Sophia laughs again, and I want to pull out my phone and record the sound, ready to replay it over and over when I'm back at the brownstone tonight.

"Sounds like a sensible man," Bennett says.

Jules and Leo talk wedding plans. I'm so happy for them. They're both really good people who are meant for each other, better together than they are apart. I glance at Fisher and Sophia. Will I say the same about them? The idea grates like I've put the wrong key in a lock.

Sophia turns to me. "So, what's your story, Worth? You the strong and silent type?"

I frown slightly. Is this my chance to impress the woman next to me? Or should I say something so she hates me and focuses on Fisher —the man her best friend thinks she's best suited to? "I'm not sure what type I am," I say, choosing neutrality over either strategy. "I think I should know all the options before I commit."

"Oh," she says. "A commitment-phobe, then," she says.

She'd never think that if she knew the thoughts I'd been having about her since I laid eyes on her.

"So far we have Strong and Silent and Commitment-phobe," I reply. "What are my other choices?" A smile tugs at the corner of my mouth and her cheeks pink.

"I'm being rude," she says. "I'm sorry."

I shake my head. "Now *I'm* sorry if that's how I made you feel. The last thing I'd want to do is make you feel like you're being anything but... perfect." The word steals my breath from my lungs and my attention circles the word. *Perfect. Perfect. Perfect.* "I was trying to draw this conversation out for as long as possible. I thought if I didn't answer your question right away, you'd talk to me a little longer."

Her smile blooms and she lifts her chin slightly. "That's a nice thing to say."

I nod. "It's the truth."

"Worth always tells the truth," Leo says from across the table. The seemingly intimate conversation we were having disintegrates.

"Always?" Sophia narrows her eyes in challenge.

"No," I confess.

"You do," Leo protests, his tone a little sharp.

"No one can ever tell the truth *all* the time. It's impossible." I glance over at Leo, but his attention is now refocused on Fisher and Jules. They're laughing at something, but all I care about is that I have Sophia's attention.

"What's the last lie you told?" she asks me.

I pull in a breath and sit back in my chair. "Someone who works for me handed in a report and I told them they did a great job."

"And they hadn't?" Sophia asks.

"No. It was a just-okay job. But it was their first time doing this type of work and I didn't want them to be discouraged, so I lied."

"You exaggerated," she says.

Our voices have lowered, and Sophia has sat back in her chair too. We've slightly separated ourselves from the rest of the table, so only she and I can hear what each other is saying.

"What about you?" I ask. "What's the last lie you told?"

That you thought Fisher was attractive when Jules brought up his picture from his Instagram? I mentally suggest. Not that I know that Jules brought up his picture from his Instagram. But Jules has clearly been laying the foundations for a connection between Fisher and Sophia.

"I told my mom I was looking forward to going back to Cincinnati next weekend."

I want to know more. I want to know everything. Where did she go to college, when did she move to New York, what she does for a living, what kind of movies she likes?

Breathe, Worth. Chill the fuck out.

"You don't like going back?" I ask.

She pauses to think about this for a second. "I do, I just don't want to go next weekend."

"But you have to?"

She shakes her head. "No, but my mom asked me to come back, which she never does."

I nod. I understand the feeling of obligation that comes with family, but also, I wonder if she thinks her mom is going to give her bad news. Maybe I have a tendency to assume the worst, but I can only think that if her mom's asking her to go back home, there's a reason—and it's unlikely to be celebrating a fresh coat of paint on their picket fence. But if she hasn't figured that out, I don't want to bring it up. The last thing I want to do is create anxiety when there's no solution but time.

"What do you do?" I ask, trying to change the subject.

"I work for Saks," she says. "In their finance department. It's boring as hell, but I get a good discount."

I laugh and catch her watching me the way I watched her when she blushed—like she's fascinated by me.

Is it wishful thinking on my part?

I glance at Fisher. He doesn't seem to notice that Sophia and I are talking. Frankly, if he was into her, she wouldn't have had an opportunity to ask me to pass the butter. Fisher is super charming when he's interested in a woman, and far from subtle.

"What about you? How do you spend your days?" she asks.

"I invest in startups and small businesses."

"You're a hero investor?" she asks, her voice lifting. Her chin juts slightly, emphasizing her full lips.

She's insanely lovely.

"I'm not sure I've been called a hero before."

Her eyebrows pulse up, and I want to cup her neck and press my lips to her forehead. What the hell is the matter with me? "Angel," she says on a laugh. "I meant *angel* investor."

"Angel, hero, Worth—you can call me anything you like," I say, physically incapable of *not* flirting with her.

Her breath catches and she bites down on her lip. I can't take my eyes from her, even though I know I should look away.

She's meant for Fisher, not me.

I shouldn't be so transparent in my attraction to her. This is not who I am. I'm calm and considered and thoughtful. But something about her sweeps all of what I'm *supposed* to be from the table and leaves... I'm not sure what.

"Do you enjoy it?" she asks.

"I do," I say. I don't want to bore her with my business dealings. She works in finance and clearly isn't enthusiastic about it.

"Tell me why. Is it your calling? Do you do it to fill the time, or because you're good at it?"

I pause, wondering if she's just being polite or whether she really wants to know. Her eyes widen and she nods, answering my unasked question.

"For lots of reasons. I like meeting different people. I like sizing them up and trying to figure out whether they've got what it takes to succeed. I enjoying hearing about really innovative ideas and solutions for problems I never even knew existed. I like spotting issues in the businesses people are trying to build and helping them solve those issues. I like... helping people."

We stare at each other wordlessly for a beat, then two.

"I've never heard anyone talk about their work like that," Sophia says eventually.

"Like what?"

"Like you love it. Like it's your life's passion. Like it's part of who you are."

"Really?"

She nods. Her long lashes brush her cheeks when she blinks. "It's... I like it."

Something heats inside me. I can't get enough of this girl. I'm vaguely aware that this conversation, just between the two of us, is probably not what Jules had in mind today. But I'm acutely aware that I can't bring myself to do what I normally would: put Jules' feelings ahead of my own and join the discussion with the wider group. I'm greedy for Sophia. I want her all to myself.

"I'm glad," I say. "It's true."

Jules raises her voice slightly—something about a rooftop—and it catches Sophia's attention.

The spell between us is broken. We both refocus on the group.

For the first time ever, I resent the presence of my friends. But how can I? Without them I wouldn't have even met Sophia.

"I don't want it to be... like a business function," Jules says. "I think if we have a big wedding, you're going to feel obligated to invite people for business reasons."

"You need to have a destination wedding," I say, like I haven't been completely distracted by the woman next to me for most of this brunch. "That solves the problem."

"Not really," Sophia replies. "Destination weddings still have big invite lists—you just kind of hope not everyone comes." She's right. Of course she's right.

"An impromptu destination wedding," Fisher says. I try not to smart at the fact that Fisher has solved Sophia's wrinkle in my suggestion. Maybe they *are* the perfect fit for each other and this feeling in my gut for Sophia is food poisoning or something.

"Vegas," everyone around the table choruses.

Fisher's suggestion is a winner. Good for him.

There are huge discussions about whether we can fly to Vegas today or next weekend. After calendar-checking and Bennett managing to get ahold of Byron, it's agreed that the following weekend we should have brunch again, which *might-slash-will* turn into an impromptu wedding.

"Oh god, no," Sophia says. I turn and sweep my eyes down her body, wondering what the crisis is. "I'm in Cincinnati next weekend."

"You are?" Jules says. "But it's Thanksgiving in a couple of weeks. You don't normally go home that often."

I don't think I've ever been to Cincinnati. Maybe I should visit.

That's where she grew up. Got braces. Had her first kiss. I grin to myself. I'd love to see a picture of her when she was younger.

"I know," she says. "Mom asked us all to go back—and she never asks, so we're all going. Well, Oliver's already there, but me and Noah are making the trip."

"Will your dad be there?"

"I have no idea. But I won't be able to make brunch next weekend," she says. "I'm sorry."

My mind races ahead, wondering if I could arrange a plane to take her from Cincinnati to Vegas and back.

"The next weekend, then," Jules says, interrupting my internal planning. "That's a little more realistic if I want to get a dress anyway."

Cells are pulled out again and calendars rechecked. Everyone agrees that two weekends from now, Bennett is going to take us all to Vegas, and Leo and Jules are going to get married.

All I'm focused on is the fact that I'm going to have to wait two weeks until I see Sophia again.

TWO

Sophia

The farther I am from New York City, the more anxious I feel. It's not that I hate going back home—of course I don't. I love my family. I had a picture-perfect childhood in Cincinnati, Ohio. My two older brothers still adore me, my mom still bakes cookies on Saturdays and works at the library three days a week, and my dad was and is—and has always been—my best friend. He's always worked so hard to provide for us, and even now that his kids are grown, he still spends a lot of time on the road for work. When he was home, though, I had the world's best dad.

It's just... I love New York. I love that everything's always changing and there's a different story around every corner. In Cincinnati, no matter how much time passes between my visits, everything's exactly the same as it always was.

I don't know what has me feeling uneasy about being back this time, but as I round the corner onto Silver Streak Drive, my pulse quickens. I take a deep breath trying to head off what feels like a panic attack—which doesn't make any sense at all. Home is a place I love. I shake my head and put my car into park outside the house I grew up in. Maybe it's delayed altitude sickness or something. Once my bag is unpacked and Oliver has told me I'm looking old and I've threatened to knee him in the balls, things will be just fine. We'll quickly revert to our teenage selves and everything will be back to normal within the hour.

Mom's is the only car in the drive. Dad must be on the road. I wonder if he'll struggle to stay in one place for long when he retires.

As I slam my rental car door shut, Mom appears on the stoop, beaming. She's wearing a blue frilled apron I made her for Christmas when I was eleven. How that thing hasn't disintegrated, I don't know. Underneath, she wears jeans and the pink sweater with red hearts I bought her last Christmas.

I grab my bag from the back seat and head over to her.

"Hello, sweetheart." She scoops up my face and looks at me for a beat, her eyes gleaming or glassy, I can't tell, then pulls me in for a hug.

"Hi, Mom."

Her hug goes on a little longer than usual, and I drop my weekender to wrap my arms around her. I come back three or four times a year for birthdays and holidays, but I'm here now because Mom *asked* me to come back. She said she hadn't seen me for the longest time. I didn't think anything about it at the time, but now, standing here in a longer-than-usual hug, it hits me that I'm here for a specific reason I don't know about. The temporary reprieve from that anxious feeling in my gut ends abruptly.

"Good to have you here," she says.

"Is everything okay?" I ask.

"Of course, sweetie. Your brothers are inside and I'm just—" The oven timer interrupts her. She laughs. "I'm about to take some cookies out of the oven."

Noah appears in the doorway and takes my bag, just as I bend to pick it up. "I'll take it upstairs," he says, kissing me on the cheek.

I shrug, a little unnerved that he's acting so nice. "Sure. Thanks."

I glance at Mom. She just raises her eyebrows. "You're all growing up. There was a time when if you'd left him alone with that bag, it would be full of slime when you saw it again."

"I still wouldn't put it past him to have a bucket of slime waiting upstairs."

She laughs and leads me into the kitchen. It's just the same as it was when I was last here for Noah's birthday back in August. Pretty green-checkered curtains at the window, yellow walls, and cabinets that look slightly more chipped every time I visit. There's even the same vase of gerberas on the counter. I distinctly remember thinking they were new on my last visit, and how nice it was that Dad bought Mom flowers. I reach out for the petals and I realize they're not real. Wow, I really thought they were fresh.

"Where's Dad?" I ask.

Mom pulls out a tray of cookies and slides them onto the counter. "These smell absolutely delicious. I've added coconut."

Oliver appears and goes to the refrigerator, where he pulls out a beer. "You want one?" He takes off the cap and offers it to me.

"Sure, thanks." I take the bottle.

"I'll have one too," Mom says.

Oliver and I exchange a look. Mom never drinks, apart from a glass of champagne at New Years and a glass of wine on her birthday and Christmas.

"You want a *beer*?" Oliver says as I hand Mom my drink. She wipes her hands down her apron, takes the bottle, and has a swig.

Shit, is that what she's going to tell us? Does she have an alcohol problem now?

"Mom—" I'm interrupted before I can ask her if she's about to enroll in a twelve-step program.

"Are you all getting hammered?" Noah says as he appears out of nowhere. It wouldn't surprise me if we found out one day that Noah is in the CIA. He's everyone's friend, but I wonder if anyone really knows him. We exchange a quick hug, he ruffles my hair like I'm a dog, and I push him away.

"Come on, kids," Mom says. "Let's all sit." She pulls off her apron and takes a seat at the small white kitchen table. Today there's a chair for all of us, since Dad isn't here. When Dad was home, we'd fight to the death not to have to sit on the stool. The obvious solution would have been a fifth chair, but Dad was home for dinner so infrequently that it never seemed worth crowding the kitchen with an extra seat.

Mom pulls a pizza menu from the drawer and we all sit. Noah grabs a beer from the fridge and comes to join us around the table. "I thought we'd order pizza. A treat. It's good to have you all home."

I glance at my brothers to see if they're finding my mother's offer of pizza as strange as I do. Not that we don't eat pizza, but the first night we're home, she always cooks.

"Good to be home, Mom," Oliver says from opposite me. "I'll take a pepperoni."

Oliver doesn't seem to think it's weird that Mom isn't cooking. Maybe it's nothing, and I'm just overthinking everything.

I download a delivery app on my phone and place all our orders. Mom insists on proof the order has gone through because the only time she ordered through the app and didn't call, the pizza didn't turn up. I hold up the order confirmation and Mom nods her approval.

"I have some news," Mom says, as if this announcement is the next thing on her agenda after gather her children, have a beer, and order pizza.

I knew it. I *knew* something was off.

"What's up?" Oliver asks.

"I'm divorcing your father," she says matter-of-factly.

As my brain catches up to what she's saying, Oliver topples backwards off his chair and hits his head on the basket of potatoes stored by the refrigerator. He's an athletic guy. How did he just take that kind of tumble?

I stand as Mom and Noah both pull him up.

"Shit, are you okay?" I ask.

He rubs the back of his head and nods. We all retake our seats and refocus, staring at Mom. Was she joking?

"You're not serious?" Oliver asks.

"I am," Mom says. "It's time I start treating you like the adults you are now. I'm divorcing your father."

What does us being adults have to do with Mom divorcing Dad? Like we're not meant to feel anything because we're over eighteen?

"How does Dad feel about this?" Oliver asks.

"I haven't seen him since I told him."

I let out a strangled yelp. "You told him over the phone?" My mom is always so empathetic. It seems totally out of character for her not to at least tell my dad the devastating news face-to-face. "What did he say?"

She shrugs. "I don't remember exactly." She doesn't remember? How is that possible?

"But he doesn't want a divorce?" Noah asks in a quiet voice I know means he's keeping his feelings submerged under the surface. The more upset he is, the quieter he gets.

Mom sighs. "I don't know. I haven't known exactly what your father wants for a very long time. I'm not sure I ever did."

My anxiety is back. My breathing is labored and I'm feeling light-headed. What is she saying? "Why? After all these years?"

"This is the next phase of life," she says, tilting her head and looking at me with pity in her eyes. "The next chapter."

"But there must be a reason," Noah says.

Mom glances down, picking at the label on her beer bottle. "I wanted you to have the best possible childhood. The best memories. The most loving home. I hope that's what I was able to give you. Your father too—" She stops speaking and shrugs. "In his own way."

"And we did," I say, glancing at my brothers. I silently urge them to agree, like if we're effusive enough in our positive recollections, she might change her mind and *not* break our family apart. "I have the best memories of being a kid. There wasn't anything about it I would change."

"Really?" Mom asks. "Nothing *at all* you'd change?"

"Well, it would have been nice if Dad hadn't had to work so much, so he was around more, but—that's life, isn't it?"

"It didn't stop us from having the best childhood ever," Oliver says.

I glance at Noah, urging him to agree, to encourage Mom not to give up, but he's looking at Mom. "Tell us why," Noah says.

She presses her lips together and looks up at him. Something passes between them, like they know something Oliver and I don't.

"I want something different for myself," she says. "Now that you're all making your own way in the world. I want something more."

"More than Dad?" I ask. My dad is the most charming, funny, charismatic man, and he's worked his ass off for this family. What's the *more* she wants? Does she want to move to London and shack up with Idris Elba, or whoever a woman hurtling towards sixty sees herself shacking up with?

"You need to be honest," Noah says. "We need to understand."

A long silence settles on the table. We're all waiting for Mom to tell us what she wants, what's happened, and why she doesn't want to be married to Dad anymore. An ember of anger starts to simmer in my gut. How can she do this to him—to all of us?

"Will you keep the house?" My voice is a twisted shriek as I imagine the For Sale sign in the yard. All the memories we made here would disappear if she sold the house.

Noah reaches for my hand. I can't remember him ever holding my hand before. My mouth goes dry. I'm staring at Mom, willing her to give me the answers I want to hear.

She pulls in a deep breath. "I discovered some time ago that your father was having an affair."

It's like someone's reached down my throat and pulled out a lung. I can't breathe.

An *affair?* Dad was always devoted to my mother. Wasn't he?

My brothers are silent, and Mom doesn't say anything else.

That can't be it. I want to know everything.

"Okay," I say. "But relationships survive affairs, don't they? I mean, you've been together for so long. Is it worth throwing everything away for?"

She offers me a pitiful smile. "The affair never ended. In fact, it might have started before we met." She shakes her head. "I really have no idea. But your dad wasn't *on the road* for work all the time." She emphasizes *on the road*, like it's code for something.

Maybe it is.

My vision starts to blur, the image of Mom and my brothers merging in front of me.

Oliver's jaw is slack and his mouth is open, but Noah doesn't look as shocked. He's got one hand on mine and the other around Mom.

"It's okay, Mom," Noah says.

"No, it's not okay," I snap. "Can you stop giving us bits and pieces of I don't know what and tell us what's going on?"

Mom squares her shoulders. "Your father has been seeing a woman in Dayton for years—twenty-five at least. He splits his time between here and there. He's done it for most of our marriage. When I found out, you were three years old." She nods at me. "I had a young family and a part-time job. So I made it work." She shrugs. "Sometimes I'd pretend it wasn't happening and that he was on the road for work. Most of the time, I convinced myself that you can't get everything you want out of life, so I should be happy with my wonderful children and my beautiful house and my generally happy life. I just didn't get a whole husband. Other times, I'd cry myself to sleep at night."

My head is spinning and my stomach turns inside out. I pull at the collar of my sweater, desperate for air. I don't know which mind-blowing revelation to focus on. It all seems so bizarre, so completely removed from the reality I grew up with.

"Are you sure?" I ask. It seems so farfetched that Dad—our father, who'd chase us around the yard with the hose in the middle of summer, who would stuff broccoli into his ear to try to make us laugh if one of us had a bad day at school, who cried when I left for college—could spend his time around someone else's dinner table too.

"I'm sure," she says.

"Does he know you know?" I ask.

She lets out a cynical laugh. "He's known since the day I found out. She was pregnant by then."

"The... mistress? Pregnant?" Oliver asks.

"You have half-siblings," Mom says. "Two, I think. A boy and a girl."

"You're telling us Dad has another whole *family* in Dayton?" Oliver asks, but Noah stays quiet.

Completely quiet.

"Noah," I say, my voice laced with suspicion. "Did you know?"

He pulls in a deep breath. "No, I didn't *know*."

Well, that's something. At least my brother wasn't lying to me, too.

"I *suspected* something," he adds. Even though my stomach is on the floor, it drops further.

Mom reaches for Noah's arm and he pats her hand.

"I saw him once," Noah says. "In Dayton. Danny's mom had taken us to a skatepark there while she went to Costco, and he was there, on the other side of the bowl. I was practicing my drop-ins, and there he was."

Mom lets out a strangled, "Oh god."

"I knew I shouldn't have seen it," Noah says. "He was holding some kid's hand. A girl, I think. They both had ice creams. I was frozen for... I don't know how long. Eventually I called out to him and pressed down on my board. But when I got up the other side, he was gone."

My mom's hand slips across her lips and she shakes her head.

"Next time I saw him, I expected him to say something but he didn't. So neither did I. I've thought about it for years. Almost asked him about it so many times. Something always stopped me before I could get the words out. Like I knew I'd be breaking the spell if I spoke it out loud."

My insides pinch. I'm so sad Noah's had to keep this to himself all these years.

"I had no idea," Mom says, which totally pisses me off, because it couldn't have been beyond her imagination that something like this could have happened. Why couldn't she have been honest? With all of us. With herself.

"Why didn't you just divorce him?" I spit the words at her like darts.

"And then what?"

"And then you don't live a lie," I say. "Then you tell your children the truth."

Noah squeezes my hand like he knows my anger isn't anger at all, but deep wounds, raw pain, cuts so deep I don't know they will ever heal. Every fragment of childhood memory is disintegrating, like someone's erasing my hard drive. I can *feel* the deletion in my brain. Washing Dad's car with Oliver and having the world's best water fight in the middle of it. Family holidays on the lake, where the five of us would pose outside the cabin every year, each picture taking a spot on the hallway windowsill. My parents at my graduation, holding hands, tears in their eyes.

None of it was real.

And now it's all gone.

THREE

Sophia

As I close my hotel room door, I finally allow myself to drop the fake smile I've worn since boarding the plane from New York to Vegas.

There's no way I can tell my best friend, who is about to start married life, that my father has had a secret second family for the last twenty-five years. No bride wants to hear about a seemingly fairy-tale marriage actually being a total sham. So I've been practicing my best fake smiles for the last week—since I learned my parents weren't who I thought they were. That they are secret keepers. Cover-uppers. Liars.

I don't know what's real anymore.

I need my best friend. I want to cry and crawl under the covers and never come out. I long for something real. Something sure.

But my best friend is getting married, so it's fake smiles, short skirts, and celebrations.

I abandon my suitcase in the hallway, kick off my shoes, and pull out my phone. I've been ignoring calls and texts from Noah and Oliver all week, but maybe my brothers are who I need. We've never been "group chat" siblings. Maybe it would be different if I'd had sisters, but with two brothers, the extent of our relationship when we're not physically together is sharing jokes. Memes is where it begins and ends for us.

But no more.

I quickly create a group chat and type.

Hi, hope you're both still alive.

It's about as gushy as I get with my brothers.

Noah replies right away.

I'm avec pulse. Anyone heard from Dad?

My stomach twists. I don't want to hear from Dad. I'm not sure when I'll ever be able to speak to him.

Does he keep a schedule? Does he make sure he spends equal time with all of us? Or did we get him for more time because there were three of us and he only had two children in his other family? Or did he just spend more time with the family he preferred?

And was that us? Or them?

I think I'm going to vomit. I rush to the bathroom and grip the sides of the sink, trying to keep down everything threatening to spill out. If I don't, I'm worried I'll never stop vomiting.

There's a knock at the door, but I ignore it. My mind is full of my dad and his other family and whether he'd chase his other kids around the yard with a hose, or paint them head to toe with the paint he was supposed to be using on the shiplap like he did to Oliver one summer. My tummy hurt from laughing so much when I saw Oliver completely covered in white paint.

Mom hadn't been so amused. The paint was water-based, but he had paint in his hair for a week.

There's more knocking at the door.

"Sophia!" Jules calls.

Shit.

I straighten, wipe my mouth with the back of my hand, and head to the door.

"Hey," she says as I open the door, her eyes dancing and excited.

"Can I get ready in here? Leo is on the phone and has the TV on, but I just want to listen to Taylor Swift and have some fun." She's wearing a robe with a towel on her head and pulling a carry-on suitcase.

"Absolutely!" I wonder if the words sound as fake as they feel. I just want to be left alone to disappear. "I don't know about you, but I'm feeling twenty-two," I say, trying to muster some enthusiasm.

She looks so happy. I can't think of anyone who deserves it more. "Whoop! I brought champagne."

Now *that* I can get enthusiastic about. Alcohol might help take the edge off my mood.

"You haven't even unpacked," she says, as she organizes glasses for our drinks.

"Oh yeah, I was just texting with Noah."

"Oh," she says. "How is he?"

I don't want to talk about my brothers. I don't know why I brought up Noah.

"Good. Tell me what you're wearing."

She describes the options and I listen intently, because if I let my mind wander, it's only going one way. I want to head a full one hundred and eighty degrees in the opposite direction.

We clink champagne glasses and I manage to glug down half a glass in two mouthfuls. And it does soften my edges a little.

Zip, zip, zip. Jules opens her makeup bag and sits in front of the full-length mirror opposite the bed. "I promise I'll tidy up after myself," she says. "Who knows who you might bring back tonight."

I choke out a laugh. Exactly no one. Men clearly can't be trusted.

"I think I'm still getting over Jamie," I say. I know it's not true, but I need a reason to not be looking for my soul mate as far as Jules is concerned. I'm not sure how it happened so quickly, but Jules has been turned into a lover of love. I don't know if that makes her Aphrodite or Cupid. But she's obsessed with the idea that I have to find the love of my life, just like she's found the love of hers.

"Jamie? Really? I would have thought the fact that you two were long distance would make it easier to get over him."

I sit on the edge of the bed and consider her statement. Jamie worked on superyachts and was based in Florida. We only saw each other every few months or so—he was always at sea and I have my life in New York. I thought we made it work because we loved each other. But maybe it was just familiar to me—a man who was never around.

"Do you think Jamie was cheating on me?" I ask her.

Jules snaps her head around. "What makes you think that?"

"He was away a lot of the time. He had every opportunity."

"But so did you, and you never did."

Just like my mom. I accepted the scraps.

"I'm not doing long distance again," I say. I don't want another man in my life who only wants to be there part of the time.

"I think that's a smart decision," Jules says. "It's not sustainable in the long run. And anyway, you should want to be with each other for the everyday-life stuff." She grins like she's downed that entire bottle of champagne, and I can tell she's thinking about Leo. All I can think about is my dad and how he can't have liked being with us for the everyday-life stuff. Not enough to not be with someone else and have an entire family with them.

I try and swallow down the feeling of loneliness that washes over me.

"Well, Fisher lives in New York City, so you wouldn't have that problem with him," she says, grinning into the mirror.

I sigh. "I'm not sure Fisher's my type."

She frowns as she applies her brow pencil. "You two got along well at brunch, didn't you? And on the plane."

Brunch seems like such a long time ago. I don't remember much of Fisher. I remember I was sitting next to him, but on the other side was Worth.

Worth is who I remember from brunch. Worth, with the cool blue eyes and intense stare. Worth, who was confident and oh-so-masculine with his stubbled jaw and deep voice that I felt between my thighs whenever he spoke.

Worth, who said I could call him anything I liked, and has me wondering if he really is a hero.

I could do with a hero right about now, but the only person I can rely on to save me is myself.

That's when it hits me: Worth wasn't on the plane. Is he not coming this weekend? Not that I should care. I don't need any romantic entanglements. Ever. Again. I just felt so drawn to him... If not for the bombshell my mom dropped in Cincinnati, my mind would probably have stayed as full of him as it had been after brunch.

"I *get along* with most people, but I have a slightly higher bar for the people I want to share body fluids with."

"Ha ha," Jules says. She's flitting between using the hair curler and applying her mascara. Her process is so haphazard, I can't watch too closely or I'll get stressed out.

"Are you okay?" I ask her.

"Of course. I'm excited about being here. And marrying Leo. Can you believe I'm getting married?"

I smile at her. She's so happy. I don't want to ruin that for her. "I can. You deserve all the happiness in the world." I wonder if I'll ever be able to tell her about my dad. Because the next thought in her head will be, *Do you think Leo could do that to me?* It's a question she'll ask herself before she eventually asks me.

And what can I say?

There's only one answer: I never thought my dad could do that to our family.

The last thing I want to do is undermine Jules' trust in Leo. Not ever. So maybe this is a secret I have to take to the grave.

"You'll get to know him a little better on this trip," she says.

For a moment I think she's talking about Worth, but then I remember she doesn't know that Worth starred in the dream I had the night after brunch. The one where he was bare-chested, wearing a blue-and-black flannel shirt—unbuttoned of course—and jeans tight to his muscular thighs.

Even now, despite what's happened with my dad, I'm feeling like I need some air just thinking about how Worth might look with fewer clothes on than is polite for dinner.

Oh, but he wasn't on the plane.

"Yeah," I say. "I'll get to know everyone a little better." I'll be fake-smiling my way through this entire weekend.

FOUR

Worth

I've never considered myself a weak man. I like to confront my problems head-on; avoidance is just another form of weakness. But there was no way I was going to share a ten-passenger Gulfstream with Sophia. I didn't trust myself. So I made an excuse about a meeting and flew commercial to Vegas. On my own. With only the thought of Sophia for company.

I checked into my hotel suite, ignored the group chat going off every five seconds, took a shower, changed, and headed down to the private room where I booked dinner for us all. There's no best man this weekend, but I've made sure we have transportation at our disposal, the restaurants are booked, and Leo's favorite wine is available at all times. Bennett figured out the plane. Fisher has got VIP passes for every club in town, and Jack organized suites for everyone. We all have our part to play.

We're here to celebrate our friend and brother getting married. I couldn't be happier for him.

The Monday after the brunch where I met Sophia, we had our

normal get-together. I kept my ear to the ground, waiting for Fisher to mention Sophia, but he didn't. I know for a fact that if he were into her, I would have heard about it. I'm not sure if that makes my infatuation better or worse. Maybe she's super into him and will be disappointed when nothing happens.

If I don't speak to her again, I'll never know. And despite the fact that avoiding Sophia reveals a weakness inside me I don't want to confront, it's taking all my strength to stay away.

I arrive at the private dining room in the restaurant early. I'm not putting name cards anywhere, but I want to make sure I'm seated at the other end of the table from Sophia. I pull three jewelry boxes out of my pocket and set them beside three of the place settings—a keepsake of the weekend. It's a ploy to direct the women of the group to the seats farthest away from mine—a way to make sure Sophia's not sitting near me tonight. That's all. It's not like I'm buying gifts for a woman I met once. It's nothing like that.

At a bar in the corner of the room, I order a whisky neat. I'm going to need a couple of drinks to get me through tonight.

I tip back the whisky and enjoy the burn as it trails down my throat. That feels better already. But it doesn't stop my pulse straining in my neck when I hear the rattle of the door handle.

I turn to see Bennett and Efa.

I slide my drink onto the table next to the seat I've claimed.

We greet each other and everyone get drinks. Fisher and Jack arrive together. They're *always* together.

My heart begins to throb in my chest and I grip my glass unnecessarily tight.

She'll be here in a minute.

I'm not sure what frightens me more: that I'll feel the same need for her—the same visceral urge to possess her that I did when we first met—or that I won't, and those feelings were a temporary, passing madness.

"You okay, Worth?" Efa asks. "You seem a little..."

"More uptight than usual?" Bennett suggests.

"I'm not sure you should be lobbing stones from where you're standing in that glass house," Efa replies.

Bennett grins and shrugs, then Fisher asks about the menu. I've escaped further scrutiny. For now.

The door opens and I know before I glance over that it's her. My vision tunnels until Sophia is all I see. She shifts slightly in her tight black dress. Her collarbones are visible above the fabric and my fingertips heat with the need to press against them, up her neck, over her lips. Her blonde hair is up, with wavy tendrils framing her face, her lips a soft pink. Need coils in my gut.

What's wrong with me?

What's with this woman?

It's like I've taken some kind of drug and my thoughts are no longer my own. I'm possessed. I have this unshakeable feeling I'm meant to be with her. I don't know if it's because I've thought about her way too much these last two weeks, even dreamt about her a couple of times, but I feel like I know her. Like she knows me.

But it's all in my head.

Our gazes catch and her expression turns from anxious to happy. She steps toward me, places her hand on my shoulder, and without thinking, I place mine on her waist as we greet each other with a kiss on the cheek.

"Worth," she says in my ear. Desire spreads through my veins. "You're here."

Suddenly I wish I hadn't arranged the seating the way I did. I want her next to me. All night. All the time.

"You thought I wasn't coming?" I like the fact she noticed I wasn't on the plane. We're a small group, so it's not like my absence wasn't obvious, but it still has me hoping that she's thinking about me in the way I'm thinking about her.

Except I shouldn't be hoping.

She's meant for Fisher. Even if he's not interested in her, she might have her sights set on him.

Her hand leaves my shoulder and reluctantly I pull my fingers from her waist.

She smiles up at me. "You weren't on the plane."

"I had a call," I lie. "So I flew commercial. But I wasn't going to miss this."

She looks up at me, her head tilted, her gaze so intense I feel it in my bones. She doesn't say a word. I'd pay a million bucks to know what she's thinking.

"Let's sit," Fisher calls out, and the moment is broken.

Everyone heads to the table. I sit where I planned to. Sophia's at the other end of the table, directly in my line of sight. Despite the distance between us, I still *feel* her in every cell of my body.

"What's this?" Jules asks, holding up the navy velvet box.

There's a bit of mumbling as Efa and Sophia discover their boxes. They didn't act as the placeholders I'd hoped, but Sophia is still at the opposite end of the table from me. Not that it's tempered my distraction.

"Just a small memento of the weekend," I say.

"Worth!" Jules says, opening the box.

I glance down at my plate, but it takes everything I have not to stare at Sophia as she opens her box. Does she like it? Will she wear it? All I could see when I came across the necklace was Sophia—the blue of the sapphire a perfect match for her eyes.

"Oh god, Worth. It's *gorgeous*," Efa says. "Thank you."

Jack groans. "Typical Worth, showing the rest of us up buying gifts."

"I'm sure no one will mind if you buy more gifts for tomorrow," I say.

I finally glance over at Sophia. She's staring right at me. But she's frowning. Is she angry? Without breaking eye contact, she stands and rounds the table toward me, holding the jewelry box.

Without thinking, I stand as she approaches. Her hand slide over my shoulder again and I pull in a breath, enjoying the heat of her palm She lifts up on tiptoes and presses a kiss to my cheek. I close my eyes in a long blink. "It's the most beautiful thing I've ever seen. It's so generous of you."

I'm left speechless. I can't move. She's so close, I breathe in her scent of jasmine and honey. I feel the heat of her body under that black dress. I desperately want to pull her closer still and tell her how I feel—how I am completely bewitched by her.

She steps back. "Will you help me put it on?" She hands me the box and spins so her back is to me.

I feel myself lengthen. The things I want to do to this woman.

I'm vaguely aware that despite the fact we're the only two people in the group standing, no one's paying attention to either of us. That's how I like it. I don't need additional scrutiny at this moment. I take the necklace from its box.

"You shouldn't feel you have to wear this now. I—"

"I want to," Sophia says, silencing me. There's no doubt in her words.

I'm careful not to touch her as I drape the necklace around her neck and do up the clasp.

"Done," I say. She spins back to face me.

"How does it look?" she asks.

I glance up at her eyes, down to her lips, and then to the necklace that sits so perfectly between her collarbones.

"You're perfect," I whisper.

Her mouth parts and she shakes her head. We're silent for a beat. Eventually she says, "Anything but. But the necklace is. Thank you."

She turns and I sit. My entire body is vibrating. I don't know if I'm going to survive this weekend.

I'LL RAISE suspicion if I start downing shots at the table, but I need something to calm my nervous system. A cold shower is probably the healthier option, but not readily available.

I head to the bar in the main restaurant and order another

whisky. This will make it better. It will make her fade into the background. I need to remember, I barely know this woman. She might torture small animals in her spare time. Or protest against women's rights. She could be a monster. Except, I don't think so.

Maybe I need to get laid. That's what Leo's always telling me. Maybe he's right. Maybe this is a buildup of lust and I'm just channeling it toward Sophia.

"Hey," a woman's voice says from beside me.

I snap my head around. *Sophia.*

The exact person I'm trying to avoid.

"You getting extra drinks doesn't seem fair."

"What can I get you?" I ask.

She leans across me, her hand on my arm, and says to the bartender, "Can I get a shot of tequila?" She turns back to me. "What are you doing?"

"Drinking whisky. You?"

"But why here and not back at the table?"

I shake my head, like I don't have an answer.

"I was on the way to the restrooms," she says, though I haven't asked. "It's... a lot." Her necklace catches my eye when she nods, and I stare at her collarbones.

What. Is. The. Matter. With. Me?

"A lot?" I ask, trying to follow her thread.

"The group. And Jules really wants me to like Fisher. And I want to focus on her wedding. Maybe she's nervous and trying to distract herself by setting me up? I don't know."

"You don't like Fisher?" I ask, intrigued whether there are things she's not saying, lines to be read between.

She sighs as the bartender slides the tequila in front of her. She ignores my question and takes the shot in one.

She winces, still managing to look beautiful.

"I don't know if it's because you don't seem to want to impress me, but it makes me want to... tell you stuff."

How could she have read me so wrong? Not want to impress her?

If I thought it would make me remotely interesting to her, I'd buy the whole town we're standing in.

"What kind of stuff?" I ask.

She glances between my eyes and my lips, then takes my whisky from my hand and sips. Fuck. Watching her, her hands around the glass I've just been holding, it's like she's got her fingers around my dick. It shouldn't be provocative, but it completely is.

Her lips are wet with whisky and I long to taste the heat.

"Everything," she says eventually.

"Start with something," I say, bracing myself for something terrible. What is it about me that makes me think the worst is always about to happen?

"I don't like Fisher," she confesses.

My muscles unlock, and I sigh with relief. "He's a good guy." Despite how I feel, I still need to defend my friend.

"Oh," she says, her eyes wide, "I'm sure he is. I don't mean I think he's an awful person. I just don't feel a connection to him. You know what I mean?"

I don't think I could have answered her question affirmatively before I'd met her. I didn't really understand what "a connection" meant. I've never felt the inescapable, visceral response that I do with Sophia. "I do," I say, trying to keep my tone neutral.

"I just don't want to upset Jules."

"Be honest with her," I say. "She's your friend."

She presses her lips together in a forced smile. What's that? I want to dig deeper and explore why she feels so uncomfortable.

"How was Cincinnati?" I ask, remembering that last weekend she went back to see her family. I felt like there might have been some bad news delivered during the trip.

Her eyes leave mine and she looks over my shoulder. "It was… revelatory."

I leave space and silence for her to fill, but she doesn't say anything and she doesn't meet my gaze.

"You want to talk about it?" I reach over and sweep a tendril of hair from her face. She focuses on me.

"Maybe," she says. "To you. But not now. Let's meet back here after the entrée. I'll need another shot. I should go." She fingers her necklace. "Thank you for this." I'm not sure if she means the necklace, the conversation, or the offer to talk.

Back at the table, no one seems to notice we were both away at the same time. I slip into my seat and begin to talk to Byron, who just arrived.

"How's Colorado?" I ask, my voice hushed, because I'm not sure who knows about what he's doing there.

"It's good," he says. "Not quite what I expected, but really good. In fact, I was going to talk to you about it a little more. I thought you might want to get involved in some way."

I raise my eyebrows in surprise. Byron is notoriously private about his business dealings, and he doesn't partner with anyone who wants any kind of say. He'll take investor money, but no one has decision-making power other than Byron.

"Let's talk some more," I say. "You seem to be spending more and more time there."

He swallows his steak. "Yeah. It feels different being back there." Byron always vowed he was New York or nowhere, but things have clearly changed for him. "Do you think you'll always live in the brownstone?"

I pull in a breath and my gaze finds Sophia for the first time since we came back to the table. "I don't think I can make definitive decisions about my future when it's not here yet."

Byron chuckles. "What a Worth thing to say. Although, I can't see you being anywhere but the brownstone."

A month ago, I might have agreed with him. But now?

Fisher comes over and crouches between our chairs. "What are we doing after this? Poker? Or should we take Leo to see some naked ladies?"

I groan and Byron rolls his eyes.

"Leo's seen enough naked ladies to last a thousand lifetimes," I say.

"Poker, then," Fisher says, nonplussed.

"I can do poker," Byron says. "Worth?"

"Maybe," I reply.

"Maybe Worth wanted to see naked ladies," Fisher says with a grin. "It's about time you lost your virginity. Happy to tag along, if that's what you want to do."

"I can't think of anything worse than going to a strip club. And anyway, it's not like Bennett, Efa, Jules, or Sophia will want to go."

"We don't all have to do the same thing," Fisher says.

"You're not into Sophia?" I ask him.

He shrugs and glances over at her. "She seems like a nice girl..."

Byron laughs. "That's a weird way to say 'no, I'd rather go to a strip club.'"

"I don't *not* like her. But honestly, as one of my best friend's wifes' best friends... I don't want to go there."

Emotion bursts in my chest. Relief at Fisher's words. But also frustration that Sophia is so close to Jules. It would have been way easier if she'd been a stranger. Overriding both these feelings is a deep sense of understanding that *I* will go there, no matter the consequences. It's like my fate is sealed.

There's no keeping away from Sophia now. I want her. There's no more avoiding her. No more pretending I don't feel as strongly as I do.

I catch her eye across the table and she excuses herself.

Entrees are over and I have... somewhere to be.

I head out a few minutes later and spot her by the bar, standing in the exact same place I stood, speaking to the bartender. He's laughing at something she's saying and I flush with envy. I want all her attention. Fuck, when has a woman made me feel so primal? Sophia makes me feel more of every damn emotion that exists.

"Hey," she says, as I approach.

"Hey," I reply.

"I got you whisky."

"You trying to get me drunk?" I ask.

Her mouth parts as if she's about to speak, but she doesn't. She shakes her head. "I'm trying to get *me* drunk."

I pick up my glass and raise it. I'm less concerned about her seeing the heat of desire in my eyes. Now that I know Fisher isn't going to be upset, things have shifted for me.

Her cheeks pink and blood rushes to my cock. Jesus, I want to see those cheeks pink some more, her skin covered in sweat, her breathing labored because she just came for the third time underneath me. My heart starts to pound and she dips out her tongue and bites down on her lip like she can read my thoughts.

She sips on her tequila this time, then slides it back to the bar.

She's in no rush to go back to the table. I'm going to have a few more minutes with her.

"Do you keep secrets, Worth?" she asks.

"What kind of secrets?" I ask.

"The kind of secrets you don't tell anyone."

"Don't we all?"

She shakes her head. "Nope. I agree with what you said that we all lie—no one tells the whole truth all the time. But secrets? Big secrets? Not everyone keeps those. Do you?"

Her question is pointed, but at the same time, I can tell it's not aimed at me. "There are things people don't know about me."

"Like what?" she asks immediately.

I pull in a breath and search for an answer. "People I work with don't know where I live."

"You deliberately don't tell them?"

I pick up her tequila and taste it, wanting to be closer to her, wanting my mouth where hers has been. "Yeah. My assistant knows. But generally, I don't want people I don't know well knowing where I live."

"What about people who do know you well? Your friends in there." She nods toward the private dining room. "What don't they know about you?" She's trying to mask her questions behind a singsong tone and a smile, but she's digging furiously for something.

"I don't deliberately keep things from..." I trail off, hearing the lie before I have a chance to say it. My feelings for Sophia—no one knows about those. "I might be careful about *when* I tell them some stuff, but I don't deliberately hide things from my closest friends, no."

She pulls in a juddering breath, then takes the tequila from me. Our fingers brush and our gazes lock. She looks away as she downs the rest of her glass.

"What about you?" I ask. "Do you keep secrets?"

She looks at me, a flare of panic in her eyes. "Not usually."

"But sometimes you do?" I ask. What secrets is she keeping right now?

"Like you said. It's about timing. But no, I don't keep secrets from my closest friends. From my family." It feels like she has more to say, so I keep quiet. "Sometimes I wonder what normal is. Is it normal to keep secrets? Is it normal to tell your best friend everything? Maybe I'm the asshole, you know? Maybe everyone else's normal is different. Don't we all go around thinking *we're* normal, and if people aren't like us, they're not normal?"

"Hmm," I say. She's saying nothing and far too much at the same time. "*Normal* is an interesting word. Everyone is different."

She sighs. "I guess. But there are parameters of normal. Like, I don't care if you're on the subway and you're dressed in Chanel or as a hot dog. But if you're naked, I've got a problem with that."

"Yeah, naked on the subway doesn't sound like a good life choice."

She shivers. "So gross—for the people having to see you, but also, can you imagine sitting on a seat? Stop. I can't think about it."

I smile. I like listening to her. I like hearing how her brain works.

She takes my glass from me, letting her fingers linger a second when they meet mine. My heart rate trips at the feel of her skin against mine.

"You're right, *normal* is a provocative word. I guess I just want to know what most other people do. Like most people tell lies—to protect others, or themselves."

"But you're not like most people." I want to say more. I want to tell her she's like no other woman I've ever met. That she's beautiful and open and has an intensity about her that makes me sit up and want to understand her. That when I'm with her, I want more. I want to spend every moment with her. I want to study her like a work of art. I want to touch her, feel her. I want to *know* her.

She blushes at my words. If only she knew what I wasn't saying. If only she knew what I *wanted* to say. Am I keeping secrets from her?

It's all about timing.

"Do you think most people keep secrets? Like, big secrets? From people who are close to them?"

I remember what she said before. About Cincinnati being *revelatory*. "What did you find out in Cincinnati?" I ask.

Her eyes widen, panic flashing in her gaze. "We should go back." She takes a swig of my whisky.

"You can talk to me, you know?"

She nods slowly. As silence stretches out between us, she seems to relax inside of it. "I know I can."

Her words fill me up. I want her to talk to me, to tell me what she's thinking. I want to know about the secret she discovered, and who kept it from her.

She turns and I catch her arm. She snaps her head back.

"I like talking to you," I say.

"I like talking to you," she says. "Very much."

I want to keep her here. Talking to me. Sharing her secrets. With me.

FIVE

Sophia

I shove my feet into my sneakers and hook my crossbody bag over my head. Efa has made all the arrangements for today and has kept the details a secret, which I hate. Her only direction was to wear comfortable shoes. I just hope there's not a paddleboat involved. Nothing good ever happens on a paddleboat. I don't have many lines in the sand, but paddling on water is one of them. Also, I don't want to get dirty, or be in a situation where I might fall. Apart from that, I'm very relaxed about what we're doing today.

I turn in front of the full-length mirror and look over my shoulder at my ass in my jeans, then roll my eyes at myself. Why do I care what my ass looks like? Who am I trying to impress? I don't know how I can even think about a man without wanting to set him on fire at the moment, but somehow, instead of making me panic or question him, Worth makes me feel like I'm the center of the universe. He's so calming. So solid.

Maybe I'm making something out of nothing, but there seems to be an intensity between us when we're together, like we've known each other from a previous life. He seems to see right through me. He didn't just remember I'd been to Cincinnati—he instinctively knew something had happened there. It's like he can read my mind, even though I've only known him a matter of hours.

But my mind is all over the place at the moment. I don't need to complicate life any more than it already is. Worth doesn't seem complicated, but any more feelings than I'm already feeling are too much.

As I head down to the hotel lobby, my phone buzzes. I pull it out of my bag and "Dad" flashes on the screen.

I feel my body heat three more degrees. It's like my anger is my own personal electric blanket, set to high.

He knows I know. He's called three times in the last twenty-four hours. He wouldn't do that unless it was serious, like I discovered he had a second family the entire time I've been alive or something.

I type out a message on the group chat with my brothers, asking if either of them has heard from Dad. Even typing the word "Dad" is difficult, and I'm sure I press the letters into the phone with more force than necessary.

The elevator stops and the doors open at floor twelve. Worth appears.

Despite being in the desert, his presence is like a cool breeze wafting in from the north. My jaw unlocks and my shoulders drop. I'm not sure why I'm having such a physical reaction to this man. Okay, sure, he's probably the best-looking man I've ever laid eyes on, but I can't just think he's hot. That can't be it.

"Hey," he says, the single word pushing everything else out of my brain.

"Hey," I say, inexplicably feeling like an idiot. "Are you... prepared?" I ask. And god, I hope it's not paintballing.

"Always," he replies.

"Do you know what we're doing today? It's not paintballing, is it?"

Slowly, he shakes his head. "Not a clue."

I sigh and slot my phone back into my bag.

The elevator doors open onto the lobby. Jules, Leo, Bennett, and Efa are already there, waiting for us.

We're the third couple.

A frisson of *something* snakes down my spine and I glance at Worth, who's checking his watch.

"I love that we're all so punctual," Jules says. "And this is actually perfect. You two can be a team."

Efa tugs at her shirt and whispers something into Jules' ear. Jules replies under her breath.

More secrets. I feel the rage rise in my stomach, and I have to turn away. What the hell are they talking about?

"You okay?" Worth asks from beside me.

I pull in a deep breath and take in the aroma of leather and pine. Apparently this is Worth's signature scent. I'm basically sniffing Worth. But it works to allay my growing anger, and I shrug off whatever's going on with Jules and Efa. I pull my face into a smile. "Teammates!" I say.

At least I'm not being paired with Fisher. That could be awkward. It's not that he's not a great guy—he's been nothing but charming to me. But he's... not my type. Then again, no one's my type at the moment.

Worth lifts his fist to offer me a fist bump and I can't help but grin. He's an unlikely fist bumper, but I press my knuckles to his. He's so dry, so deadpan, that my grin turns into a laugh.

"Teammates," he says.

Fisher and Jack arrive. Leo gets a call to say Byron will be late because he's on the phone to Acapulco.

"But this is better because we're all teams of two," Jules says. "It's fairer this way."

"Fairer for what?" I mutter under my breath.

Worth puts his hand on my back. It's just a touch, but it's like he's got a magic wand. I don't know if it's what he intended, but the gesture makes me feel like I have someone in my corner. And I haven't felt that since I found out about my dad. I never felt I *needed* that until I found out about my dad.

"So, are you ready for some fun?" Efa says. "You know the one thing we don't have for this wedding tomorrow? Something old, something new, something borrowed, something blue. Your mission—and you will choose to accept it—is to find the most innovative, creative things to satisfy the brief!" Efa's grinning at us like she just invented a cure for world hunger. I have to fight the urge to eyeroll, which instantly makes me feel horrible. Why can't I just be happy—push away the lies my dad told me for my entire life?

"We can find a bar if you prefer?" Worth says quietly as Efa hands out written instructions for our quest.

"Jules and Leo, you get *new*, Bennett and I are going to take *old*, Sophia and Worth, you take *borrowed*, Fisher and Jack, you can have *blue*."

I look up at Worth and his cool, blue, intent gaze. "Maybe we can work in a bar stop. Or maybe our thing can be a bottle of tequila, which we sample to make sure it tastes okay, and let Jules and Leo borrow a shot each from the bottle."

Worth smiles, but there's a question in his eyes.

"You haven't told them the prize," Bennett says.

"Oh yeah! The prize is, you get Bennett as your personal butler for the day." Efa actually jumps in excitement.

"What happens if you and Bennett win?" Fisher asks.

Efa gives a one-shouldered shrug. "Then I get to have Bennett as my personal butler for the day."

Worth chuckles beside me. It's catching and I find myself smiling. "We have to win this," he says to me under his breath.

"Who's judging?" I ask. Obviously, I need to understand my audience.

"Byron," Efa says. "Or if he finishes what he's doing and actually joins a team, we'll ask a hotel employee to judge so it's fair. We have four hours," Efa says. "Oh, and final thing. You have a spend cap of one hundred dollars."

Everyone groans.

"That makes it almost impossible," Bennett complains.

"No, it means you have to use your brain and creativity, rather than just your wallet," Efa retorts. She glances at her watch. "You're just eating into precious time. See you all back here at one thirty for lunch."

"Plenty of time for tequila." Worth grabs my hand and pulls me toward the exit.

We climb into a waiting SUV, and I don't even have time to ask whether this car was actually meant for us.

"Borrowed?" I say. "Isn't that the hardest one?"

"Everyone else is probably thinking the same thing. We'll figure something out."

"I suppose the first thing we should ask is whether either of us has anything on hand that would qualify," I say. "And for the record, I don't."

"Let's just drive the length of the Strip," Worth says to the driver. And then to me, "We might get inspiration on the way."

Worth's knee nudges against my thigh. I wonder if it's normal to feel that touch across my entire body. The guy exudes a certain quiet confidence I don't think I've come across before. I suppose Leo has it a little. Although he's much more gregarious—more the life and soul of the party. Worth is more reserved, which somehow makes him sexier. His calmness makes me calm. Like nothing is going to faze him, no matter how difficult life gets. I wonder how he'd react if he found out his father had a second family he knew nothing about.

My phone beeps, alerting me to a message from Oliver about Thanksgiving. How can he even think about Thanksgiving right now? I click into the message.

Do you think we're still celebrating Dad's sixtieth birthday on Thanksgiving?

What's he talking about? He can't think we're all going to sit around the kitchen table like one big happy family.

Noah replies.

I hope so.

I feel the furnace inside me stoked. How are my brothers casually texting about being with Dad on Thanksgiving like it's nothing?

Thanksgiving has always been a holiday we go all-out for, because it's Dad's birthday around the same time. Dad usually made it home and would cook. Some of our happiest memories with him were from Thanksgivings over the years. I can't think about any of it now. Not my brothers, not Thanksgiving, not the fact that my dad is a liar. It's too much, I feel like I'm going to combust if I give any of it more attention. I want to push it all down and make it disappear.

I shove my phone into my pocket, sigh, and glance out the window at the passing cars and chaos. "This is my first time in Vegas."

"It is?" he asks. "Huh. I wouldn't have thought that."

We're basically strangers, but I like the idea that he's thought about me enough to form any kind of judgment.

"But not for you?" I ask.

"You know. Guys love their weekends in Vegas." He sounds unenthusiastic, and I like him more for it.

"You're not one of them?" I ask.

"Not really my scene."

Most guys in their early thirties would consider Vegas an adult playground. The gambling, the drinks, the women. "You don't like to party?"

"I like to spend my time with people who I like equally drunk or sober."

I smile. "Yeah, it's easy to like people after a few shots."

"I prefer New York," he says. "Or the Catskills."

"A closet lumberjack?" I ask. "I wouldn't have guessed."

A small smile curls at the edge of his mouth. "I just like the peace."

"Which is why you live in New York," I say.

"I think it's okay to like both. New York isn't everything and neither is the Catskills, but together, they come pretty close."

My stomach churns. Is that what my dad thought? That my mom, brothers, and me weren't everything, so he had to go out and get more—so he could have everything?

"You okay?" he asks.

I nod. "Fine. We just need to find something borrowed."

Worth leans forward to ask the driver something. "Can you do a tour of the main attractions? The Welcome to Vegas sign, the fountains at the Bellagio, the chapel where Britney got married, that kind of thing?"

I can't help but dissolve into giggles. "The chapel where Britney got married? That's what you want to see?"

"You said you'd never been to Vegas. I thought you'd want a thorough introduction."

"Bellagio is just here," the driver says, pulling into the drive.

"If we had a pretty perfume bottle, we could borrow some water from the fountains," I suggest. "That might work."

"It's an idea," Worth says, though his frown tells me it's not the best idea he's ever heard. He grabs an unopened bottle of water from the side pocket of the car and slides out of his seat. He turns and offers me his hand to help me out of this car.

"One more than you've had." I take a step down, but instead of releasing my hand, Worth links his fingers through mine.

Like we're a couple or something.

A crackle of desire courses through me, and I wonder if he feels it too.

"That's true," he says, leading me along a pathway like he knows exactly where he's going. "So let's collect some water, and if that's all we're left with when our time's up, we don't have to come back." Rather than let go of my hand, he unscrews the lid of the water bottle with his teeth and empties the water out on the path.

"So a tour of Vegas and a treasure hunt at the same time?"

"I'm all about multitasking," he says. I know he's making a joke, but someone should tell his face.

Is it weird that I find it low-key adorable how dry he is?

People seem to appear from everywhere and we're all headed in the same direction. Worth clearly knows where he's going and squeezes my hand in reassurance. Despite the fact that it would be easier if he let my hand go, he doesn't.

The fountains come into view, except they're not... fountaining. Worth walks up to someone in security and they have a conversation. Music has started playing and I can't make out what they're saying.

"This way," Worth says, leading us to the front of the fountains.

"Are we allowed here?"

Worth doesn't respond, but the fountain display starts as we get to the edge of the pool.

"I bet you've done this a million times if you've been to Vegas a lot?" I ask.

"I've never done this," he says. "I've passed by the fountains, and I once had a room opposite with a view of them, but I've never stood and watched them like this."

He must feel me staring up at him, because he glances down. "It's a first," he says, and then lets out a small huff of laughter.

"What?" I ask, half shouting because the music has been ratcheted up. "What's so funny?"

He glances back at me and down at our hands, and then back at the fountains as they start to spurt. "Just having a lot of firsts at the moment—" He shakes his head. "I'll tell you later."

I get the feeling it isn't the music that has stopped him explaining what he means.

We watch, hand in hand, our heads tipped back as the water climbs hundreds of feet in the air.

"Is this weird?" Worth calls out.

"What?" I call back, even though we're close enough to still be holding hands. Is it weird that it's not weirder that this man I hardly know is holding my hand? Is it weird that I feel oddly comfortable with him, like I've known him for years rather a handful of hours? Is it weird to be in Vegas at my best friend's wedding when she hated the man she's marrying for years before falling in love with him for the second time?

Yes, all of it is very weird.

"That we're watching water being propelled into the air to music?" Worth asks as he frowns.

I laugh. "Well, now that you put it like that, maybe it is a little weird."

"Do you like it?" he asks, his attention still on the display in front of us.

"I'm not sure."

He chuckles. "Me neither. I don't *not* like it." Then he turns and looks at me, and my nipples pebble beneath my bra like I'm naked and his gaze is trailing across my bare skin.

"I like being here with you," he says.

It's not what I was expecting him to say. It's so direct. To the point. And I have no doubt he's telling the truth—like he's totally transparent and I can see right through him and can tell he's not keeping anything from me and doesn't want to. On a laundry list of sexy things about Worth, that might be number one.

"Samesies," I reply, then close my eyes, trying to wish away the past five seconds. Samesies? Am I eleven?

He lets out that half-laugh again at my clumsy response, and I open my eyes. Once again, Worth has surprised me. I half expected him to be offended. But I get the feeling Worth isn't telling me anything to get a specific response. He's saying it because it's true and he doesn't want me not to know. His shoulders are broad in more ways than one.

I feel his fingers curled around mine. The heat of them. The strength of them. The way they feel so protective. They feel like truth. Right about now, that's exactly what I need.

We stay watching the fountains for a few more minutes. The spray occasionally mists my face, the cooling sensation of the water a balm against my heated skin.

"We should get this water," he says.

I agree, but I don't know how. There's a barrier between us and the pool where the fountains are.

"You stay here," he says. "I don't want you to get in trouble."

"Worth!" I say. "Don't—"

But before I can finish, he's off. He slips effortlessly through the crowd to the other side, where the balustrading ends. Then he jumps over a barrier like he's some kind of Olympic athlete, and extends his arm, plunging the empty water bottle into the pool.

I scan the crowds, looking for security closing in on him. There's a security guard coming up behind him, but Worth has got what he needs. He screws the lid on the now-full bottle before making his way back across the barrier. The security guard meets him on the other side. The two of them have an exchange of words that ends in a handshake.

Worth looks up and meets my eyes as he stalks back to me.

"You got caught," I say.

He shrugs. "What are they going to do, arrest me for stealing water?"

"Borrowing," I correct him.

"Exactly. We can bring it back the day after the wedding."

When we get back in the car, he hands me the bottle and I tuck it into the pocket in the back of the front seat. It's not a great option for borrowed, but at least we have something.

"Let's do the Vegas sign now," he says to the driver. "We need to up our game."

When we reach the sign, we hop out of the car.

"I'll take your picture," he says, pulling out his phone. I adjust the collar of my shirt, hoping it's straight, then hold my arms outstretched. He pushes his Wayfarers to the top of his head and holds up his phone.

"You're fucking beautiful," he says as he takes the pictures.

My stomach rises and falls and I don't know what to say. But again, he's not looking for a response.

"Now your turn," I say as he lowers his sunglasses.

He shakes his head, slings his arm around my shoulders, turns us, and holds out the phone for a selfie.

I stare at the still image he's just captured.

We both look so happy. He looks so gorgeous, anyone would think he was a movie star or a model or something.

"Come on," he says, scooping up my hand and pulling me into the car. "Next stop."

"Do you think we need to get someone to loan us something?" I ask as we pull back out onto the street. "Or do we buy something and loan it to Leo and Jules?"

"Either would qualify. What could we buy for a hundred dollars?" he asks.

"What about the necklace you gave us," I suggest. "I could loan her that. It's the most expensive thing I own. But she does already have one exactly the same."

A smile curls around his lips at my lame suggestion, and I have the urge to press my fingers against his mouth, feeling the way it moves under my touch.

"Is she looking for expensive or thoughtful?" he asks. "Meaningful?"

"I don't have anything with me." I have a trinket box at home with things inside that might have qualified: a shell I found by the lake the first summer we went to the cabin, a small ceramic duck I took into all my exams in college, and the silver dollar coin my dad gave me on my sixth birthday. He told me it was magic. For years, when Dad went away, I'd take the silver dollar everywhere I went. I'd turn it over and over in my hand, thinking of my father working hard for us, sacrificing his time with us so we could have the life he wanted for us.

But it was all a lie.

That dollar has the Statue of Liberty on one side, her hand thrust in the air. On the other side is etched a boat with the words, "The Love of Liberty Brought us Here."

That coin wasn't magic—it was an excuse. It was a symbol of his worship of liberty and freedom. But he didn't want freedom from governmental tyranny. He wanted to live free from responsibility and loyalty. He twisted what should be great to fit his selfishness and cowardice.

"You okay?" Worth slips his hand over mine, and I nod.

"Did you get bad news in Cincinnati?"

His question takes the breath from my lungs, and I snap my head around to look at him sitting across from me in the car. The colors and sounds of the Strip are shut out, and all I can think about is how Worth is inside my head.

"I don't—I can't—I have—yes," I say finally. "I got some bad news. But I don't want Jules to know," I say quickly. "I don't want to take the attention away from her and Leo's weekend."

"So you haven't told her. And she won't hear it from me."

I nod, grateful for his promise. "Thank you. I am... processing things and..." I think about how Worth has been so honest with me. Should I tell him? "Being with you is..." He waits for me to finish the sentence, but I'm not sure how it ends. "You're like the fountain. Pretty to look at, even though I'm not quite sure I should be finding you pretty and cooling. An ice pack for my bruise." I realize I'm acknowledging the attraction between us, but it's hard not to between his hand-holding and his focused attention. The way he called me beautiful.

"A distraction maybe," he says, and there's no tinge of bitterness to his words.

"Maybe. I don't know." If I hadn't been to Cincinnati last weekend, I think I may have been more flirtatious with Worth. I have no doubt he finds me attractive, and usually, that's the only cue I need to be into someone. But I'm holding back this time.

Maybe I'm thinking too much about this.

The driver points out the big hotels as we travel down the Strip. Worth and I sit in comfortable silence. We travel into downtown Vegas, which feels more like a normal town, but a little flashier.

"On your left is the Clark County Marriage License Bureau," the driver says. "Open until midnight for those couples who like to do things last minute."

"I don't think I'll ever get married," I say.

"Really?" he asks. "Why?"

I sigh. "Because I've always thought my parents had a perfect marriage and we had a perfect childhood, and now my parents are getting divorced because my dad's been a complete selfish idiot." My voice cracks as I finish my sentence.

Worth pulls a tissue from the box in the door and hands it to me.

"I don't want to be sad. I want to be mad."

"There's room for both," he says.

I like the way he doesn't ask any questions. He doesn't sound horrified or outraged. He's allowing me to have all the space I need.

I lay my head on his shoulder and he pulls me closer.

SIX

Worth

I can't remember the last time I enjoyed not doing anything in particular. I thrive on having a sense of purpose, but spending time with Sophia is... a revelation. I normally enjoy being productive. Helping. Hanging out with Sophia is different. I feel a sense of lightness that I'm not used to. She's going through some stuff, but being with her doesn't feel heavy. Or maybe she's not heavy when she's with me.

I button up my black shirt and tuck it into my slacks. After lunch I came back to my room to make a few calls before dinner, but I feel like I lost my right arm not having her by my side this afternoon. She would have looked good draped on my bed or on my knee while I talked some business associates off the cliff.

I press the button for the elevator, and as the doors open, before I can see who's in the elevator car, I know it's going to be her again. It's a weird feeling, but there's a surety that comes over me I haven't known before.

"Hey," I say as the doors open.

She half frowns, half smiles. Utterly breathtaking. "How do you always seem to know when I'm in the elevator?"

"It's just my good luck. You look beautiful." My eyes slide down her body as I step into the car. She's wearing a tight-fitting black dress with a deep V in the front that gives a glimpse of cleavage. Her hair is in a loose braid over one shoulder and she's wearing black boots with a high heel. It's a sexier look than last night, and I'm here for it.

"Can we have our time-outs tonight?" she asks. "At the bar, just the two of us?"

If I had my way, I'd spend the entire evening in time-out with this woman. I growl in appreciation of what she says and slip my hand to the small of her back. The elevator doors open and I guide her out.

"Oh, and I got something for the competition," I say. I hope she doesn't think it's showy, but I don't want Jules to be disappointed with our offering.

"You mean, something that might beat the water from the fountains at the Bellagio?"

"It depends how you look at it. I've brought the water, in case you want to go with that. We were a team. It should be a team decision." I pat the pocket of my slacks.

"Oh, so you're not just pleased to see me, then?" she asks on a grin.

"Never doubt that, Sophia. I'm always pleased to see you."

I reach into my other pocket and pull out the jewelry case. There's a sense of déjà vu from last night.

"We had a limit of one hundred dollars. Whatever's in there is bound to have cost more than that," she says, though it doesn't stop her from gently taking the box from my hands. She opens the lid and gasps at the solitaire diamond earrings within, each five carats. I think she likes them. "Jesus Christ. How much did they cost?"

"Nothing," I reply truthfully. "I called in a favor. They're on loan."

"How did you ever think that water from the Bellagio was going to beat these?"

"Well, the earrings are prettier, for sure," I say. "But there's no sentiment there."

"There's hardly sentiment in recycled water from a tourist attraction."

I chuckle. "Maybe not for you, but I'll remember this afternoon for a long while."

Her cheeks pink at my admission. We're in this no-man's-land where we both know we find each other attractive, but there's been no crossing of any lines. Yet. There's been no kiss, no hands on bare flesh, no bite. No whimper.

And given her... vulnerability at the moment, I'm not sure it will happen. Not this weekend anyway.

But there's an ache inside me that grows every time I see her. Every time I'm near her. It's like I've found someone I've been unknowingly searching for, and now I have to be patient a little longer. She needs to feel it too.

And I have to square things away with Fisher. I know he's not interested in Sophia, but I still have to make sure it's okay.

"We should give Jules both and she can decide," Sophia says.

"Are you ready to be beaten in this quest thing of Efa's?" Jack asks as we meet him at the entrance to The Angel Rooms. We're having dinner in the hotel again, though we're in a different restaurant tonight.

"Absolutely," Sophia says as I nod. We share a knowing look. We didn't find anything amazingly creative, but I did have one of my favorite days of my life. So I definitely won. Just not as far as Jack's concerned.

Jules squeals as we enter the room. Sophia and I part and go to opposite ends of the table, though I'm willing her to stay close tonight instead of keeping away. I've given in to my feelings. There's no denying them.

Once we're seated and have placed our orders, Efa announces we're each to reveal our offerings. I don't like to lose and I'm relieved we have something better than Bellagio water to set out in front of us at the table.

I'm sitting next to Fisher. I need to tell him tonight, even if things don't go any further with Sophia.

"Sophia and Jack, why don't you swap seats so you're each next to your partners," Efa says.

My chest lifts at Sophia being referred to as my partner. She feels like that on so many levels. But why? How? It's not like we've been dating... at all. But the moment I laid eyes on her, something inside me slotted into place. I feel a sense of peace I can't remember ever having before. None of it logical. None of it makes sense. And yet it completely does whenever she's near.

"Hey," she says as she sits next to me, giving me a sideways glance.

"Hey," I reply.

I glance across at Fisher. I need to speak to him.

"Okay, let's do 'old' first since it's Bennett and me and we were a complete disaster."

The vibration of Sophia's giggle reverberates against my thigh. "They ain't seen nothing yet," she whispers.

"Turns out a hundred dollars doesn't get you a lot in Vegas," Efa goes on.

Around the table there's a mumble of agreement.

"So, Leo and Jules, here is your something old." Efa produces a smooth, shiny rock. "I wrote your names and the date of your wedding on the back. Then Bennett varnished it."

"I never had you down as a crafter," Fisher says, chuckling.

The image of Bennett hunched over a table, varnishing a rock, is going to last a long time.

"Fuck you," Bennett says. "At least we put in some effort."

Jules is flapping at her face. "You guys are going to make me cry. Thank you so much." She gets up and hugs Efa and a reluctant Bennett. Then she takes the stone and hugs it to her chest.

"That was a good idea," Sophia says to me. "We should have thought of that."

I roll my eyes. "How would we feel right now if we were going to give them another stone?"

Sophia laughs. "Like losers."

"Okay, so what did Worth and Sophia get?" Efa asks.

Sophia and I glance at each other conspiratorially. "We have two options," I say.

I pull out the antique hip flask filled with water from the Bellagio. After lunch, I got the driver to take me to an antique shop and I picked up the silver flask for ninety dollars. I may well have paid ten times that amount for the pen I grabbed at the same time. I wanted to make sure I was following the rules. I hope Sophia's not too pissed at me. I just couldn't slide a Fiji water bottle onto the table. "This contains water borrowed from the fountains at the Bellagio. Alternatively"—I produce the earrings from my pocket—"we have earrings on loan from Bulgari."

Jules glances at Leo, and Sophia reaches for the earrings.

"They're really pretty," Sophia says as she opens the case and sets them down on the table.

"Wow," Jules says. "They're beautiful. I'm not sure I'd want to give them back."

"I'm sure I could arrange for you to keep them," Leo says.

Sophia pats me on the leg, excited, and I feel a sense of satisfaction for playing a part in her happiness.

Fisher and Jack's blue is a blue ribbon fashioned into a bow that could be affixed to the inside of Jules' dress. Leo and Jules broke the budget rules and splurged on a tennis bracelet.

Bennett and Efa win, and I can't bring myself to be mad about it. Spending the day with Sophia, just the two of us, more than made up for losing the game.

After the appetizers arrive, Sophia disappears from the table, and after a couple of minutes, I make my excuses and try to find her.

She's at the bar. Today, she's waiting, grinning at me, practically jumping up and down.

"She loved both," she says.

I nod, wondering whether or not it's possible to feel so much for someone you'd never laid eyes on three weeks ago. "Yeah, it turned out okay."

"I don't even care that we didn't win." She sighs. "I had such a good time today."

I slide my hand through my hair to try to stop myself from grinning like an idiot. "Me too."

"It feels good to be away," she says. "Like the version of me here can forget about things going on in Cincinnati. This me can be a little wild. A little crazy."

Our eyes lock. I want to kiss her so badly it actually hurts, but I don't want to overstep. She's going through a lot. "I want to kiss you," I admit.

Her hand slides over my chest. "I want that too. Very much."

I cup her face and press my lips against hers. The buzz I feel whenever I'm around her intensifies. She feels warm under my hand, soft and perfect. I take her bottom lip between my teeth and she gasps, pressing her body against mine.

I'm totally fucking one hundred percent *in* for this woman.

My tongue slides into her mouth and I feel myself falling deeper and deeper, like each touch binds us together, tighter and tighter.

Her hands slide up my sides and I shudder. Fuck, I want her. I want to feel her soft skin, all over every dip and curve. I want to run my tongue against every inch of her flesh and I want to fuck her in the fountains at the Bellagio.

But I know that at the end of it, I won't possess her—she'll possess me.

She pulls back slightly and our kiss breaks off, but she doesn't step back. Instead, she wraps her arms around me and puts her face to my chest. "Did everyone see?" she asks.

"We're in the middle of a bar, so anyone who saw me definitely thought I was the luckiest guy in Vegas."

I feel her smile against my shirt.

"We should get back to the table."

I sigh. She's right, but I don't want to move.

Fuck, I haven't spoken to Fisher yet. That has to be the next thing I do. "Yeah, we do," I say.

"I have to go to the restroom first." She drops her hands and steps back.

"See you back at the table."

I get back to the private room and catch Fisher's eye. I lift my chin and indicate with a sideways nod of my head that I want to speak to him.

"You okay?" he asks as we slip out to the restaurant lobby.

"Yeah. Just want to talk to you about something. You're not interested in Sophia, are you?"

He frowns. "No, I told you, getting involved with her would be messy."

I push my hand through my hair. "Right. So, I'm *very* interested in Sophia. Is that a problem?"

His eyes widen and a smile explodes on his face. "Worth! Dude, I'm happy for you. Is she into you?"

"Yeah."

"Of course she is. I mean, look at you, rich, handsome as fuck and there's no one more caring. Have some fun." He shrugs. "Or marry her. Good luck to you."

The words *marry her* ring in my ears.

We *are* in the wedding capital of America.

He slaps me on the back, and I feel like I've ticked that off my list. The only other possible wrinkle in our group is Jules. As Sophia's best friend, she's bound to be protective, but she wants her friend to be happy. I can't believe she would be anything but supportive.

"Just one more thing," I say, "don't mention it to anyone. Not even Jack. This is Leo and Jules' weekend. I don't want to take the spotlight off them in any way."

He taps his nose. "Sure thing."

We slip back into the dining room and the rest of dinner passes without incident. Sophia and I hold hands secretly under the table, but neither of us goes to the bar. Maybe we were both waiting for the kiss, and now that it's happened, we know that when dinner is over, it will happen again. There's no need to rush.

"So what's next?" Leo asks.

"Strip club?" Fisher asks. "It *is* the night before your wedding."

Leo, Bennett, and I groan.

Jules whispers something into Leo's ear.

"Then that's what we'll do," Leo says to her. He turns back to the table. "Jules and I are going to the Bellagio to watch the fountains. You guys can go to the strip club, play poker, whatever."

My blood starts to hum in my veins. That means I get to spend the rest of the night with Sophia.

"I'm definitely up for poker," Fisher says. "Anyone else?"

"Happy to witness you lose a lot of money," Jack says. "I'm definitely down for poker."

"Byron says he might make an appearance at the tables," Fisher says, scrolling on his phone.

"Bennett and I are going to make good use of the shower," Efa says with remarkably casual candor. "Unless you want to play poker?" she asks him.

"Rather than fuck my fiancée? I don't think so," he replies.

"What about you, Sophia?" Jules asks. "You want to come to the Bellagio with Leo and me?"

Sophia shakes her head. "I think I'll have an early night. Or maybe I'll watch the boys play poker or—something. Don't worry about me."

Everyone gets up and we file out of the dining room. When we reach the lobby, everyone disperses in different directions, leaving Sophia and me standing by ourselves.

Just how I wanted it.

SEVEN

Sophia

Kissing Worth was like nothing I'd ever experienced before. His lips erased everything in my mind so I could only think about him and how his hands felt against me. It transported me somewhere I didn't have to think, to worry, do anything but *be*. I want to hold on to the feeling forever.

"Shall we take a driver down the Strip?" Worth asks. "If you haven't seen it at night, you should probably cross it off your list."

"You're really selling it to me," I say.

"Never said I'd make the best tour guide."

I tilt my head. "But you are anyway."

Our ride is waiting. Hanging out with billionaires gives a different perspective on life. Nothing seems off-limits. Everything is right there, ready for you to pick up, drink in, enjoy.

"Were you always rich?" I ask as the driver pulls out onto the Strip.

"Absolutely not. My dad died when I was fourteen, and even though we'd never been rich, I'd never thought much about money.

Then after he passed…" He pulls in a breath and I smooth my hand over his thigh. He catches my fingers and slides his between mine. "Things got more difficult. In every way."

"Did your mom work?"

"She was a nurse, but she was hit hard by my dad's death. She… didn't cope very well."

"I can't even imagine." In the week since I found out about my dad's betrayal, I've struggled to understand why my mom stayed with him. But maybe his complete absence would have been worse than his partial presence. She says she wanted us to have a good childhood, but how did she pull that off? How did she manage not to let it eat her up?

"But we're all through the other side. My little sister just graduated from Yale."

"Yale, huh? That's amazing. How many siblings do you have?" It feels like I've known this man my entire life, but I don't know anything about him really. I just know that he feels like solid rock compared to the waves of my rage.

"Two younger sisters. My parents had me young, when Dad was still in college. So they waited a while before having Avril and Poppy. My dad died when Poppy, my older sister, was six."

I think about Worth as a fourteen-year-old, having spent the first decade of his life the only child of two young parents, then to get two siblings and lose a father all in a short space of time. It must have been so difficult for him.

"You think that's why you became successful?" I ask.

"I do. I knew my mom couldn't take care of herself. And Avril and Poppy were just babies. I knew it was down to me."

His words feel like a drag on my insides. What a burden for a child of fourteen. "Your mom was depressed?"

"Couldn't get out of bed most days. Dad had a life insurance policy that paid out and took care of the house. And it took care of some of the bills, like medical insurance and daycare. But I knew it wouldn't last forever, and it wasn't going to cover college or a new car or a new roof. So I did what I needed to do."

"Worth," I say, trying to convey how sorry I am for what he went through.

"It was a long time ago. Anyway, we should talk about something more suited to the Vegas Strip," he says.

"Like how you're the kind of guy a girl should marry in the Little White Wedding Chapel and never let go?"

"We'll end the evening that way." His tone is completely serious, without any trace of humor. He checks his watch. "We have an hour and a half before the wedding bureau closes. Let's get a drink at Ghostbar first. The views from there are the best we're going to get."

I can't help but laugh at his lack of enthusiasm, and a small smile curves around his lips. I'm not sure if he's smiling at my amusement or something else. I feel so safe with him, I want to know every expression he has and what they all mean.

GHOSTBAR IS on the 55th floor of the Ivory Tower, with sweeping views of the Strip. It feels like we're overlooking a fireworks display, bursting with color and light.

Worth has bought a bottle of tequila that looks like it cost more than I earn in a year and tastes even better. I'm two shots in, and with Worth by my side, it feels like everything other than *right now* is ten thousand miles away. I don't need to worry about any of it.

"It feels like we're flying above the city up here," I say. "It's so much brighter than New York."

"Flashier," Worth says.

"Yeah, but there's more energy, like it's a dream version of New York where you can create your own reality."

"Where you can get married to a perfect stranger?" he asks.

"Exactly," I say. "I totally get why people get married here on a whim."

"You wanna try it?" he asks me, fixing me with a look that tells me he's totally serious.

"Do I wanna try what?" I tease. I know what he's suggesting, but I want to hear him say the words.

"Wanna marry me?"

It's ridiculous, but the question pulls at me, like my instincts are all reaching toward Worth and the promise of more.

"I think I do!" I say. I bite down on my lip, knowing how crazy that sounds.

"You said you would never get married."

"Not in my real life, but this is Vegas."

I bend, pour us two more shots, and hand one to Worth.

"What about when we get back to New York?" he asks.

I shrug and throw back my shot. "Let's worry about tomorrow, tomorrow." I'm sure twenty percent of the Vegas economy is based around undoing the bad decisions of the night before. Right now, I just want to prolong this feeling of freedom—freedom based on truth and not lies.

"I've made a lot of money by making sure I take opportunities when they're presented to me." He tips back his shot.

He pulls out his wallet and puts a lot of money on the table, not bothering to count how much. He picks up the tequila bottle, scoops up my hand, and stalks toward the exit.

The driver doesn't even bat an eye when Worth asks him to take us to the wedding license bureau.

"Didn't we drive past there this morning?" I ask Worth. "You think our driver knew we'd be coming back?"

"Maybe," Worth replies. "Maybe JJ can see this thing between us."

"This *thing*?"

"The thing we feel. You feel it, just like I do," he says. "Like we've known each other for decades, like I can see what you're thinking before you say it. Like I can feel when you enter the room without even looking around."

I close my eyes in a long blink as my heart expands in my chest. It isn't just me. He feels it too.

"Maybe you didn't get it right away at that brunch. I did. The moment I laid eyes on you, I just..." He shakes his head. "I can't explain it other than to say that I knew I'd know you a long time. Maybe for forever."

My breath hitches in my throat. He's so earnest and open. I want to climb him like a tree and kiss him... everywhere.

"I felt it here in Vegas," I admit. "And I was disappointed you weren't on the plane. I thought you weren't coming. So I guess I did get it at the brunch."

"I didn't travel on the plane because I thought it would be obvious to everyone how much I felt for you. And you and Fisher..."

"Had no connection whatsoever," I finish the sentence for him.

"Right, but he's my friend and I didn't know that yet, so I was trying to distance myself. To give you both space."

I lean over to him and place a kiss on his cheek. "No more space necessary."

He growls and slides his hand around my back. Just as he starts to pull me onto his lap, the car stops and the driver announces we've arrived.

"It's just past eleven," the driver says. "You'll be out in ten minutes. I'll be waiting."

I laugh. He's obviously done this before.

And he's almost right. Worth and I emerge less than fifteen minutes later, with a marriage license with our names on it.

"Are you sure you want to do this?" I ask. "You don't strike me as the kind of guy who gets married on the fly."

"I'm not," he says as he opens the car door and gestures for me to get in. "But I'm sure. Are you?"

I look him right in the eye. "I'm sure." And even though I shouldn't be, I'm completely and utterly certain that I want to do this.

He slides in next to me and the driver turns the car around. "Do you know where you want to get married? Little White Chapel is obviously the most famous."

"We can't go there," I say. "That's where Leo and Jules are getting married tomorrow."

"Right," Worth says. "Is there anywhere you recommend?" he asks the driver.

"We just had the New York Loves Vegas Chapel open up just this week. That might suit you folks. Plus it's probably not that busy, being new and all."

Worth and I stare at each other, dumbfounded by the idea of a new chapel opening up with New York in its name. "Sounds like it has our names written all over it," Worth says. "Let's do it there."

We pull over to the side of the road, where the New York Loves Vegas Chapel boasts a skyscraper instead of a steeple. It's ridiculous and perfect at the same time.

"I might need a swig of tequila right about now," I say, reaching for the bottle.

"We don't have to do this," Worth says.

"I know," I say. "I want to. I just need a little kick to remind myself that I'm in Vegas and the real world doesn't exist." I take a swig and follow Worth out of the car.

I take his hand and nod my head in the direction of the entrance to the chapel.

"I'm serious," he says. "This is fun and silly and not in either of our natures, but it's legally binding. We don't have to go through with it if you don't want to."

"I want to," I assure him. I step onto my tiptoes and manage to press a kiss to his jaw. It starts an ignition button in him, and he strides toward the chapel with me barely keeping up.

Our driver was correct. There's no line. After filling out some paperwork and flashing our new license, we're standing in front of the altar opposite each other.

"I didn't know your last name was Huntington," I say.

"I'm not expecting you to take it."

I start to laugh. This is ridiculous. I'm marrying a man whose last name I just discovered. This is not the kind of girl I am. I'm from the Midwest.

"Good," I manage.

"You're not going to ask me to take yours, are you?" he asks, his frown deepening.

I tilt my head as if I'm considering it. "I think Worth Jones would suit you, if that's what you're asking. It's not as sexy as Worth Huntington though."

His eyes turn to molten heat and he dips to kiss me just as the minister interrupts us.

"Are you ready?"

Worth looks into my eyes as he speaks his vows. His expression is serious and earnest, as if we're really pledging ourselves to each other.

I suppose we are.

For now.

I repeat the vows next, promising to take Worth as my husband, to have and to hold.

I zone out for a second. I'm completely up for *having* Worth. He's gorgeous and built like a redwood. But if we have sex after this ceremony, doesn't that consummate our marriage and make an annulment more difficult?

Worth squeezes my hand. Any concerns I have melt away.

"To have and to hold," the minister repeats. "From this day forward."

"To have and to hold, from this day forward," I say, gazing into Worth's eyes and knowing as sure as anyone can be sure that this is the most honest, caring man I've ever met.

As the minister pronounces us husband and wife, Worth cups my face in his big hands and kisses me, like I just made him the happiest man on earth.

I think the feeling might be mutual.

EIGHT

Worth

It sounds ridiculous, but I feel different—even more protective of Sophia, if that's possible. I just got married on the fly, but it's as if I spoke vows in front of all my friends and family, in a ceremony that took two years to prepare, to a woman who I'd known for five.

I slide my hand up the back of her thigh as we get into the elevator. She hits floor fifteen and I growl, because the idea of waiting fifteen floors until she's naked seems interminable.

"I want you," she breathes against my cheek as I press my lips to her neck.

I dip my hand between her thighs and my fingers hit lace just before her knees buckle.

"How much tequila did you drink?" I ask. We can get unmarried, but we can't un-have sex. I want her fully lucid when I fuck her.

"Why?" she asks breathlessly.

"I want to know if you're..."

"Oh," she says, her tone almost alarmed. "I'm one hundred and twenty percent consenting to this. Like, I'm going to be pissed if you don't fuck me."

I laugh as the elevator doors slide open.

"My room is right here," she says, taking a key from her purse.

"In front of the elevators?" I ask and pull in a breath, wondering how loud she's going to scream when she's underneath me.

She lets us in and kicks off her shoes as soon as we get through the door. Then she spins to face me.

"Where do you—"

"Everywhere," I say. I take the shoulders of her dress and pull them down. The fabric falls in a pool at her feet.

I have to close my eyes in a long blink, I'm so overwhelmed at the sight of her naked.

"You're fucking beautiful," I say, opening my eyes. "Fuck." I'm going to have to keep it together tonight. I already never want this to end, and it hasn't even started.

She starts to unbutton my shirt. I pull at her nipple, the tip of my thumb flicking the hard nub, and Sophia gasps at my touch.

"Worth," she whispers, hands stilling. "Don't break me."

"Never," I say, and shrug off my unbuttoned shirt. I pull out my wallet from my pants and toss it on the desk, making a mental note to remember where I left it. That's where my condoms are.

"You're so tall," she says.

"You like it."

"I really do." She nods in appreciation, and I kick out the legs of the desk chair, strip my pants off, and sit.

I'm hard, straining at the ceiling, and Sophia looks at my cock like she's hungry.

Fuck, I can barely wait to slide inside her.

I pull her toward me and she sits astride, so we're facing each other.

"Now we're the same height," I say, cupping her face. "Almost."

Her fingers thread into my hair and we kiss. I pull her closer still, so she slots against me, the lace of her underwear the only barrier between us. Her nipples scrape against my chest and her hips sway on my lap, grinding closer and closer, and it's so fucking good, I can barely stand it.

Sophia's right—being together feels freeing. In my previous relationships, I felt stifled and caged in, but I'm married to the woman on my lap and I've never felt so light and liberated.

She stills and pulls back. "Promise me one thing, Worth."

"Anything." Blood is pounding in my veins like it's trying to set an Olympic record, my heart is clattering against my chest, and my dick is so hard I'm not sure I'll survive putting the condom on.

"No lies. This might be over tomorrow or next week or never. We might stay together, raise kids, and grow old together. But no matter what happens, don't ever lie to me."

"I promise," I say. "I'm going to take care of your heart, Sophia." Gazing into her eyes, I realize they aren't just blue, but have purple flecks that look like flowers unfurling under the sun's heat. I know we're not going to be over tomorrow. Or next week. The more I get to know this woman, the more I'm going to fall for her.

She takes my palm and presses it over her panties. They're soaked through. It calms me to think she's been waiting for this moment too, thinking about it, fantasizing about it.

I can't do anything but grunt in appreciation. I want to feel that wetness on my tongue, around my dick, down my chin.

"They need to come off," I hiss.

I'm dizzy with need for her. I want to fuck her so hard she won't stand for a week, and I want to take my time, smoothing my hands over her body, placing chaste kisses to every dip and curve of her. I want it all.

I can't remember ever wanting anyone or anything in the way that I want Sophia right now. So much of my life has been about avoiding disaster, I don't think I've ever let myself get pulled in by someone this way. I want her to the exclusion of all else—and this tunnel vision means I'm not looking out for potential problems on the horizon. Right now, the world could burn for all I care.

She stands and shimmies off her underwear.

I hold out my hand. "I'll take those," I say.

"My underwear?"

I nod. I toss them on the desk. Then I clamp my hand around my cock and pull it up and over my crown. "Come sit," I say.

She bites down on her lip and her mouth flushes red.

I shake my head slowly. "I'll be gentle," I say.

"You might break me in half."

"I'll go slow," I say.

Her eyelids flutter, like she's imagining what I might feel like filling her up. My heartbeat pounds in my ears: *now, now, now.*

I have to work backwards tonight. I need to fuck. I need to come. We both need that. Then I can lick and suck and bite and we can do it all over.

"Do you have a condom that will fit?" she asks, her expression genuinely worried.

I grab my wallet and pull out a condom, rolling it on in record time. "Come sit," I repeat.

I hold out my hand and she takes it tentatively, stepping forward, climbing back on my lap, lifting herself up.

Her breasts sway in front of me and I cup one in my hand and squeeze. She groans as I pinch the puckered flesh.

She hooks her feet back on my legs so she's kneeling over me. My crown finds her entrance.

"Please go slow," she says.

"It's going to feel so good," I promise her.

"Promise?"

"So good," I say. "You're going to come so many times tonight."

I run my fingers up her spine and her back arches. The crown of my cock sinks into her.

She lets out a small, startled scream.

"That's right," I say. "Open up for me," I say.

Just her warmth on my tip has me half crazed. She feels so good.

I run my hands over her ass and pull her down a little farther, sinking deeper into her. She lets out a low, guttural moan.

"See how good that feels?" I ask, my jaw tight, my dick hard as a fucking baseball bat.

Her eyebrows are knitted together, like she can't quite believe what she's feeling, but she nods. "So good," she whispers. "So big. So hard."

Jesus, she's going to kill me.

She sinks down farther onto me, her hands gripping my forearms like she might fall apart if she doesn't hold on.

But I won't let her.

I just don't know how long I can let her set the pace here. I want to flip her over the desk and fuck her right onto the Strip.

She pulls up a little and our eyes meet. She sinks down, lower this time. I send up a silent prayer of gratitude. She feels so fucking tight, so warm. So mine.

And she is mine. My wife. I'm fucking my beautiful, sexy, tight wife.

Or she's fucking me. For now.

She starts to move with more confidence, lifting herself up and sinking down on me, lower each time, punctuated by moans and gasps. Her hands move to my shoulders and she tips her head back. Whisps of her hair trail against my thighs, setting every nerve ending in my body on high alert.

Finally I sink to the hilt inside her, and she lets out a breath.

"I can't believe you're inside me," she gasps. "I feel so full."

I slide my hands over her hips and pull her toward me. "You feel fucking gorgeous," I say.

She smiles shyly at me and begins to move her hips. Her movements are small but the sensations are explosive. I don't know if it's because she's setting the pace, or because we just got married, or because I feel so fucking lucky to be anywhere near this woman, but being inside her is intense. Like this isn't *just* sex. It's much more than that.

"What are you thinking about?" she asks on an exhale.

"How good you feel," I respond. "How fucking lucky I am."

She moans and pushes deeper onto me.

I press my mouth to her lips and start to move her hips. I need more of her. Right. Now.

"Worth," she whispers into my mouth.

"We both need this," I growl.

"But I'm—" She doesn't finish her sentence. Instead she convulses around me like her orgasm has been waiting, just an inch away, for an hour.

The vibrations on my dick break through all my defenses and my orgasm rushes through me. I push my hips up, animal instinct taking over, driving me to bury my come deep.

Damn that fucking condom.

She collapses in my arms. After a moment I stand, scooping her up. I dispose of the condom and take her to the bed.

Now I can get to work.

I lay her out, body limp and satiated. For now.

I crawl between her thighs. Her pussy is still swollen from my dick. This time I'm going to make her come on my tongue.

"Worth," she says, propping herself up on her elbows. "You don't have to do that."

I frown. "I want to," I say.

She doesn't look convinced. "Are you sure? I just—"

"Am I sure that I want to taste you, make you wet, feel you vibrate around my mouth, make you come? Yeah, I'm fucking sure I want to do all of that."

She still doesn't look like she's convinced.

"It's just..."

"What? You don't like it?"

"I do, but I just don't climax like that. I don't want you to be offended."

I can't help but laugh. Partly because she's being so goddamn polite, but partly because she's very much mistaken. She's going to come so hard, they're going to hear it over at the Bellagio.

"Just relax. I don't want you to come," I say.

She slumps down onto the bed and I prop myself up from where I'm situated between her legs. "Do you hear me? No coming. If you dare come on my tongue, I'm going to flip you over and fuck you so hard, you're not going to be able to walk down that aisle tomorrow, do you understand?"

She nods her head, and I settle back down between her thighs. I slip my hands under her ass, licking slowly up and down her folds, enjoying the way she shifts underneath me, half trying to resist, half wanting more. I circle her clit with my tongue, flicking and pressing before pushing deeper. I can taste her juices. She's so wet, so slick under my tongue, across my chin. I'm growing hard against my stomach again.

I push my thumb into her and she moans, my fingers spreading her folds so I can get closer, deeper, have more of her. I twist and pull my hand, alternating fingers, pushing two in, curling and pressing, my tongue licking over and over and over. She's writhing underneath me, the movements that started so small and unsure now growing into something primal. She's losing control.

Her fingers grip my hair and she calls out my name. "Worth."

I withdraw my fingers and my tongue. "I said no coming."

"Worth. Please," she begs.

She tries to grab my hair, but I dodge her. "Do you hear me, Sophia? No coming."

She nods hopelessly.

I go back to work and she's helpless in seconds. I feel her body tense, her back arch as she rocks her pussy against my face. Her breathing goes jagged and she tries to move away from me. She's trying to resist her orgasm. But I want her to come. I want her to suffer the consequences. I'm going to fuck her so hard, she's not going to be able to stand.

I pin her down, my palm flat over her lower stomach, holding her in place while I lick and suck until her entire body is vibrating as she climaxes on my tongue, just like she told me she couldn't.

NINE

Sophia

Worth's friends describe him as the kindest, wisest, most dependable man in New York.

I've discovered he's all those things. He's also the dirtiest.

I've never really enjoyed a man going down on me. In my previous experiences, the guys never knew what they were doing. They didn't do it for long enough, and I always felt pressure to come two minutes ago—like slow-building pleasure was an inconvenience.

It's not like that with Worth.

He *instructed* me not to come.

Instructed me. Commanding and domineering. It's... unexpected.

I haven't known him for long, but Worth doesn't strike me as a man who commands anyone to do anything. He's the ultra-polite guy who tips thirty percent and helps old ladies cross the street.

Except this Worth—*bedroom* Worth—isn't polite at all.

He presses down on my lower stomach, and I gasp. What's he doing? He's sliding his fingers into me, his thumb rubbing against one part of me, his tongue on every other part. I'm lost in sensation.

His instructions were clear—I'm not to climax under any circumstances, but I don't have a choice. He's doing things to me I'm not sure are legal. There's no way I can stave off the orgasm that's been circling me for the last few minutes.

I take a deep breath, trying to give myself a few more minutes, but it doesn't work. He needs to stop touching me like that. Stop doing the things he's doing to me with his tongue.

The thought dissolves as soon as I have it. I don't want him to stop anything. I want to stay like this, my legs around Worth's neck for the rest of my life. I cry out. The pleasure is so intense, so deep, so enveloping, I can't feel where I end and he begins.

I try to twist, to remove myself, to get out from underneath him so I don't break my word and climax, but he's got me pinned to the bed. There's no escape.

The thought is the final string left of my resolve and I call out his name as I surrender to my orgasm and convulse under his tongue.

I haven't moved, but my heart is telling me I just ran a marathon. I can't catch my breath. I'm boneless and limp.

"Oh dear." Worth's voice comes like a roll of thunder. "You promised me you wouldn't come, but I can taste your climax on my tongue."

Oh god, I've never found a man as sexy as I do Fully Clothed Worth, but Naked Worth, chastising me for climaxing in his mouth, might have the ability to make me come without even touching me.

"Worth." My voice comes out dreamily, like I'm waking up from anesthesia or something.

"You know what that means, don't you?" he asks, his face dark and serious. I squirm with need. His cock is rearing, hard and huge in front of me, and I can't wait to feel it again, even though the idea is mildly terrifying.

Because Worth is packing.

He's not the guy in the friend group that screams Big Dick Energy, but I guess his dick is so big, he doesn't have any need to prove anything to anyone.

He was so sweet and gentle to me the first time, before my first orgasm. It was just what I needed. And I guess he gave me what I needed just now, because I've never come from a guy's tongue before.

Worth seems to know me in the bedroom, better than *I* know me in the bedroom.

A small smile curls my lips. "It means, I win?" I suggest.

He lifts his chin. "How's that?"

"Because you're going to fuck me so hard, they're going to hear me over at Ceasars Palace?"

He growls, the sound so fucking masculine, I can barely stand it. He grabs my ankle, flips me over and pulls me to the edge of the bed. My toes touch the floor, my stomach on the mattress, and Worth is between my legs.

"Face down," he barks and grabs a pillow. "Cover your mouth."

I take the pillow and lay it under me, as I'm vaguely aware of Worth putting on another condom.

I let out a small, contented sigh and then my body tenses as he spreads my legs farther apart.

"Ass up," he says.

Shit, I hope he's careful. He might very well split me in two, although I'm so wet, I could probably take anything right now.

I moan as he circles his crown at my entrance, dipping it down my sex before sliding it back up and in. Right. Up. To. The. Hilt.

I scream, but not in pain—in pure pleasure.

"Face in the pillow." Intensity laces his words.

He pulls out and I bury my face in the pillow and scream again. He just feels so good. He fills me up so completely, there's no room for anything else in my body, not even air.

"You feel that?" He slams into me again. "You're going to feel it all day tomorrow. Every time you move, you're going to feel the scrape of my stubble between your legs, the pinch of my fingers on your nipples, and my cock driving into this pussy.

"I'm going to sit next to you tomorrow," he hisses out between gritted teeth, "and we're going to watch our friends get married and all you're going to be thinking about is how long it's going to be until I'm fucking you again."

"Yes," I choke out. I know it's true. The instant I laid eyes on Worth, I felt a spark of something. The more time I spent with him, the more time I wanted to spend with him. He's sexy and kind and thoughtful and wise.

And he's *phenomenal* at fucking me.

My hands grip the bedsheets and he thrusts in again with a grunt. The sound travels through my body and connects right between my legs.

He leans over my body, not breaking his rhythm, slamming into me over and over.

I reach back, wanting to feel him, wanting more from him, like that's even possible.

He slides his arms underneath me, giving me the connection I want. He uses the contact as an anchor, holding me still so he can fuck me harder. I'm trying everything I can not to come, but I have nothing left.

I'm breathless.

I'm exhausted.

I'm utterly boneless.

Then one hand snakes down and his fingers round my clit. I explode on contact. The stubble on his chin scrapes my cheek and he half licks, half bites my jaw. "Good girl."

Somehow he turns me around and positions me on my back on the bed.

"You're so beautiful, Sophia," he whispers into my ear as he leans over me.

He slides into me again and it's like the first time I ever felt him inside me. I'm impossibly full. Every part of me feels him.

"Too much?" he asks, his gaze dipping from my eyes, down to my open mouth, and then back up.

I shake my head. It's not too much. It's exactly enough and I can't imagine ever wanting it to end. All at once, images of my life back in

New York flash into my brain, and it feels empty, like they're black and white, because he's not in them too. We got married on a whim. There was something between us and we were in Vegas and we could worry about the consequences tomorrow. At this moment, though, the only thing I'm worried about is that he'll want a divorce. I don't want my black-and-white life back in New York. I want a life in full color.

Sweat gathers at Worth's hairline. It's good to know he's not a machine. I press my fingers down his back and he rears up, like I've just turned him on so much he can't stand it. His back is tight and hard, just like every other part of him. He seems bigger out of his clothes. Taller and more muscular than I'd expected.

He pushes into me and a moan escapes my throat. My climax was lying at the foot of the Red Rock Canyon sixty seconds ago, but Worth has managed to bring it to life again. I shift underneath him and he hisses out a curse.

I bite back a smile. It's good to know that this man hulking over me, who seems to be the god of sex, isn't completely immune to my moves.

I squeeze his cock as he pulls out of me and he fixes me with a stare.

"Are you trying to make me come?"

"I'm trying to make you feel a small fraction of what you make me feel."

"I couldn't feel anything more than I do at this moment. You would just have to bite down on that lip again and it would push me over the edge."

I can't help myself. The idea that I could have power over this *oh-so-powerful* man is too tempting. I lick my lips and bite down.

He groans and thrusts up, up, up before collapsing on top of me.

I don't even catch my breath before he's moving. Cool air hits my body, goose bumps smattering my skin. I yearn for him back. In only seconds, I miss how he keeps me covered, keeps me warm, keeps me safe.

I hear the sound of something hitting the trash and then the tear of a condom wrapper.

Again?

His thighs hit mine and he lifts me and throws me back onto the mattress. He crawls over me, his eyes greedy.

"I'm hard again," he growls. "What are you doing to me?"

He lifts my knee and looks between my thighs, like he's inspecting me. And I'm his to inspect. It feels like he peeled off every layer of me until he got to the core. Like he sees everything, all of it, even parts of me I didn't know existed.

He knows me.

His eyes lock on mine as he pushes into me, and I feel a mixture of relief and rapture and total goddamn bliss.

"Feel that?" he asks. His jugular pulses in his neck and his jaw tightens.

I smooth my finger over his lips and sigh. "I feel everything." I've never done drugs, but I imagine this is what it feels like—everything brighter, more, better.

"It's fucking perfection."

I'm mesmerized by the rhythm of his hips pushing into me, over and over, the muscles in his arms flexing as he holds me in place. He's big in every sense, but so gentle. So kind. So incredibly sexy.

He grinds deeper and it catches my breath. "Worth," I gasp. "It's so deep. So deep."

He pushes in again and heaves out a breath like he can't quite believe what he's feeling.

Sliding his hand up my body, his gaze flits between his fingers and my eyes. Every touch ratchets up my bliss and I feel like I'll pass out if he doesn't stop. He anchors his hand on my waist and shoves up inside me. His sharp, fast movements shift things and I lose control.

I'm vaguely aware of the noises I'm making, but I can't stop. I can't worry about who can hear. I can't do anything but feel.

He leans over me, his stubbled cheek against mine, and whispers in my ear, "I want to do this forever."

My orgasm starts to vibrate around his dick and pushes outward, down, deep in my belly, and across and over my entire body.

He groans in my ear and tenses on top of me, his orgasm hitting a second after mine.

I wrap my arms and legs around him, wanting to pull him closer, wanting to float up and into him. Wanting to stay just like this for as long as I can.

TEN

Sophia

Jules looks absolutely gorgeous sitting in her robe, sipping a glass of champagne while a makeup artist perfects her bridal look.

"Considering how hard we've partied the last couple of nights, we all look fantastic," Efa says, putting her earrings in. They're small diamond studs. Bennett is just as rich as all the rest of them, but it's nice that she's chosen such modest jewelry.

"You look fantastic because you're thirteen," Jules says.

"We are practically the same age," she says.

Jules and I share a look. "The beginning of your twenties looks very different to the end," Jules says to Efa.

"It does for you," I say. "You're off the market. About to be a married woman."

"You're next," she says.

I smile. Worth and I haven't spoken much about the wedding. It was a spur-of-the-moment decision. It wasn't like we were committing the rest of our lives to each other.

But the sex last night? I can't help thinking that if we hadn't said those vows before, it wouldn't have been so intense.

Or maybe it would, given the size of Worth's dick.

I bite back a smile.

"So it's definitely a no to Fisher," Efa says. It's not a question, more a summation. "And Jack definitely isn't ready for commitment. Have you thought about Worth?"

My cheeks burn like the sun. I hope I've got enough makeup on to hide it.

"He's a really great guy," Jules says.

"A great guy," I say.

"Not really your type, but that might not be a bad thing," Jules says.

I sigh. "Yeah. Not my usual type." I'm not lying. I normally would have chosen someone who was... absent. Looking back at my previous relationships, I'd picked men who were very much like my father. Jamie was physically absent, as he lived in Florida and worked on yachts. He wasn't even in the same country for a lot of our relationship. He could have had ten other girlfriends and I would never have known. Other guys I've dated were similar. They worked nights, or were focused on their bands' gigs, or whatever. There was always a reason for me to take a back seat in their lives.

I wasn't the priority for any of them.

Maybe it was because we were in our twenties and that's how it was meant to be. Or maybe it's because that's how I *thought* it was meant to be. My role model was a man who had another family in the next town over. His focus was never just us.

Jules is right. Worth is nothing like any of the men I'd dated before.

"So do you like him?" Efa asks. "Even if he's not your type. I mean, Bennett was very definitely not my type, and he's the love of my life."

Efa and Jules stare at the mirror, their eyes on me.

I shrug. "Maybe," I say.

They both *ahhh* at the same time.

"He's so nice," Efa says. "Bennett always goes to him for advice."

"Leo is the same. He says Worth is the dad of the group. That shouldn't put you off though. He's lovely."

And has a huge dick and knows exactly what to do with it, I don't say.

"Marriage material," Efa says.

I take a swig of champagne to cover any reaction I might be having. The last thing I want to do is let it slip that Worth and I got married last night. I don't want the focus on anything but my best friend and the man lucky enough to marry her today.

My phone buzzes once, then twice. I'm thankful for the distraction.

It's the group chat with my brothers.

Noah: Mom just called me to ask me if I can do decorations for Thanksgiving.

Oliver: What decorations?

Noah: For Dad's birthday.

"What?" I ask out loud.

"You okay?" Jules asks.

I smile and shove my phone back in my pocket, trying to ignore the pounding of my heart. "Fine, just my brothers being dicks." This is the last thing I need right now. Why would we be celebrating Thanksgiving with Dad? We're going to be with *Mom.* How is anyone considering this?

"When are they going to settle down?" Jules asks.

My dad never settled down. His genetic offspring probably never will, either.

"Don't wish that on a woman," I say.

"I think we're done," the makeup artist says.

"Dress time," I say, thankful for the focus being off me and my brothers and Worth.

"Have you thought about a honeymoon?" Efa asks.

"Leo wants to go to Paris, but we both have work. We'll do something in the New Year." Jules shimmies off her robe and I take the dress from where it's hanging against the door.

"Life will be a honeymoon for you both," I say, unzipping the dress cover.

"Awww, that's such a nice way of looking at it," Jules says. "You're turning into a romantic."

Efa and I help Jules into her dress. It's not a typical wedding dress, but this isn't a typical wedding. It's simple white satin and hits her mid-thigh. It's backless but long-sleeved—elegant and sexy. If it were black, it would be perfect in New York, which means it's perfect for Vegas.

"It's gorgeous," I say.

"I love the way your hair is down," Efa says. "So sexy and relaxed. Leo is going to love it."

"Oh he does. He's seen it."

Efa squeals. "He's seen your dress?"

"It's not like we're doing anything else the traditional way."

There's a knock at the door, and I jump out of my skin.

"You okay?" Jules asks me. "You seem a little on edge."

"I'm fine," I say, heading to the door of the suite. "Was just so caught up in admiring the view. I'll get the door."

Luckily, Jules is getting dressed in the bedroom area, which can't be seen from the door. I pull the door open and come face-to-face with Worth. The painted-on smile I've been trying to perfect all morning morphs into a real one.

"Hey," I say. He looks hot as all holy fuck. The tux suits him. Maybe it's because I know the body hiding beneath that sharply cut suit, but I've never seen a better-looking man. He's had a shave, and his hair is pushed back. He looks like an Italian model or something.

"Hey," he replies, grinning at me. We didn't have much time to talk this morning. We were up most of the night *not* talking, and only woke with the alarm. Worth gave me a kiss that made me wet and needy, then left. "I have this for the bride." He produces a jewelry box and hands it to me. These boys sure do like to spend their money on jewelry. "It's from the groom," he says.

"Worth?" Jules shouts from the bedroom. "What's going on?"

"Just delivering a present," he calls back. "Which can also double as a status check. How close to ready are you?" He looks me up and down, his eyes heating as his gaze trails the length of my body. "You look good enough to eat," he whispers. "I'll look forward to every bite later."

I throb between my legs, ready for him instantly. I bite down hard on my bottom lip.

He growls and reaches for me, his hand skirting the inside of my thigh, traveling higher and higher.

"Worth wants to know how long we'll be?" I call out, trying to hide the strain in my voice as his fingers find the lace of my underwear.

"We're just zipping her into her dress," Efa calls. Worth's finger dips into my panties. "We're two minutes away from being done."

Worth removes his hand and puts his index finger in his mouth, then removes it with a pop. "Mmm," he hums. "So sweet."

Then he turns and strides down the hall, leaving me weak-kneed and flushed.

I let go of the door and turn, straightening my shoulders and swallowing. "I'm fine," I whisper under my breath.

"Leo sent you a gift," I say as I walk back into the bedroom area. I hand her the box.

Her eyes widen. She opens the red box to reveal a row of diamond stars forming a bracelet. We all gasp. It's beautiful.

"He has really good taste," I say.

"Well, it's not like there's much bad at Cartier," Jules says.

We help her fix the bracelet on and she gives us a twirl as we record her on our phones.

"Your last moments as a single woman," Efa says. "Do you have anything to say?"

I suppose I'm not technically single at the moment? I can't

remember what my last words were. They were probably, yes, I'm sure I really want to do this.

"I can't wait to marry my best friend and soul mate."

"It's about time," I say.

Worth might not be my best friend—I haven't known him long enough—but as crazy as it sounds, there's something nudging at my edges telling me he's important. More important than anyone I've ever had in my life.

ELEVEN

Worth

I can't take my eyes off Sophia. I've spent the entire morning trying my best not to touch her, and I don't know how much longer I'll be able to hold back. I'm out of self-control.

"To the beautiful bride and the groom, who will spend the rest of his life knowing he doesn't deserve her." Bennett finishes his speech with a typical flourish.

We're all having a drink in a roped-off area in a bar after the ceremony before we go for a late lunch. Jules admitted to Leo on the way back from the ceremony that she wanted to end her wedding day in New York, so we're not staying the night tonight. Bennett has arranged for the plane to take us back this evening.

I can't help but wonder if Vegas has been a spell cast on Sophia and me, and whether going back to New York will undo what's been done between us on this trip. We're married, but we've never dated. How are we supposed to navigate that? I don't want to go backward, but I don't know how to go forward. I feel a deep connection with

Sophia, who is without a doubt the most beautiful woman I've ever laid eyes on. But it's more than that. Or at least I think it is.

All I know is that I don't want to divorce her or have our marriage annulled. You can't start getting to know someone by divorcing them. At the same time, I don't want to freak her out and come on too strong. She's been through a lot recently and doesn't always know which way is up. A wrong move from me could lead to her going cold. That's the last thing I want.

Our group has split into three. Sophia and Efa are standing by the velvet rope, admiring Jules' bracelet. Leo, Jack, and Byron are by the private bar, just a few feet away. I'm standing with Bennett and Fisher, where I've got a direct line of sight to Sophia. I didn't deliberately arrange my sightline to have such an exquisite view, but my subconscious was all over it. I'm as mesmerized by her today as I've ever been. She flipped a switch in me as soon as we met, but now? And after last night? I'd do anything for her.

On the other side of the rope, a guy interrupts the girls and speaks to them. I narrow my eyes. I can't quite tell if he's asking them a question or making a pass or what. My phone buzzes and I take it out of my pocket.

It's my sister.

"I have to get this," I say to Bennett and Fisher. I step to the side, still facing Sophia. The guy is still talking to them, and they've all adopted blank expressions of disinterest. What the fuck does he want?

"Hey, Avril."

"How's my favorite big brother?" she asks.

My heart sinks. If Avril is being nice to me, there must be something seriously wrong.

"Busy. What's going on?"

"You're in Vegas, right? Poppy told me. And Vegas puts people in a good mood, right?"

"Just come out with it."

"I'm going to lead with the positive."

It must be really bad, but I stay quiet.

"I posted my own bail," she says.

"What?" I hiss into the phone.

I step farther to the side, keeping Sophia in view. The guy outside the rope seems to be inching closer to them. Sophia looks a little bit uncomfortable, but not seriously. She'd just move if he was an issue, right? I'm not sure I know her well enough to have the answer to that question. I know all three women can handle themselves, but I don't want them to have to. I look around and see if this guy is with anyone, but no one seems to be missing him. Why doesn't he just fuck off?

"I'm kidding," Avril says. "I haven't been arrested. But I *have* been put on academic probation."

"Academic probation?" I whisper-shout into the phone. "You're smarter than your entire class put together. What the fuck is going on?"

The guy with eyes for Sophia leans farther toward her and she backs away a couple of steps.

"I thought Vegas was meant to put you in a good mood," Avril whines.

"What kind of mood—" I cancel the call, as the guy the wrong side of the rope reaches across to Sophia and grabs her arm, trying to pull her back toward him.

How dare he even *think* he can touch her.

It takes me less than a second to reach her.

I step between them and tower over the guy, looking down at him, Sophia safely behind me. "Get. Your. Hands. Off. My. Wife." I fist my hands as they itch to punch the shit out of this creep.

He steps back, wide-eyed, his palms facing me in surrender. "Woah, dude, you need to get her to wear a ring. I thought she was fair game."

The comment makes me sick to my stomach. "Leave or get thrown out. Your choice."

He rolls his eyes, tosses back his drink, and walks away.

I turn, and even though I can feel the stares of everyone in our group on me, I slide my hands up Sophia's arms. "Are you okay?"

She nods. "I'm fine, really. You didn't need to—"

"I know. But guys like that—" I suck in a breath through my teeth. "That kind of thing isn't happening to you. Not on my watch. And now, it's always my watch." I press a kiss to her forehead.

And then reality seeps in.

Bennett clears his throat. Sophia turns, and I take a breath before looking up. He has his eyebrows raised. "Anything you want to tell us, Worth?"

Shit. This is just what Sophia and I didn't want—attention to be taken from Leo and Jules.

"Sorry, guys. I just saw that guy grab at Sophia and I had to step in."

"You want to rewind to the bit where you told him Sophia was your wife?" Leo asks.

Sophia lets out an anxious laugh from in front of me. "Yeah, Worth was just being protective, weren't you?"

"You are a terrible liar, Sophia Jones. Did you marry Worth?" Jules asks.

Sophia lets out a manic laugh. "We only just met."

I start to chuckle. "I think the jig is up, Sophia."

She slumps in front of me. "We didn't want to steal your thunder, so we didn't mention what may or may not have happened last night at the New York Loves Vegas Chapel."

Jules squeals. "Sophia! How could you have not told me the instant you—" She stops and turns to me. "And how long has this been—" Then she turns in a slow circle, pointing her finger at everyone in turn. "Am I the last to know?"

"Sophia has become... very important to me very quickly," I say. "I felt a connection at the brunch, but things are very new."

"We kissed for the first time thirty-six hours ago," Sophia says.

"When were you going to tell me?" Jules says. "Do you like him?"

"I'm standing right here." I wave at her.

She shoos me away and steps toward Sophia. "We need a debrief. Also, how did a kiss turn into a wedding?"

Sophia glances back at me. I'm not sure what she's going to say. Does she want me to step in to explain?

I start to speak but Sophia interrupts. I'm more than happy for her to take the lead. "It was just a spur-of-the-moment decision."

"Are you annulling?" Efa asks, and it's like someone's hit me in the stomach with a mallet.

"It just happened late last night," Sophia says. "We're here celebrating you two. We both want to focus on that."

"Awww, I love how you said that," Jules says. "*You both*—like you're a couple. Well, you are. You're married." She raises her glass. "Congratulations!"

Byron sidles up to me. "Everything okay?" he asks under his breath.

I nod.

"Sure?"

"Absolutely sure."

"It's just... not like you to make a decision like this on the fly."

I nod. "That's true."

He holds my gaze. "Would you tell me if there was something wrong?"

I pull in a breath, considering my response. "Probably. But there isn't anything wrong." I glance over at Sophia, who's talking to Efa and Jules in hushed tones. I know I'm biased, but she's so fucking beautiful, I ache for her. I can't wait to get back to New York and have some time with her on our own, without having to sneak around behind our friends' backs. "I like her," I say.

"I like my car. I didn't marry it."

"Which car?"

He narrows his eyes at me, like he doesn't understand the question. "I like all my cars." He tilts his head. "The new Lambo is probably a favorite."

"Bet you'd marry it if you could."

He fixes me with a stare.

"What?" I ask. "You started it."

"My point is, you don't go around marrying every woman you like."

"It's true, I don't."

"So, what's the plan?" he asks.

I catch Bennett's concerned gaze from where he's talking with Fisher, Jack, and Leo. They've obviously sent Byron in here to figure out what's going on. Dad's gone rogue and they don't know what the fuck to do about it.

"Do I need a plan?" I ask.

"Are you going to get it annulled? Divorce her? At least make her sign something to say she's not going to take all your money?"

I scoff. "She's not going to take my money."

"Worth, do you realize you barely know this woman? Did you do it as a dare or something?"

I sigh. "On a whim. We're in Vegas. Why not?"

Byron's mouth presses into a hard line. I can tell he's got the urge to punch me. But I can't give him answers I don't have.

"I don't have it figured out yet," I say. "Things will unfold."

"Have you hit your head? Are you on an acid trip? What the actual fuck is going on?"

"Avril's on academic probation. So I've got to sort that shit out when I get home. Looks like the building on Ninth I invested in is more of a money pit than I suspected, given Mason has fucked off with five hundred grand."

"Fuck, Worth. That doesn't sound good. So you were trying to escape and decided to get married? I mean, I get having an emotional reaction and everything, but maybe next time try and work it out at the gym, rather than enter into a potentially life-changing contract."

"I didn't get married because of Avril or Mason. I got married because I like Sophia. I really like her and... I went with my gut."

There's a beat of silence before Byron says, "Nothing much I can say to that, is there?"

"Nothing you need to say."

"Just promise me you'll come to me if you feel out of your depth. I know you're used to handling anything and everything, but it doesn't mean you have to do it alone. We're all here for you."

I clink my champagne glass against his. "Thanks."

"And congratulations," he says, an eyebrow raised.

I grin and glance over at Sophia. If she's the biggest mistake I make in my life, then so be it.

TWELVE

Sophia

Traveling private is the worst. I'm officially ruined when it comes to flying commercial.

We get to the bottom of the steps on the tarmac in New York to find six blacked-out SUVs waiting. We all say our goodbyes like we're never going to see each other again, and everyone peels off into their waiting vehicles. The first one is for Jules and Leo. The second for Bennett and Efa. The third for Fisher, the fourth for Jack, the fifth for Byron.

"The last one is ours," Worth says, as he pulls up the handle on my carry-on he just brought down the stairs.

My heart starts to thunder in my chest. *Ours?* We've known each other days. When did anything become *ours?*

"I thought we could talk on the way back to Jersey," Worth says, his tone relaxed.

"You're inviting yourself back to my poky little apartment?" I ask.

"No, I was going to see you home and head back to the city."

My stomach swoops at the thought of him leaving me, but I'm not sure I want him to stay either. I'm a confusion of feeling. I left New York having spoken to this man only once. Two days later, I'm coming back married.

This is ridiculous.

"Oh," I say.

"Let's not overanalyze this," he says. "I have a car. You need a ride."

I bite my cheek, but in the end I can't resist. "Debatable after last night."

He raises his eyebrows and I laugh.

"Can't a girl make a joke around here?" He's right, we're sharing a car, not picking out china.

We head to the car and slide into the back seat. There's a privacy screen between us and the driver, which makes me feel a little more comfortable.

As the car pulls away, Worth slips his hand into mine. The flip-flop feeling in my stomach quiets.

"I had a good time," I say, wanting to break the silence but unsure what to say.

Worth pulls in a breath like he's about to make a confession. "Me too." He rubs his thumb over the back of my hand. "I like you." His phone vibrates, but he ignores it. "What do you say we go to dinner this week?"

"You're asking your wife to dinner?" How is it possible that I'm someone's wife? I suppose it's just a legal technicality, but it feels so strange. "To discuss a divorce?"

"No," he says quickly. "I want to spend time with you. Explore this a little."

"This?"

"Us," he says.

That word again. Us. Us. Us.

"Explore things... in case we want to stay married?" I ask.

"Maybe," he says. "I don't have any definitive answers for you, Sophia. All I know is that I look at you, and I don't want to look anywhere else. I like that you're a ballbuster, but you seem unsure about a lot of things all the time. You didn't want to get married, but you married me. You're a mass of contradictions, but I feel drawn to you in a way I can't explain. And there's no denying the sexual chemistry. The way I see it, we don't have to make a decision about anything. So let's not. Let's sit with this. Let things evolve."

I sigh. He makes it sound so easy, but I have a thousand questions. What do I tell my parents? Or my mom and my brothers? Do I wear a ring? Do I tell people?

"We don't need to tell anyone," he says. "It's no one else's business. And then we live life."

"And date?" I ask. He nods, like it's the easiest solution in the world. "Exclusively date?" I ask. I don't want a slot on this man's roster if I'm actually married to him.

He looks at me for a beat. "Of course. Why would I want to spend time with anyone else, when I can spend time with you?"

Joy and relief surge in my chest. How does he always say the right thing?

I give a little shrug. "Okay, then. Let's date. Exclusively. But can we look at the options around an annulment? Just so we're aware."

He nods. "I'll speak to my lawyer."

His phone vibrates again, and I can't help but wonder if it's a woman—someone he sees regularly or just to scratch the itch. The guy is gorgeous, rich, and kind. Any woman would want Worth. They'd be fools not to.

"Do you need to get that?" I ask. "I mean, I'm not going to get mad if you want to tell her you got married in Vegas."

His eyes catch on mine and he turns the phone screen toward me. "My sister Avril. She called me in Vegas to tell me she's been placed on academic probation, despite having an IQ of one-sixty." He sighs. "So I gotta go talk to the dean or make a donation to something."

"You do? Why?" I ask.

"So she doesn't get thrown out of Columbia."

"But why is that your problem?"

"Because Avril makes it my problem."

His body has tensed since he started talking. I don't want to push it, but I still don't get why it falls to him to clean up his sister's mess.

I squeeze his hand and the car stops. I realize we're outside my apartment building. "You want to stay?" I ask him.

His eyes search mine as if he's trying to find the answer. "I do," he says earnestly. "I'm just not sure I should. I don't want to fuck this up by pushing too hard."

I laugh. "Worth, we're married. Staying over is no big deal."

Besides, I want him to stay. We can start talking about divorce tomorrow.

THIRTEEN

Sophia

Worth's phone goes off again as soon as we're through the door. He flashes me the screen, wanting to reassure me that it's Avril again and no one wanting a sample of his dick—not that I could blame them.

"Take it," I say. "She obviously wants to talk to you. I can get unpacked while you do."

He scoops a hand around my waist and pulls me toward him, placing a kiss on my forehead. He answers the phone.

"Avril. Unless you're going to tell me you're now off academic probation, there's nothing to talk about." He listens for a second. "You're pregnant?" he bellows into the phone, and I wince, taking my two suitcases into the spare bedroom to unpack everything. My apartment is less than five hundred square feet, so it's not like I can't hear him, but there's an illusion of privacy. "Are you fucking ser—" He stops mid-sentence, obviously listening to something his sister is saying. "Well, an Ivy League education isn't teaching you the definition of what a joke is. Maybe you need to go look it up. Because giving your brother a heart attack isn't funny."

I press my fingers to my lips to stop myself from laughing. He sounds like he's a dad chastising his daughter, not a brother talking to his sister. Worth lowers his voice and they fall into easy conversation while I unpack. When I take out the black cocktail dress I married Worth in, a frisson of excitement runs through my body. I never thought my wedding dress would look like that.

"Sorry about that."

I spin and Worth is in the doorway. He runs a hand through his hair. He looks tired.

"Let me make you a drink. Or a peanut butter and jelly sandwich. Or we could order in?"

He checks his watch. "It's nine. Let's order."

"Sure, what do you like?"

"You," he responds, and my smile unfurls like a flower under the attention of the sun.

"To eat," I admonish him.

"You," he replies. It's his turn to smile now.

"Door Dash doesn't deliver me. You pick something. I'm going to shower."

He growls as he scrolls on his phone. "Want company?"

"Next time. I'm really hungry."

In twenty minutes, we're sitting opposite each other at the bistro table and chairs Jules bought when we first moved in.

"Is this weird for you?" I ask. I wonder if he has a chef to cook for him. He's bound to have a housekeeper.

"What?"

"Being in this tiny apartment and sitting around a table that's as small as a postage stamp. I've been to Jules and Leo's place—"

Worth laughs. "My place isn't like Jules and Leo's. Although, who knows how long they'll be there."

"You think they'll move?" I ask.

"It doesn't seem to be the kind of place Jules would call home."

I burst into laughter. "No, considering she used to call *this* place home."

"I mean the look and feel of it. Where they live now feels like Leo's apartment. It's got nothing to do with size or how... fancy it is." Worth shrugs. "After my dad died, we couldn't afford much."

"How did he die?"

"It was a traffic accident. Drunk driver."

"And they were so small, they don't really remember him?" I have so many incredible memories of my dad, it's difficult to fathom what life would have been like without him. Even though he wasn't with us all the time, when he was, he was at the center of our world. I can't imagine not having that.

"No, from their perspective, they grew up in a single-parent household with an annoying older brother."

"I bet they don't think you're annoying," I say.

"I'm sure they'll tell you themselves when they meet you."

"Did you work it out with your sister?"

"I'm meeting her tomorrow so we can formulate a plan. God, I hope she's not trying to drop out. She's so close to graduating."

I take this opportunity to get up and put myself in his lap. "Hey," I say.

"Hey," he replies.

"So... you wanna make out?" I ask him, my eyes dropping to his lips and back up to his eyes.

"Yeah, I wanna make out," he whispers, pulling my shirt up and over my head and running his hands over my bra. "This is pretty."

It's my nicest bra, bought in a Saks sale at seventy percent off thanks to my employee discount. It still cost me a fortune. "Thanks. It's Italian."

He reaches around my back and snaps the clasp open, then takes his time dragging the straps down my arms. He sets the pile of lace aside gently, always considerate, then pulls my legs to either side of his thighs.

We've been here before.

"I'm naked," I say.

"Not naked enough." He cups my breasts, pushing them up,

squeezing my nipples. I feel myself getting wet. I'm just so ready for this guy *all the time*. He sucks a nipple into his mouth, licking and grazing his teeth over the sensitive skin until I'm writhing on his lap, grinding myself against him. He's hard through the denim of his jeans and I'm impatient for him. I need him so deep that I can't think about anything other than catching my breath. I arch my back at the thought that it won't be long.

He unzips my skirt at the side and pulls it off over my head so I'm naked other than my panties, while he's fully clothed. I reach down to rub my hand over his erection, but he catches my wrist.

"No," he says. Firmly.

I gasp. Not because he's chastised me, but because I like it.

He slides his index finger into my mouth, wetting it, then pushes it through my folds, over my throbbing sex.

He shakes his head. "So wet already. Is that what I do to you?"

I nod my head.

"You can't wait to feel my cock sliding in there, can you?"

I whimper, and he removes his hand.

"Answer me," he instructs.

"No," I choke out.

"No what?"

"No, I can't wait to feel you inside me, Worth."

He growls appreciatively, lifts me, and somehow manages to remove my panties. I'm astride one leg now instead of both.

"I want to see how wet you are." He grabs my ass and pulls me toward him, my pussy dragging over the denim of his jeans. He pushes me back and inspects the damp patch on his leg. I bite down on my lip and drag my gaze from his pants to meet his eyes.

"More," he says simply.

I start to rock back and forth on his leg. It feels better than it should. Maybe it's because I can feel Worth's breath on my skin, or because I'm imagining his muscular thighs getting wet through the denim. Maybe it's the way his eyes flare with heat at my movements.

I'm so under this guy's spell, I'd do anything he asked right now.

The rough cotton drags over my folds, catching my clit on every move forward.

"Worth," I cry out. My breathing is jagged, pushing out each breath like I can only just make it.

"You're doing so good, Sophia."

My entire body tightens at his encouragement. I try to keep up my rhythm, pulling and pushing, darkening the material of his pants.

He kneads my breasts, pinching my nipples so hard it makes me dizzy. And even wetter.

I'm so close, and he's barely touched me.

"Good girl, Sophia. You can come now."

His words unleash something in me, and I shudder as my orgasm radiates from where my pussy connects to his leg all through my body. Groaning, I collapse on his chest. He pulls me close as I try to piece together what just happened.

He scoops me up, still slumped across him, and carries me into the bedroom. I lie on the bed as he quickly undresses. The sight of his gloriously hard cock makes me quiver. I can feel renewed wetness between my legs.

He drags me to the edge of the bed and kneels of the floor, sinking his face into my pussy like he's devouring me. Another time, in another life, I would have resisted him. But I know I can't. The only choice I have is to give in to every single thing I'm feeling. Worth is in complete control of my body and mind, and I trust both in his care.

FOURTEEN

I stand and look up at the monolithic problem in front of me. I knew something wasn't quite right about Mason Wright. I just didn't expect him to be a thief.

"Why are we meeting here?" Avril nudges me in the arm like she's been here all along and hasn't just arrived.

"You're not late," I say.

"Nothing gets past you, does it?" Avril says. "You can even tell time."

I ignore her and take in the twenties-era, twelve-story building on the corner of Forty-Sixth and Ninth.

"What's so interesting about this place?" Avril asks.

"I own it, and I'm not sure what I'm going to do with it."

"What a terrible dilemma," she says dryly. "Did you buy it by accident?"

"I invested in it. We should be six months into demolition and reconstruction by now."

"Demolition?" she says incredulously. "Why on earth would you rip down a building like this? It's beautiful."

"You haven't seen the structural report. It would cost as much to fix as to demo, so we got our permits to do just that. I thought we were moving ahead."

"But you're not?" she asks.

"Well, the developer has moved to South America. With my money. At least the property was in my name."

"God. How much did he take?"

"We're figuring it out, but I think around half a million." It's my own fault. I should have sent someone from my team on every inspection. He'd been paying off the architect to send me false updates, and I'd been too busy to follow up.

"Jeez. I hope you reported everyone involved."

"I have. And anyway, it's only a little less than I'm paying for your and Poppy's education."

I don't need to be facing her to see her eyeroll.

"So tell me why you're here," I say. "Shouldn't you be in class, given you're on academic probation?"

"Not until this afternoon. Are we going inside?"

I've fired everyone who was working on the project with Mason and brought in a team of people I trust. Apparently it's safe to enter, so we go inside.

"What was it before?" Avril says, turning three hundred and sixty degrees. "It's beautiful."

"Beautiful?" I scoff. "It's a literal construction site."

"But look at the crown moldings," she says, pointing at the thirty-foot ceilings. "Oh god. And that staircase. It's like it belongs in a palace."

"Hardly," I mumble. "Those stairs should be a bank of elevators by now. No apartment building should be without one."

"Seriously? You were tearing this down to make apartments? Where's your soul, Worth?"

"Run off to South America with my half a million dollars," I reply.

"It would look incredible with a marble floor. And you'd have to do a royal-blue rug. No! Electric blue. You could really go old school and restore it to its glory, but add in a curveball here and there. Let's see through here."

I follow Avril as she leads the way through abandoned piles of rubble and random bits of timber.

"This is gorgeous. The bar is still in good shape. Do you have the original plans?" she asks. "Or any photographs of the hotel before it... ended up like this?"

"How did you know it was a hotel?"

Avril laughs. "It wasn't a family home with these dimensions. And I bet we can find a ballroom somewhere around here. Oh god, Worth, it's great. You can't pull it down."

Of course I'm going to pull it down. That's been the plan for the last three years. "It's all settled. I've got all the permits and a team of new architects on board." I don't really know why I'm here, other than to allay my guilt over being so hands-off before. Mason was my choice and my investment, which means the blame for him fucking off to South America lies at least partially at my feet. I don't want to make the same mistake again.

"You should restore it. Make it a hotel again. It would be worth a fortune."

"It'll be worth a fortune when it's eighty-three apartments."

She sighs. "No soul. I thought you were looking for a hotel in New York."

"I bought one in Boston." Although I can't remember how long it's been since my last visit. I need to be more on the ground in all my investments, but I'm spread thin at the moment.

"Sell that one," she says, like she's playing Monopoly and not million-dollar real estate.

"I'm not selling it." I never wanted the Boston hotel in the first place, but Bennett, Byron, Jack, Fisher, Leo, and I had all agreed to buy a hotel after we sold the business we created at school together. Now we hold an annual competition to see which one—or who—is most successful. A little friendly competition to strengthen the glue that holds our friendship together. Only, I couldn't find a property in New York that made commercial sense and hadn't been snapped up by one of my friends. So I ended up with a property in Boston and dutifully lose the competition every year.

"So tell me about academic probation," I say as we head into what might have been a dining room. Or maybe a lounge. It's difficult to say.

She sighs. "I don't know, my soul isn't in it."

"Does your soul *need* to be in it?" I ask. "Don't we just need your brain to be in it?"

"Ha ha. I just don't think economics and I are... meant to be."

"You're not dating. You just need a degree. Even if you don't do anything economics-related, a degree will be useful."

"I could come and manage this project for you. Help with design and decision-making."

"The decisions are made. The plans have been approved for well over a year."

Avril folds her arms. "I don't like economics," she says. "I want to do something creative. Coming here just makes it worse, because I see ten jobs I could be doing and really enjoying. Instead, I'm stuck in a classroom, wondering whether I'm destined to become just another empty wannabe banker who would do anything for a dollar."

You won't just find Avril's name next to the entry for *exaggeration* in the dictionary—you'll also find a full-color photo.

"You're telling me you want to drop out in your junior year? With nothing to show for it except your brother's empty wallet?"

She sighs. "Oh please. You've got more money than god. And what's the point in being rich if you can't use your wealth to help others? To feed your sister's soul."

"You're ridiculous," I say. I don't even know how to respond to her. My mind is too full of other things. I want to see more of Sophia.

She's busy tonight, and I hate the thought of spending the night without her. I'd be happy for her to move in so we could really get to know each other, but I know she's not ready for me to suggest that.

During the brief moments when I'm not thinking about Sophia, I'm consumed by thoughts of this Ninth Street disaster. I really don't want to take on a project like this—at least not when I have to be involved at the literal ground floor.

And now there's Avril.

I'm used to having solutions to everything, but today it's raining problems and I'm out of umbrellas.

Sophia was surprised that Avril being on academic probation was a problem for me personally. I suppose in a normal family, it would be my parents' problem, but we're not a normal family. Will I always play a pseudo-parental role in my sisters' lives? I'm not sure I know how to relate to them any other way. I should be encouraging both of them to be more independent.

"You need to stay in school—"

Avril groans from the other room.

"Let me finish," I say. "It doesn't make any sense for you to quit when you don't have any idea what you're going to do. It's not like you have anything lined up."

Avril appears in the doorway. "I hate it, Worth."

"So find something you want to do. Something you're passionate about. This is your life, Avril. It's not my responsibility to figure out what you want to do with it."

"I told you, I can help you with this place."

I sigh. Is she just looking for an easy out? I can't tell. I need more data. "Then write me a plan. No whining. No excuses. Write me a plan for this place or whatever it is you want to do if you drop out of Columbia."

"I don't need your permission, you know. I could just drop out."

I fix her with a stare. She knows she needs my okay to leave the Ivy League school I've been paying for.

"Okay, what kind of plan?" she relents.

"Tell me what you're going to do. What experience and qualifications you need. I want a career plan from you. And don't half-ass it. Do it properly. You need to sell me on this."

A smile twitches at the edges of her mouth. "You'll consider it?"

"I'll consider the plan. But if it's bullshit, it gets tossed, just like the ten proposals I get per week that I don't think are worth my time. And you stay in school. But if it's good, then, like I said—it's your life."

She bounces on her toes. "This is going to be the best plan you've ever fucking seen."

That's all I've ever wanted for my sisters—a life plan. I don't want to see them disappear into nothing like my mother did after my dad died. I want them to have something to get up for every morning. For Mom, we weren't enough. If Avril and Poppy find something to be passionate about, there will always be a light at the end of every tunnel.

It takes me a little by surprise when Avril slips her arm into mine and rests her head on my shoulder. "Thank you, Worth. You won't regret this."

I hope she's right.

FIFTEEN

Sophia

I'm impressed with myself, and it's not because of the pink cocktail dress I'm wearing. Despite going out with some of the girls from work last night, I did not booty-call Worth. And I managed *not* to tell the girls I got hitched in Vegas, even when I was three drinks down. I deserve a ten out of ten.

This dress isn't right. I pull another from my wardrobe—my last option. I just don't have a wardrobe that screams *I'm married to a billionaire.* I don't know what Worth likes. Not that I'm dressing for him. Except, maybe I am. He seems so into me, I feel like I need to live up to who he thinks I am.

My phone buzzes. It's Worth.

I answer. "Hey."

"I'm buzzing your buzzer. Can you let me in?"

"Shit, it's broken. I'll come down. I just need to decide what to wear."

"Whatever you've got on is fine," he says.

"Oh okay, jeans and a white tee okay for you?"

"Completely fine," he says. "You'll look beautiful in anything. I'll be waiting."

I groan and hang up the phone. He always says the sweetest things. But surely he can't mean that we can have our first date when I'm wearing jeans and a t-shirt.

I put on a black cocktail dress—which is Holly Golightly meets Zara—grab my bag and pink coat, and head downstairs.

Worth is leaning against a black SUV. He wears a long gray coat with the collar turned up, because it's fucking freezing. He looks so hot, I want to suggest skipping dinner and going back upstairs.

But I want to get to know Worth. He's a good guy. He's also my husband. Our marriage is essentially just a piece of paper—it shouldn't mean anything. And yet... it does. I'm just not sure what.

"Pink suits you," he says as he greets me with a kiss.

"Would you have said green suited me if my coat had been green?"

"Absolutely. Because green does suit you."

I grin up at him. I don't think I've ever felt so adored. I've been love-bombed before, but that's not what Worth is doing. I haven't known him long, but I know him well enough to understand that he doesn't say anything he doesn't mean. He adores me. And instead of it making me deeply uncomfortable, I kinda like it.

"You look hot. But then, I did marry you, so I guess you know that already."

He pulls me closer to him and growls in my ear, kissing my neck. "We should leave now or we won't make it to dinner."

We slide into the car and Worth takes my hand in his right away.

"I saw my sister yesterday," he says.

"How was that?" I ask. He obviously has a very close relationship with his siblings. I don't want to say anything I shouldn't.

"She wants to drop out of Columbia."

"Because she's on academic probation?" I ask.

"More like she's on academic probation because she wants to drop out. She says she doesn't like studying economics."

"Oh. Well, that's a bigger problem. It's nice she came to you, though. Isn't it?"

He sighs. "I don't know, honestly. She obviously wants my approval to drop out." He glances across at me, and I try to keep my expression neutral. "Because I'm older, and because once our dad died, our mom wasn't particularly engaged, both my sisters put me in a parental role."

He's a problem solver for more than the people he invests in, but he seems to like it. "*Put* you?"

He's silent for a beat while he thinks. "Maybe not consciously, but that's the role I'm in. Partly because I was the one who made sure they had their packed lunch and clean clothes a lot of the time. I made their doctors' appointments and nursed them when they were sick. But also, because I have the money now to pay for their education or whatever else they want to do with their lives.

"You *parented* them? Because your mother was sick after your dad died?"

He takes in a juddering breath. "I knew if I didn't step up, we'd all end up in foster care. I wouldn't let that happen. So I got on with it. Lucky for everyone, I was fourteen and smart. Mom had her good days." He pauses. "And her terrible days."

Pain flashes across his expression, and I squeeze his hand. Worth is the dad of the friend group and oh-so-sensible, because that's what he knows. It's what his family needed from him.

"I'm so sorry, Worth. How is your mom now?"

"Good," he says simply. "She moved to North Carolina as soon as Avril turned eighteen."

"You still see her?"

"Yeah. But we're not close. Her light went out when my dad died. She wasn't the same woman after his death, and part of me will always resent that, I think. She gave up so completely. I know depression isn't something people can control without help, but it felt like she didn't even try."

"Sounds like you didn't have much of a childhood," I say quietly.

He smooths his thumb over the back of my hand. It's all the confirmation I'm going to get that I've hit the nail on the head.

"Your sisters clearly adore you."

"And hate me in equal measure."

"What do you think about Avril dropping out of Columbia? Do you approve?"

"I'm not sure my approval matters. If I don't, and I put pressure on her to stay, she's just going to fail her courses. If I approve... I asked her to write me a business plan for what she's going to do if she drops out."

"A business plan you'll approve?"

He chuckles. "Maybe. I just want her to have a plan. To have something to get up in the morning for. I don't want her to drift."

It hits me right in my chest that Worth and his sisters lived with the understanding that they weren't enough to get their *mother* up in the morning. I can't imagine how painful that must have been. How painful it probably still is, to this day. "You're such a good role model, Worth. I have a feeling she's going to surprise you."

He turns to me. "It's possible. The road ahead is full of bends and curves. I didn't expect I'd be sitting next to my wife en route to our first date, but here we are. Which reminds me, we need to figure out when we can have our second date. Are you free tomorrow?"

There he is, that driven, intense man, never far from the surface.

"I don't have enough clothes for us to date every night."

"Enough clothes?"

"Yeah, like, for going out. I don't go out six nights a week."

He narrows his eyes like he's considering his response. "And you don't want me to pay for a new wardrobe."

I laugh. It's not a question, but it's nice he knows I'd never accept that. "Absolutely not."

"We could have a sweatpants date? You haven't been to my place. Come over. I can have a chef prepare dinner and pretend I cooked."

I laugh again. "I'd like that."

"Are you going to Cincinnati for Thanksgiving?"

My blood turns to ice at the thought. "I was supposed to," I say.

"But?" he asks.

"I don't know if I'm going to go now."

"My sisters and I usually go to Tavern on the Green. If you're in New York, I'd love for you to join us."

"Thank you. Thanksgiving is complicated," I say. "It's also my dad's birthday. I need to figure out what I'm doing and where I'll be." I start to feel itchy. I don't want to miss out on being with my family for the holiday, but at the same time, my family isn't my family anymore. Everything's changed. And the fact that Dad will be there? Mom probably thought keeping up with tradition would be normal in some twisted way, but the opposite is true. And what about Dad's other kids? Shouldn't he be with them?

"I'm pretty good at running through pros and cons."

"I'll bear that in mind," I say. I'm not ready to tell Worth everything going on back in Cincinnati. I don't want him to think I'm bringing him problems to solve. I don't want to be a burden. He's my lover. My very new husband. I want to enjoy that for a while. But I do start mentally composing a text telling Mom I won't be home for Thanksgiving.

SIXTEEN

Worth

Even though my sisters and I argue and get annoyed with each other, we're tight. They were little when things started falling apart, so they don't remember when we were good as a family—but they understand the bond we have. We don't talk about it. We don't need to.

But it's why I'm slightly on edge at the idea of introducing them to Sophia.

Sophia is running a little late. I've told her to text me when she's on her way. I'll come out of the restaurant to meet her, so she doesn't have to walk in on her own.

I press send on my message and look up to find Poppy and Avril approaching the table.

"Happy Thanksgiving," they both chorus.

"I have a present for you," Avril says, dropping a roll of paper on the table. It's tied up with a bow. "I'm going to spoil the surprise and tell you it's my business plan for dropping out of Columbia, and it's also a midterm report saying how I'm up to date and passing all my classes with a grade point average of three point two and rising."

"So why do you want to drop out again?" I ask as my sisters slide into the seats either side of me.

"I never wanted to drop out because I was failing. I was failing because I want to drop out."

She's right. It's an important difference.

"You need to read the report," Poppy says. "It's great and what we all need."

"What we *all* need?" I scoff. "I'm pretty sure I need my sister to graduate from the Ivy League school I've been paying for."

She puts her hand on my arm. "Just keep an open mind," Poppy says. "I think you'll be surprised."

I groan and check my phone. No message from Sophia. "I'll read it like I'd read any other business proposal."

"Perfect," Avril says. "You're always harder on us than you are on everyone else, so that should work in my favor."

I raise my eyebrows. "I can't remember the last time I paid for college for anyone else but you two. Can you order some drinks? I'm going to call Sophia and see where she is."

"Sophia," Avril says. "I can't believe you're actually introducing us to a woman. I thought you might be gay. Bennett is absolutely gorgeous."

"I'd take Jack if I had to pick one of them," Poppy says. "And if I had to pick two of them, I'd take Fisher as well."

"We are all gay," I say. "The wife and girlfriend thing is just an elaborate beard operation."

"Called it," Poppy says.

I roll my eyes and stand, only to lock eyes with Sophia as she walks into the restaurant. "Wow," is all I can say. She looks incredible. She's wearing a huge smile and her hair is in a braid, with curls falling around her face. She's in a jade-green dress and she seems to shine.

Her gaze flits to my sisters, but I can't keep my eyes off her.

"Hey," she says as I slip my hand around her waist. She presses a kiss to my cheek, holding back more than she normally does. I know it's because we have an audience.

"Sophia, this is Poppy and Avril." They greet each other with hugs and Avril switches seats so Sophia can sit next to me,

"We're excited to meet you," Avril says. "We've never met one of Worth's girlfriends. Just his boyfriends."

Lucky for me, Sophia starts to laugh. "Is that right? Bet none of them rocked heels like I do."

My sisters laugh, and I smooth my hand over Sophia's leg. She's passed their first test. No doubt there will be more.

"Worth just admitted that his friends' wives and girlfriends are just beards."

Sophia shrugs. "Well, I don't think gay men are quite as good with their tongues as your brother, but I might be wrong."

Avril clamps her hands over her ears and Poppy's jaw drops onto the table.

"I would say that's game, set, and match to Sophia. Can you two get over yourselves?"

"I'd love a martini," Sophia says, looking around for a waiter.

"Please god, if I take my hands from my ears, will you promise never to speak about my brother's..." Avril screws up her face like she's just smelled sour milk. "Anything, ever again?"

Sophia smiles a genuine smile. She doesn't seem irritated or offended, just mildly amused. "I'll promise the only thing I *can* promise: I'll meet your energy."

Jesus Christ, she has balls of steel. I don't know why I was worried about her walking in here alone.

"Fair enough," Avril says, uncovering her ears and calling over a waiter. "I need a drink."

Sophia turns to me. "Two older brothers. This is life around our kitchen table. You learn to keep up."

As if I wasn't completely obsessed with this woman already.

"So how long have you two been dating?" Poppy asks.

"Not long," Sophia answers. "But long enough to know we really like each other."

My chest hollows out and fills with lightness at her words. I do really fucking like her. I more than like her. It's so good to know she feels the same way.

"He's a good guy," Poppy says. "Interfering? Yes. Controlling, yes. Bossy? Absolutely. But he's also kind and loyal and honest."

"And a great brother," Avril says.

Sophia laughs. "I have no doubt that's true. Did she give you a copy of her plan as your Thanksgiving gift?"

"Oh, you have Avril down."

Sophia is only a little older than Poppy, and they seem to hit it off immediately, talking about art and architecture and the bars of Manhattan.

"I'm obsessed with New York," Avril says. "Completely obsessed. I kinda wish I'd done an art history degree so I could work at the Met. I want to work in a New York institution."

"J.P. Morgan is a New York institution," I say.

Avril rolls her eyes. "That's why I really don't want Worth tearing down the Ninth Street property."

"What's your plan?" Sophia asks her.

"I want to *create* an institution. An old-school New York hotel. I think it's coming back in style—all the maximalism of the Gilded Age. It's such a different vibe to the clean, modern lines of some of the newer hotels and the lack of soul in some of the big chains. I think he should restore the building, but add touches of modern luxury."

"Sounds gorgeous," Sophia says. "Are you into interior design?"

"I mean, I'd like to be," Avril says, her gaze flitting to me and then back to Sophia. "I'm at college for economics. It's just not me. I want to do something more creative."

Sophia nods. "I get that. I work at Saks, but in the finance department. I thought it would be the perfect balance between the business side of things and the creative side of things. But there's not much creativity in finance."

"I love Saks," Avril says. "That's a New York institution for you."

"I'm living the dream," Sophia says unconvincingly. "Ultimately, it wouldn't matter who I worked for. The work I do day to day doesn't excite me."

"I get it," Avril says. "That's why I want more than a job. I want a family business. Poppy would kick ass on the finance side."

I snap my head to Poppy. "You're in on this too?" I ask. "I thought you were enjoying the bank?" I thought that it was just Avril I had to worry about. I didn't realize Poppy wasn't happy.

"I do enjoy it," she says. "But I'm a tiny cog in a huge wheel. I'm basically an admin manager. I don't get much exposure to the meaty stuff." She shrugs. "I work at one of the top banks. It's the job I wanted when I graduated college, but two years in and the shine has rubbed off. A bit like what you're saying about working at Saks."

I groan and tip my head back. In the beat of silence that follows, a phone vibrates. I swipe mine from my pocket but no one's called.

"Is that your phone?" I ask Sophia.

She pulls it out of her bag, which is hooked onto the back of her chair. "It's just Oliver. Probably wants to wish me happy Thanksgiving."

"Get it," I urge her. "We're not eating yet."

She's reluctant, and I'm not sure if it's because she doesn't want to appear rude or if there's something more behind it.

She shrugs. "I'll call him back later."

The phone stops and she goes to put it back in her bag, but a text notification pops up almost immediately. She swipes to read it.

Her face turns white. "Actually, I will just call him back."

"Everything okay?"

She doesn't answer. Based on her pallor, there's every chance she genuinely didn't hear me. She heads out the door, phone already pressed to her ear.

"Is she okay?" Avril asks.

I glance over at the door Sophia just went through. "I'm not sure. She's got stuff going on with her family."

"I like her," Poppy says.

I nod, because of course she does. "She can handle you two, that's for sure."

"Anyone dating you has to be able to handle us. You seem serious about her," Avril says.

"I'm serious about everything. Haven't you been telling me that your entire life?"

"True, but—"

"I'm just going to check on Sophia." My chair scrapes the floor aggressively as I stand. I mutter an apology for the disturbance to the table behind me before going to find Sophia.

But when I follow her path through the doorway, she's not there.

Eventually, I try outside. She's there in the freezing cold, her phone clamped to her ear.

"What do you mean you don't know?" Her eyes are brimming with tears, panic strewn across her face.

I want to tell her we can figure this out—I can fix whatever's wrong. I just need to know what we're dealing with.

"I won't even be able to get there. It's Thanksgiving. There's no way I can get a flight."

"You need to go home?" I ask. "I can get us a flight."

She grabs my shirt like she's worried she might fall if I'm not there to steady her. "You can?"

"Absolutely. We can leave now if you want."

"Okay," she says into her phone. "I'll call you back." She hangs up. "It's my dad. They think he had a heart attack. He's on the way to the ER now. Oliver called me on the way. I just—"

I scoop up her hand. "Let's get your coat or you're going to freeze to death. I'll send for my driver and tell my sisters we're leaving. We can be in the air in thirty minutes." There's doubt in her eyes. I don't know where it's coming from. "What is it?"

She scrubs her free hand over her face. "I'm just not in a good place with my dad at the moment. I don't want to do more damage by turning up when he's not expecting me or... I'm not even sure I want to see him."

"We can make those decisions on the way to Cincinnati. If you're there, you don't have to see him, but you can be a support to your brothers."

She nods. "Okay. You're right. I should be there."

"Good. I'll go tell them we're leaving."

"Oh, I don't want to pull you away from celebrating with your sisters. You stay. I can—"

"You're my wife, Sophia. I'm coming with you."

She doesn't argue.

SEVENTEEN

Worth

I click Sophia's lap belt into place and take the seat opposite her on the plane. She's barely spoken since we left the restaurant. I can see her mind whirring, the pain in her eyes. I want to make it better.

But how?

"This is all so expensive, Worth. I don't know how I'll ever repay you."

"No repayment required. There's no way you could get to Cincinnati quickly on Thanksgiving without flying private. I'm only happy I could help."

"I still don't know if I can see him."

I want to reach for her hand, but I don't want to make her feel any kind of obligation to return my affection. Not now, when she's confessed to feeling like she's in my debt.

"You don't have to see him if you don't want to. But you can be there for your brothers and your mom."

"Yeah. Maybe. I just don't want him to die."

My insides clench. Fuck, I wish I had the power to make time stand still. I can't bear the thought of her hurting as much as she is.

"He's in good hands," I say. "The best."

"If he's going to die, I want to have said my piece to him first."

I leave space for her to tell me what exactly her piece would be, but she doesn't. She just stares at her lap.

A member of the crew comes over and offers us something to drink. "Coffee," I say. "For two. And something sweet to eat."

Sophia offers me a small smile. "Thank you. I didn't know I wanted exactly that until you said something."

"You have two brothers, right?" I ask. I want to keep her out of her own head and distract her. I don't want her to torture herself.

She snaps her eyes up to mine and nods. "Yes. Noah and Oliver."

"Who's the oldest?" I'm asking inane questions, but anything to keep her mind off what might be happening in Cincinnati. I hope we make it there in time for her to see her father. We don't know yet how serious this heart attack was, though I'm sure the doctors are doing everything they can. At least he's in a hospital.

"Noah," she replies. "He's... astute. You know?" She glances up at me and then away.

I nod, even though I don't know what exactly she's trying to say. "Sensible?" I ask.

"Yeah," she says, looking out the windows on the opposite side of the plane as we taxi to the runway. "He's more reserved than Oliver. Oliver—well, you can tell everything he's thinking just by looking at him."

I smile at her, trying to encourage her to say more.

"Sounds like the three of you are close," I say.

She frowns. "I don't know," she says, her gaze finally catching on mine. "I'm not sure of anything anymore."

Another crew member brings two coffees and a bowl of M&M's.

"You can be sure of me," I say. She needs to know I'll be here for her. The more time I spend with Sophia, the more protective, the more possessive, the greedier for her I get.

She lets out a wry laugh. "That's the ironic thing about my life at the moment. I thought our family was so close, but we're not. I love my brothers, but I'm not sure I know them. Not really. I don't know if Noah's dating anyone, or why Oliver complains endlessly about Cincinnati but never leaves. I don't know if Noah's happy. I don't know what he's focused on in his life. With either of them. We have a shared history and we're familiar with each other's faces. But beyond that?" She shakes her head. "I never realized it until recently. I thought we had this perfect, white-picket-fence family. We were the American dream. Dad worked hard to provide for us, Mom was a homemaker who worked in the library part-time when her kids got older. The only thing we're missing is a goddamned dog.

"But actually, it's not like that. *We're* not like that. It was all just... make-believe. No, not make-believe, because we weren't pretending. More like, I took it all at face value. I believed the lie so much it became the truth. But now the veneer is gone. When I look at us—our family, our history—I don't know what I'm seeing anymore. I was so wrong about so much and now..." Her voice trails off, like she's run out of words.

I don't want to pry, but I wish she'd tell me what's happening.

She sighs. "But you?" She meets my eye. "Somehow, I've known you for barely any time at all, but you're the one I feel I know the best." She blinks a few times. "It makes no sense. I haven't known you long, but it feels like I see all of you... like I *know* all of you."

"It feels like that for me too," I say.

"It's not just the sex," she says matter-of-factly, and I nod.

"It's more than that. I know."

"It feels like I can count on you."

"You can," I say. "Always."

A crew member collects our coffee cups and lets us know we'll be airborne in a few minutes.

"I'm here for you, Sophia."

She reaches across the table and threads her fingers through mine just as we begin to take off.

EIGHTEEN

If it hadn't been for Worth, there's no way I'd be pulling up outside the hospital three hours after the call from Oliver. Hell, even if it hadn't been a holiday, it would have taken me three times as long. But Worth waved his magic billionaire wand, and in a flurry of helicopters and private jets, here I am. And I don't even know if I want to go in.

"Oliver says it was definitely a heart attack," I say to Worth. "They've put a stent in apparently."

"That sounds positive."

I nod. "Yeah. I guess... he's awake already." Of course I'm relieved Dad's not dead, but I don't know if I want to go up and see him.

"That's good."

"It is," I agree.

We sit in silence. Worth doesn't push. And I don't know what to say.

I glance out the window at the hospital, knowing both my brothers are inside. With Dad. They don't seem to have skipped a beat as far as their relationship is concerned. They're just business as usual, like what he did doesn't matter. Like they don't care Dad had a whole other life that didn't involve us.

"I don't know if I want to see him."

Worth squeezes my hand but doesn't ask me why. "Do you want to see your brothers?"

Then it hits me like someone's put a fist right through my chest. Are Dad's other kids there? His other *wife*?

Shit.

"I don't know. I want to go in, then run back to the car if I'm uncomfortable."

"Well," Worth says. "Do that. I can come with you and our driver can wait here, or we can both wait here."

I glance across at him. He's so kind and thoughtful. I don't know how I'll ever repay him for today. "Thank you."

"You don't need to thank me."

I offer him a smile I know doesn't meet my eyes.

"You know, when my dad died, I would have given anything to have gotten to say goodbye. I would have told him I loved him. Even though he must have known, I didn't tell him enough. Sounds like you're going to have plenty more opportunities to tell your dad how you feel about him. But one thing my dad's death taught me was to try and live my life without regrets. I try to do things I think I'll regret if I don't. And vice versa. That means my friends tell me I'm boring and sensible and dad-like. What they don't realize is that each time they tease me, they're paying me the biggest compliment. It means I'm living my life exactly the way I want to."

"You're not that sensible," I say. "You married me after knowing me no time at all."

He fixes me with a look. "And I have no regrets about that. Never thought I would."

My heart takes a tumble in my chest and I squeeze his hand. I take another look at the hospital.

"Will you regret going up there to see him? Or is it more likely you'll regret not going up?"

He's made the decision so easy for me. Long term, any regret I have will be about not going inside.

"You're right," I say. "I'm going up."

Worth nods, like he knew I would come to this decision all along.

"I'll go on my own if that's okay. I just—"

"That's fine. But you know where I am if you need me."

I let out a slow breath. "Yeah, I do." It feels good to have him here. It feels like nothing can go seriously wrong with him in my corner.

NINETEEN

Sophia

Noah texted me directions to Dad's room. When the elevator doors open, I see Oliver right ahead of me. He's slumped in a chair, one leg over the arm, just like he does when he's watching a movie at home.

Mom is on the other side of the corridor. Part of me wondered if she'd be here, though I shouldn't have. If she's ready to host Thanksgiving with Dad at the table, she's probably on board to see him through a medical crisis. I don't know who we are as a family without Mom and Dad together.

She looks up and meets me halfway, pulling me into a hug. "It's okay, sweetie. He's going to be okay."

When she releases me, Oliver is standing. I hug him too.

"How the fuck did you get here so soon?"

I shake my head, because it doesn't matter. "Tell me what happened."

"We were just having dinner," Oliver says.

"He was at Mom's?"

"Yeah, we hadn't even touched a forkful of food." Oliver offers me the bag of chips in his hand.

"Er, no, thanks. So do we have a prognosis? Is he going to be okay?"

"He's going to be fine," Mom says, putting her arm around my waist. "They fitted a stent and did various scans and tests. They're going to monitor him for the next few days, but the doctors seem very relaxed about the entire thing."

They probably see it every day.

"Where's Noah?"

"In with Dad. I just needed to eat something," Oliver says. "Wanna go in together?"

I glance around and behind me. "No one else is here?"

"They're on their way," Mom says. "I didn't have contact details before today. Once your father could have visitors, Noah called... Rita."

I rest my head on her shoulder. "Mom."

"It's fine, sweetheart. Don't worry about me. Worry about you. And your dad. In that order."

"I figure I can hate him all I want when he's better," Oliver says, stuffing the empty chips bag into the trash and wiping his hands down his jeans. "Shall we all go in?"

"You two go," Mom says. "I'm okay out here."

My heart pinches at the shift in our family dynamic. But maybe there hasn't been a shift for my mom. Her situation hasn't really changed—she's been coping with this for more than two decades. She's at the hospital for us. She's stayed in a broken marriage for us. What sacrifices she's made. I wonder if she regrets any of them.

"I love you so much, Mom."

Her voice catches. "I love you too, Sophia."

It's like I'm fighting against gravity as I walk toward my dad's room, like I'm wading through mud or something. Oliver goes first.

"Brought you a visitor," he says, holding the door open for me.

"Sophia! I thought you were in New York." Dad looks so damn

pleased to see me, it makes me happy and sad at the same time. Why can't we just rewind to a time when he could make different decisions? He could *not* have an affair, *not* get her pregnant, *not* tell a thousand lies to his wife and kids. Why can't he love me the way I thought he did?

Noah stands and pulls me in for a hug. His embrace is so much more than *I'm pleased you're here*. It's *thank you for coming, our dad's sick, our family's falling apart, I love you*. Long seconds tick by in the longest hug I've ever shared with my brother.

I blink back tears as Noah releases me and stuff my hands in my coat pockets. "How are you feeling?" I know my words sound cold, but it's all I can manage.

"Better, much better. They're keeping me in a couple of days, but just as a precaution."

I don't move to hug him and he doesn't ask for one. "You need to stop with the bacon," I say.

He nods. "I know, I know. I have a thousand pamphlets telling me the same thing." He nods to his bedside table. "Noah picked them up for me."

"You need to read them," I say. "Maybe get a Peloton or something."

"I know," he replies, his voice quieter than usual. "There are a lot of things I need to start doing." Silence echoes in the room. I stare at my shoes. I'm so angry with him, but I'm so pleased he's okay. "I really appreciate you being here," he finally says. "I know there's a lot we need to talk about." He can barely finish his last sentence.

"You need to rest," Oliver says, sitting in the chair beside the bed. "Don't stress out about anything."

I pull in a breath. That's easier said than done. Dad has split apart his family—has been splitting us apart for twenty-five years. "We can talk when you're better," I say.

Dad catches Oliver's and Noah's eyes and nods at the door. They both get up and leave. I don't stop them. I don't really want to be alone with my dad, but at the same time, I want to hear what he has to say. I desperately want there to be something he can say to stop this anger bubbling inside of me. I need that from him.

I don't move. I stand still at the bottom of his bed.

"I have a lot of regrets," he says, "but being your dad isn't one of them."

"Is that why you sent Noah and Oliver out? You don't want them to hear I'm the only one you don't regret?" It's meant to be a joke, but it doesn't land. They're the words of innocent, fourteen-year-old me, who'd sit on the couch with Dad while he watched the game, telling him everything I knew about Taylor Swift. Today it seems like I've lost my sense of humor, and no wonder.

"We'll always be a family," Dad says.

I don't want him to see me cry, and I don't want to argue with him, but that's bullshit. We were never a family. At least, we've never been the family I thought we were.

I don't respond.

"I'm sorry—"

"Let's do this another time," I say, turning to leave. "You need to rest."

"Sophia. Don't leave. Just wait."

I stand still, facing the door.

"I love you. I love the daughter you are. I know you're upset—"

"Please, Dad. I don't want to be the reason for your second heart attack today. Just focus on resting and getting better. There's plenty of time for this conversation."

"I hope so," he mumbles.

No regrets, Worth said to me. That's what his dad's death taught him. To live life with no regrets. But wherever I turn, all I can see is regrets. If we talk about it now, the stress could kill him or at least hamper his recovery. If we don't talk about it now, I'm not sure I'll be able to bring myself to try again. I don't know which way to turn.

I release the door handle, head over to the bed, and press a kiss to my father's cheek. "I'll see you tomorrow, Dad. Just focus on getting better." I open the door and pause before turning back to say, "I love you."

No regrets.

I TEXT Worth my location and ask him to meet me. My head is so full of thoughts, my body so full of emotion, I don't think I can successfully navigate my way out of the hospital without his help.

"Are you okay?" Mom asks as I shove my phone in my pocket and slump down into the seat next to her.

I shrug.

"I think we should go home," she says, smoothing her hand over my back like she used to when I was a child. Even before she finishes her sentence, I know I can't go back home tonight. It will only make my racing thoughts worse. I need space. Distance.

The elevator doors ping and Worth emerges. I let out a breath. Somehow, he makes things less complicated.

"Mom, this is my friend Worth," I say. "He arranged for me to get here today."

She looks from me to Worth, then stands and opens her arms to hug him. "Thank you so much. It's good to meet you."

"This is Oliver and Noah." I stand slowly, like all my bones are weary. "Mom, do you mind if I don't stay at home tonight? I just need a break from thinking about this stuff with Dad."

"Not at all, sweetheart. Have you got a place to stay?"

We both turn to Worth, and he nods. I shouldn't have presumed he'd arrange a hotel. But I'm very pleased he has.

"Why don't you come over for breakfast?" Mom says. "I make great pancakes."

"Sounds wonderful," Worth says. "Can we drop you home? I have a car waiting out front."

"I drove," she replies. "But thank you. You don't want these two together in the back seat of a car, like ever," she says, gesturing to Oliver and Noah.

Mom pulls me in for a hug and I hold her a little tighter. Is this difficult for her?

"Have you two said goodbye to your father?" she asks.

Oliver doesn't look up from his phone, but he raises his hand. "I did."

"Actually, Mom, I'll Uber back. I'm going to stay a little while longer," Noah says.

She squeezes his hand. "Try and get some sleep."

Mom grabs her coat and purse, and Oliver finally puts his phone away. We press for the elevator.

When it arrives, we step aside to let a woman out.

She's about the same age as Mom, but with dark hair. I take in her knee-high boots and dark jeans, and she must feel me looking at her, because she smiles. She tucks her hair behind her ear as she navigates past us.

I stare as she goes down the corridor, checks something on her phone, then reaches for the handle on Dad's door.

It's her.

It's Dad's other life colliding with ours.

I look back at Mom, who's now in the elevator with Noah and Worth. She shrugs, like there's nothing she can do. She gave up this fight a long time ago. She grabs my hand and pulls me into the car.

"That was her," I whisper. "Noah's in there."

"Yes," Mom says.

The elevator doors close.

"What?" Oliver says, entirely oblivious to what's going on.

I look at Worth, who takes my hand. I don't know if I'd have the strength to get anywhere without him next to me. He makes every-thing easier, just by being here.

"Thank you," I whisper.

"No thanks needed," he says.

TWENTY

It's late and Sophia is entirely out of energy. Everything about her is heavy—her gaze, her footsteps, her hand in mine. I take off her coat as she steps into the hotel suite. Then I bend and take off her shoes. "Can I run you a bath?"

She shakes her head. "I just want to lie on the bed and watch movies and eat junk."

"Then that's what we'll do." She'll be asleep in ten minutes. I head to the closet. "I hope you don't mind, I had Jules pack up some stuff and I got it sent over."

"What stuff?" She turns and sees her clothes hanging in the wardrobe.

"I thought you'd want to be comfortable."

"How? I mean… that's so incredibly nice of you, Worth."

"It's nothing. I had my housekeeper pack up some things of mine too." I check the drawers. "Yeah. We have sweats. And thick socks. Perfect for a movie."

It's past midnight, but if she needs a movie to sleep, that's what she'll get.

I guide her over to the bed. I pull out some comfortable clothes and start to undress her. I work quickly, pulling down the zipper of her dress before pulling a hoodie over her head.

"I'm so tired," she says.

I nod. "It's late. You've had an exceptionally long day."

I kneel at her feet and help her into her sweatpants, then lift her onto the bed and hand her the remote. "I'm just going to change."

I do, and Sophia flicks through the TV channels.

"Find anything?" I ask.

"Nope. I need a murder mystery or something. Dark but not gory."

"Agatha Christie-ish?"

"Exactly."

I take the remote from her and scroll through the channels until I land on an adaptation starring loads of British actors. Next stop is the minibar, to gather snacks. "I have popcorn, gummy bears, or M&M's."

"Yes, please."

I crawl onto the bed next to Sophia and she shifts to be closer to me, resting her head on my chest. "You okay?" I stroke her hair away from her face as she focuses on the TV.

"You know that woman who got out of the elevator as we were leaving?"

I think I know what she's going to say, but I keep my suspicions out of my voice. "Yeah," I say.

"She's been having an affair with my dad for twenty-five years. She has two kids with him. And my mom has known for decades."

Shit. Shit. Shit.

"Fuck, Sophia. That's a lot. You just found out?"

"During my last trip to Cincinnati. My mom announced she wanted a divorce." She pauses to shove a handful of M&M's into her mouth. Once she chews and swallows, she continues. "I don't even understand why—or any of it. Part of me wants every detail, wants to hear my dad explain why he betrayed us all. Why he lied and cheated all this time. And then another part of me just wants to run away and pretend it's not happening." She takes another M&M and pops it in my mouth. "My dad has been calling me nonstop since I found out. I haven't accepted a single one. Haven't answered any of his texts." Her voice breaks. "You think that's why he had a heart attack?"

"I don't," I say.

She looks up at me. "You don't?"

"He's been living a double life for twenty-five years, Sophia. He's hidden the births of two children from his family. I'm pretty sure he's had more stressful weeks than this one. He knows you love him."

"I'm not sure I do." Her voice is clipped and hard, which is hardly surprising. It's a lot for anyone to take in.

"There's a lot to process. You haven't done anything wrong in this scenario."

"You don't think ignoring him was wrong? Or refusing to come home for Thanksgiving?"

"Your mom was hosting him at Thanksgiving?"

"Just like nothing happened. My brothers are the same—they're just getting on with it, like this is business as usual. He's still dear old Dad and we're still the perfect family, white picket fence and everything."

"I'm sure what you're seeing isn't what they're feeling. Everyone copes differently. They probably feel as paralyzed and upset as you do. There's no one way to grieve."

"Not my mom. She says she's had a long time to get used to it, and is perfectly fine with the whole, 'Can you pass the gravy, Geoff?' thing."

"Fine?" I ask. "Or trying to be fine so you and your brothers don't feel as bad?"

She sighs and opens the bag of popcorn. "That house is... I couldn't go back there. Do you mind me coming back with you?"

"Sophia," I say, my tone admonishing. "Do I mind? Of course I don't mind. I'd ask you to move into the brownstone tomorrow if I thought you'd say yes."

"Don't ask me tonight, because I *might* just say yes."

My heart inches higher and higher, and I'm so tempted to jump in and ask, but Sophia's like a pressure cooker. She doesn't need me adding any additional complications to her life at the moment.

"Let's put a pin in that conversation for now."

"I haven't told anyone," she says. "Not even Jules. About my parents or my dad's second family."

I keep my eyes on the TV, but my heart pushes in my chest at the thought of being her only confidant. "How come?"

"I found out a week before the wedding. I thought hearing about how much of a sham my parents' relationship has been for the last twenty-five years might take the shine off."

I continue to stroke her hair. "You're a good friend. But I'm sure she'd want to know."

She sighs. "I know. I don't want to burst her bubble... and, I just... when I'm in New York, I can pretend it's not real. If I tell Jules, then I have to deal with it or something. Don't say anything, okay? Not to Leo, not to any of them?"

"You have my word." Now's not the time to tell her she probably needs to share this burden with her friends—because in my experience, it's not until she starts to believe it that she'll begin to heal.

She shifts so she's sitting up next to me and leans her head on my shoulder. "Thank you, Worth. For all of this."

"It's nothing, Sophia."

She looks up at me. "Don't say that. It's more than I ever could have expected."

"Then you need to start expecting more," I say. "You deserve *everything*."

A small smile twitches at the corners of her lips, but she still looks so sad. I wish I could take it away from her. "You say the nicest things." She looks away and pulls in a breath. "You should sleep. Do you want me to turn off the TV?"

"What about you?" I ask. "You should try and rest."

She shakes her head resolutely. "I won't sleep tonight."

"Then neither will I," I say. "I won't leave you alone."

"You're right here."

"You can be near a person and still be alone, Sophia. If you're not sleeping, neither am I. I'm here to talk if that's what you want. I'm here for foot rubs if that's what you want. I'm here to play goddamn charades if that's what you want. I'm here with you, and I'm not going anywhere."

She pulls in a deep breath, and when she exhales, her shoulders settle lower than before. For the first time tonight, there's a sense of peace in her expression. If I've been able to help her with that, just a little, it's more than I could have hoped to achieve. Even though I've only known Sophia a short time and logic says it doesn't make sense, I'd do anything for this woman in my arms.

"After your dad has finished all his tests and been discharged, he should get a full physical. And a second opinion. Just so you all have a little more certainty. I have a number of contacts who would be able to help. I can arrange it if you want."

She turns her head and presses a kiss to my shoulder. "Thank you."

"I'm just pleased I could be here. Pleased I could do something."

"I don't need foot rubs or charades," she says. "Just you."

My chest expands at her words. How is it that I can count on one hand the number of times I've been on my own with this woman, but I feel so protective of her? It felt like I got hit by a thunderbolt when I met her, but my feelings have only gotten stronger since then. I love her compassion for her friends and the way she can handle my sisters. I love her humor and the way she cares so deeply. I love holding her and helping her. I just want to be with her.

I'm in so deep, I'm worried I'll never come back up if she doesn't feel the same way.

TWENTY-ONE

Sophia

Worth squeezes my hand as we exit the elevator and head to Leo's apartment—Leo and Jules' apartment. Everything's changing so quickly. We got back from Cincinnati a few days ago and Worth's stayed at my place ever since.

It feels like we've slotted together in a perfect fit.

"Sophia and Worth," Jules says as we push the door open, like she wasn't expecting us to arrive together. I don't suppose she or any of them can really understand our connection. I can't fully understand it myself. "So great to see you both."

We're the first to arrive, which isn't a surprise. Worth is a stickler for punctuality—just one of many qualities I find completely adorable.

We greet each other, take off our coats, and get drinks.

"I haven't seen you since Thanksgiving," Jules says. "How was Cincinnati?"

"How are things going in Harlem?" Worth asks Leo at almost the same time. I know he's giving me some space to talk to Jules. I have to tell her what's going on. I can't leave it any longer or I'm worried I'll undermine our friendship.

"I wasn't planning on going to Cincinnati for Thanksgiving," I say to Jules.

"You weren't? You could have come here. What did you do?"

"I ended up going at the last minute." I take a deep breath.

I tell her the whole story, from finding out about the second family, to the divorce, to Dad's heart attack, to seeing the other woman in the hospital corridor.

"And Worth was there the entire time?"

I nod. "I don't know what I would have done without him."

"I'm so relieved. But honestly, you could have told me. I would have gone to Cincinnati with you."

"I didn't want to ruin this time for you and Leo. Most people would still be on their honeymoon at this point."

"You're my friend," she says. "I want to be there for you." She pulls me into a hug. "So how are things with your dad?"

"I stayed in Cincinnati until he was discharged from the hospital, but I didn't visit him again. He needs to get better. And then... I don't know."

"You've always adored him."

"I thought he sacrificed so much for us—working so we could have a comfortable life. In reality, it was my mom who made the huge sacrifices. Staying with him, knowing about his second family, but wanting us to have a picturesque childhood anyway."

"You know, I'm kind of proud of her for divorcing him now," Jules says. "She's still young enough to fulfil her own dreams."

I haven't really thought about my mom in all this, other than the sacrifices she's made in the past. But Jules is right. She has a chance at a real life now. Maybe she'll move to New York.

"Tell me about you and Worth," she says, emptying a bag of chips into a bowl on the counter.

"Aren't we about to have brunch?"

She looks at her watch and then shrugs. "Food will be here in ten minutes. What are we supposed to do, not eat until then?"

I take a chip. "Worth's been amazing. He got me to Cincinnati on a private plane on Thanksgiving. We were at Tavern on the Green with his sisters but he didn't hesitate to come with me—"

"You met his sisters?"

"Yeah, just for a few minutes. Because then I got the call from Oliver."

"But you were doing Thanksgiving at Tavern on the Green with the fam?"

Before I can answer, Leo comes into the kitchen. "Fisher and Jack are here. Do we have that weird beer Fisher likes?"

"Did you hear Worth and Sophia went to Tavern on the Green for Thanksgiving? With Worth's sisters."

"Yeah, he just said," Leo says. "Sorry about your dad."

"Thanks," I reply.

"You don't think that's a big deal?" Jules says. "Like... I think Worth really likes her."

"He married her. Of course he likes her."

"But it was a Vegas thing. They were drunk and acting crazy."

"Yeah, sounds like Worth," Leo says sarcastically.

Jules snaps her head toward me. "Was he drunk and acting crazy?"

"We'd had a few drinks, but no, he wasn't drunk."

"He's in love with you," Jules says, and my heart bunches in my chest. I can't quite breathe. "Isn't he, Leo?"

Leo holds his hands up in surrender. "I just came here for beer."

"Try the bar," Jules snaps playfully before shooing him back toward the living room. Turning back to me, she asks, "Are you in love with him?"

"I'm getting to know him. I like him. I'm actively *in like* with him." I haven't even considered whether I'm in love with Worth. I haven't known him long enough, and there's been so much else going on. "I don't know about love, but he's a good guy. Kind and generous and smart—"

"Have you had sex?" she whispers.

I widen my eyes. "Of course."

She sits back, surprised. How can that be a shock to her? "Is it good?"

I laugh. "The best I've ever— I mean, I can't even call what I was doing before 'sex' if I'm going to make a comparison."

"Wow," she says, reaching for another chip. "It's the same with Leo. We have a connection that's..." Her voice trails off, like there are no words for what she's trying to describe.

"I know what you mean. It's not just physical."

"So no annulment for you two. I mean, if you've consummated things. Have you discussed any kind of divorce?"

"Yeah, before we left Vegas, Worth said he'd speak to his lawyers. And then we agreed we'd continue to date for now."

"So if things go well, and you don't want to divorce, you don't have to. You'd have made it down the aisle before Leo and me." She squeals. "This is so exciting. It couldn't be more perfect. You know how close Leo and Worth are. We get to double-date, go on vacation together."

My heart squeezes tighter, like it's trying to get through a too-small hole. Jules is going at a million miles an hour. I just want to take this step by step.

"We don't know how this is going to play out," I remind her. "Worth and I haven't known each other very long. We've both got a lot going on."

"Right, but you're both amazing people who are perfect for each other."

I raise my eyebrows. "You tried to set me up with Fisher," I say.

"Momentary lapse in judgment. You and Worth—you're both so kind and low-key hilarious. I don't know why I didn't put you two together from the jump."

"He's very kind. And very hot."

"Sooo hot. It's actually almost offensive how hot he is."

I try and bite back a smile just as Worth comes through the door. "How's everything in here? Are you two gossiping?"

"About your huge dick, Worth," Jules says as she slides off the counter.

Worth shoots me a look and I shake my head. Jules might think she's joking, but she's very much on point.

"I want you to know, you have my blessing. I very much approve. But look after my friend or..." Jules slices her index finger across her throat.

Thankfully the buzzer goes. I hope that's the food.

"I'll bear your threat of murder in mind, Jules. Thanks."

She pats him on the arm as she leaves. "I'm off to play hostess. Don't make out in here for too long."

TWENTY-TWO

Worth

I glance at the door as my assistant comes into my office. Her sudden appearance means I'm running late on my video call. It's her job to keep me on time, and if I don't finish a call, she'll come in and make sure it finishes. It took me a while to find an assistant who's prepared to interrupt me and tell me to finish up my meeting. But I've grown very fond of Veronica.

"Mr. Huntington, your two o'clock is waiting."

"I'm going to have to leave things here, Patrick," I say. "But I think we've got a clear way forward. Let's talk same time next week." I nod at Veronica—a reminder to her to put it in the calendar.

I end the call and stand. I need to move around.

"Shall I show in your next meeting?" Veronica asks. There's something in the tone of her voice I can't quite place.

"Yes. Who is it?" I ask.

She doesn't answer my question, which isn't like her.

Before I have the chance to call after her, Avril bursts through the door. "Brother dearest."

"Avril, you're going to have to go. I have a meeting."

"I'm your two o'clock," she says, handing me an iPad. "You left my business plan at Tavern on the Green, so I'm here to deliver it in person."

Shit. In all the drama of Thanksgiving, I'd forgotten about Avril's plan. I'd kinda hoped coming off academic probation would inspire her to finish her degree after all.

"Okay, well, I've got it now. I'll let you know when I've had a chance to look at it."

She shakes her head, a mischievous grin unfurling on her face. "I'm booked in for an hour. You're not getting rid of me until I have my money's worth." She holds out her hand to the small conference table in my office. "Shall we?"

I know Avril well enough to realize I'll waste more time trying to tell her to leave than just going with it. I sigh and take a seat.

She smiles at me, knowing she's already won her first victory.

"So," she says, "I'm here to talk to you about Hotel on Ninth Street."

She was meant to formulate a plan for her future, not talk about my business issues. "Hotel on Ninth Street? You mean... my white elephant of a building on the corner of Forty-Sixth and Ninth?"

"I could draw you a Venn diagram, but you'll get the picture soon enough."

She opens a presentation on the iPad. The front page is a fancy logo for the aptly named hotel. She swipes through to the next slide.

In the moments before she starts talking, I really take her in. She's wearing black pants and a crisp black shirt. I've never seen my sister in business casual before. Seeing her dressed like this, it hits me that she's an adult—not a kid who needs protecting. At least, not the same ways she did when we were both younger.

"I'm going to ask you to think about this project as if it's brand new," she says. "Everything that's gone before are sunk costs. We don't want them clouding our judgement. I've done a cost analysis for a new apartment building and for restoring the current building and turning it into a hotel. I've also gone through the financials your previous business partner drew up. I hate to tell you this, Worth, but they're a pile of bullshit. They had a completely illogical average cost of capital, which threw all the other numbers out of whack."

"I use the same WAC for all my investments."

"*You* might, but the guy who took your money didn't—and whoever you had look over the numbers didn't catch it."

I pull back my shoulders, feeling slightly uneasy. Did Avril completely misread the financials, or has she really discovered something? And when did she start doing financial analysis? Did she rope Poppy into this?

Did my team really miss something?

"How did you even get the historical numbers?"

"You know Veronica wears the same perfume as Mom?"

That was the last thing I expected Avril to say. "What? Ver—How do you even remember what perfume Mom wore?" Avril was only four when Dad died. Mom never wore perfume again.

"I remember. I stole the bottle out of her bathroom. Poppy and I used to wear it."

"Huh," I say. "So Veronica gave you confidential financial information about my business?"

"If you fire her, I'll kill you," Avril says. "She's amazing. And besides, I told her my plan and she's invested. Let's get to the end and you can tell me you don't love her a little bit more for believing in it."

I roll my eyes. She's so dramatic.

"Okay, so whatever, you have an issue with your finance people. You can deal with that on your watch. This is my hour." She swipes to a different screen. She's had her nails done short, in a neutral color. The last time I saw her, her nails were blue and looked like ten deadly weapons. Avril really means business. "So it turns out, restoring the current building and turning it back into a hotel isn't as profitable as your proposed development over a ten-year period. But over a twenty-five-year period, it's more profitable."

I start to speak but she cuts me off. "I know that means you have more inherent risk, but let's talk about reward."

She flips over the iPad screen, like I'm a grandpa who couldn't quite manage it myself. "This is the Huntington family legacy." The screen fills with a bronze wash over the building, and in gold, "Hotel on Ninth Street" fills the page. Then underneath, in smaller letters along the bottom of the page, reads "A Huntington Family Hotel."

I glance across at her, trying to read her expression. The next three slides are renderings of a lush, elegant hotel lobby. Then on the next page, Poppy's picture comes up, along with her biography. "Director of Huntington Investments, Poppy acts as chairman of Hotel on Ninth Street."

"I think you're too old to play make-believe, Avril. Poppy has a perfectly good job at Goldman Sachs. There's no way she's going to come work for her brother. And by the way, she doesn't have enough experience."

"Well, A, she's up for working for you. I already asked her. And B, your finance director needs to be fired. We already established that."

I make a mental note to go through the Ninth Street development financials to see if Bryan missed anything. If he did, I need to know whether there might be a reasonable explanation for the lapse. "You think Poppy is going to give up her job at Goldman? She's killing it there. Even if she's having a bit of a rough patch, she'll be partner in ten years."

Avril looks at me like I'm the stupidest man ever to have lived. "Maybe being a partner at Goldman isn't what she wants. Ever thought about that?"

"Oh right," I say. "Loads of people turn down that opportunity."

"No, you're right. If you've put in loads of time and effort, sacrificed family and friends, relationships, vacations and holidays for two decades, you're probably not going to turn it down when it's offered. But maybe she doesn't want to pay the price of partnership."

I make another mental note to talk to Poppy about how things are going at work. She'd said something at Thanksgiving, but I just thought it was normal complaining about work.

Avril swipes the screen again and reads aloud the bio under her headshot. "Avril is the creative director of the hotel. She's gradually learning all aspects of hotel management with a view to becoming the manager."

"You're at Columbia for economics," I say, incredulous. "You want to become a hotel manager?"

She sighs. "You've always worked so hard for us, Worth. Poppy and I see it, and we're so grateful. You've done it our entire lives. And it's not just about becoming the businessman you are today—you've worked hard at trying to get us to succeed, too. You've worked hard at keeping our family together. But it's time we shared the burden. This hotel would be a central point where we can all come together. You as owner, Poppy as chairman and finance director. Me as manager— one day." Her eyes go glassy as she speaks. "It means we'll all be in each other's lives forever."

I'm stunned into silence. I'm completely and utterly floored. I always thought Avril thought of me as an interfering, overbearing father figure. I assumed she'd want space, not the exact opposite.

"I want this hotel to be our family legacy. Not death. Not grief. Not survival."

How can I say no to that?

"I know I could stay at Columbia and finish out my degree, but honestly, I have almost two years to go. And in two years, I could have learned so much. I thought I could go to Boston to work in your hotel there. Or I could ask Bennett or Jules if I could work at their place while I help oversee renovations on Ninth Street."

"I'll need to think this through," I say. "And I need to talk to Poppy."

She nods enthusiastically, like she's willing a yes out of me.

"You know Mark Zuckerberg dropped out of Harvard. And Bill Gates," she says. "And Ben Affleck, although—"

"Quit while you're ahead. And anyway, dropping out of college doesn't mean you're going to become successful. They're the exceptions, not the rule."

"We're exceptions. Poppy, you, and me. You've achieved so much, Worth. But most of all, you protected Poppy and me. I know we don't talk about it a lot. But we would be in very different places in our lives if it hadn't been for you."

I take in a steadying breath. She's right—we don't talk about how bad it got with Mom after Dad's death. How I learned to make dinner by watching the Cooking Channel, how I faked Mom's signature on permission slips, the excuses I'd make up for her not attending soccer matches and ballet recitals. "Maybe," I say.

"I remember, Worth," she says. "How you'd make me my lunch. How you'd come to my gymnastics class and pretend Mom was in the parking lot making a call when the other moms asked you where she was."

I swallow. "It was a long time ago and we're all in different places now."

"Because of you," she whispers.

"So, what's this hotel thing? You're trying to repay me or something? You don't owe me anything."

"That's the best part of you. You did everything to keep our family together and you never talk about it, never throw it in our faces. You've never asked us for anything. You just keep giving more. I would never try to repay you, because I know that's the last thing you want. What I *can* do is my part to keep us together, just like you've done for so many years. I think this hotel would be the embodiment of that. A central place of connection for the three of us."

"Let me guess: you're thinking you could be my eyes and ears on the ground at Ninth Street during refurbishment, while simultaneously learning about the hotel business?"

She's no poker player. Her smile says she'd agree to anything right now. Seeing her happy like this shifts something in me. Yes, I want her to get her degree, but I never went to college until business school. It didn't do me any harm, even if I was one of three people in the history of the school who didn't have an undergrad degree before doing the MBA.

"Absolutely," she says. "I'd really like to be involved with the renovations. And the design process. I know I'm no architect or designer, but I can see space. And I have a really cool vision for the look and feel of the place."

"Right, but you wouldn't get final say on that."

"I just want to be part of the discussion. If it's our family legacy, I want to feel like I've contributed."

I've worked so hard for so long, I'm not sure how I feel about my sisters working alongside me. Everyone I work with is dependent on me for a paycheck. It means what they tell me gets filtered into acceptable form. Working with family would be different. It could be a good thing. It could be a *great* thing. But I need to think carefully before I make a decision. This hotel could bring us together, but it also could tear us apart.

"I understand," I say. "I'll think about it."

"That's all I can ask. I already have an appointment in your calendar in two weeks. You can give me your decision then. In the meantime, we're going to lunch. Let's find somewhere to eat."

TWENTY-THREE

Sophia

I've always loved New York so much that leaving for the weekend has never been a priority. Even in the height of summer, I shun the Hamptons and spend the weekends playing tourist and enjoying the empty park. All to say, going to the Catskills at the end of November isn't at the top of my bucket list. But that's exactly where Worth and I are headed. He wants to show me his cabin, and honestly, I want to see it. I want to know every part of him. Getting to know him the last few weeks has been like being on some huge treasure hunt. I keep uncovering more and more great stuff about the man I'm married to.

"I've learned that the drive up is important," Worth says from the driver's seat. He's wearing an open-necked plaid shirt, jeans, and boots. It's not a version of Worth I've seen before, but Mountaineer Worth is hot. His five-hundred-dollar haircut and unshaven jaw don't hurt, either. I plan to appreciate the hell out of the side-profile view I have of him for the next hundred miles or so.

"Important how?"

"Important because it takes time to leave the city behind. I've used a helicopter a couple of times, but it's not the same."

"It's not the same as going by car? Because it's going by air and it's quicker?" I ask sarcastically.

"Wow, you're funny," he says, his mouth twitching at the sides.

"It's nonstop jokes with me," I reply. "But seriously, tell me why a helicopter is a bad idea, other than it's terrifying and bad for the environment."

"Because in a car you're forced to move through the landscape at a slower pace. You see it change. First the high buildings disappear, then the houses get bigger and more spread apart, and in among that is the greenery. More and more trees appear. It's like they're welcoming you in, urging you forward."

"It feels like you're about to break into song. Please can you warn me if you're going to start singing?" I grin at him.

"Interesting idea. I might just want to surprise you." He slides his hand over my thigh and I snake my fingers between his. His hands are so large and strong, just like the rest of him. He's the anchor in my personal storm at the moment. He's keeping me safe and sane. "It's a gradual change," he says. "It gives you time to let go of what's in the city and embrace what's in the mountains."

I'm silenced by what he's saying. It's thoughtful and profound and just so entirely *him*. I squeeze his hand. "And what is it you want to leave behind?"

"Just the usual," he says. "Work and stuff."

"And you want to leave work behind because...?"

"I love my job. But it's a lot of... work."

"Because you have employees and they're looking to you for direction and paychecks?"

"Yeah. Partly that. And because a lot of the time I'm investing in people's dreams. In passion projects. That's a lot of responsibility."

"Do you get very caught up in the individuals?"

"I did at first. I have to separate myself a little more now." He pauses and I don't speak. Worth is a thinker, and I don't want to interrupt that. "I separate myself, which makes it easier, takes some of the pressure off, but it also takes away some of the sense of purpose. Does that make sense?"

"Yeah. So the sense of purpose comes from helping people realize their dreams, but that comes with huge pressure."

"Exactly."

"That's a conundrum. It's the same for your sisters as well, I suppose. Except the stakes are higher."

"What do you mean?" He blinks. I'm mesmerized by his long lashes and the way he shifts in his seat. If we weren't going fifty miles an hour, I'd straddle the guy and make out with him for a week.

"You help them realize their dreams. You must feel huge pressure for them to succeed."

"Huh," he says. "I hadn't drawn the comparison before."

"Really?"

He shrugs.

"What about your own dreams and ambitions?" I ask. "Are they always for other people to succeed, and then you're successful by default?"

"I've never thought about it like that."

He's so completely willing to listen and see a different perspective. For someone so powerful, he completely checks his ego. "You're a good guy, do you know that?"

He looks across at me and smiles, this huge boyish grin, and it's like the sun coming out. This man lights me up, inside and out.

"You have a pretty smile," I say.

He chuckles as he turns back to face the road. "Not as pretty as yours."

"Wow," I say as we round the corner. Suddenly we can see for miles. Trees in every color fill the view as far as the eye can see, like they're piled on top of each other, in every color, reds and golds and deep browns. There's still hints of green from the smattering of evergreens, but this is leaf-peeper heaven. I have a flash of us forty years from now making the same journey, a blanket on my knees and wrinkles at Worth's eyes. I bet he'll say *wow* every trip when he sees the leaves turning like this.

"It's beautiful," I say. "There's every color."

"Can you believe they do this every year?" Worth says. "The trunks and branches stay solid while the leaves shift and change. Eventually the branches let them fall, leaving them bare. It's such a beautiful ritual. Then that trunk and those branches grow new life the next spring, like nothing happened. It's so symbolic. The passing of a chapter can be as beautiful as the start of a fresh one."

I swallow, my throat tight. "Yeah. I guess life is full of chapters ending." It's certainly the end of the chapter where I thought my dad walked on water. That book is firmly closed.

"You don't get the new ones without ending the old ones," Worth says. "It's about survival. The tree knows it can't survive as it is. It lets go of the leaves to ensure it continues into the next year. The roots and trunk grow and expand, develop new branches, and create new leaves the next year. It's really beautiful."

The road curves and a fresh landscape unfurls in front of us, more rust colors this time, with smatterings of yellow. I can see the branches more clearly. More of the leaves have dropped.

"And the old leaves don't just disappear," Worth says. "They fall and become food for the trunk and the new leaves. The old chapters make the new chapters richer and stronger."

"I don't know if I can ever forgive him," I confess. "I know that makes me a bad person, but I just don't know if I can."

Worth tightens his hand in mine. I know he wants to help, but this is not a problem he can solve. "It doesn't make you a bad person. It makes you human. There's no pressure on you to forgive him. No one's going to think badly of you. Maybe your next chapter doesn't involve him. Or maybe it does, but in a totally different way from before."

"Mom wants me to hear him out. Oliver says the same thing."

"They're trying to make you feel better. But they're so involved in the situation that all of your needs are overlapping. You need to do what's right for you when the time is right."

"But I don't want to upset Mom or Oliver."

He shakes his head. "You won't. They love you."

"Do you think I can live in this in-between world where I'm not *not* speaking to my dad and my family isn't a family? It can't go on forever."

"You'll know when the time is right to reach out. You need to trust yourself."

"I don't trust anyone at the moment." I glance across at him, wishing I hadn't said those words. Worth has given me no reason not to trust him. He's been nothing but a gold-star boyfriend or husband or whatever he is. But I don't know if I'll ever be able to trust anyone completely ever again. Including myself. I've lost faith that what seems real is anything more than an illusion.

"Don't feel bad about whatever you're feeling," Worth says, reading my mind as usual. Sometimes I wonder if he knows me better than I know myself. "Let's just see what today brings. You can't bring back yesterday or fast-forward to tomorrow."

"Please god, no songs." My words are joking, but I can't inject my tone with the same levity. I desperately want resolution, but none of the roads available give me the ending I want. Because what I want is my father to have been the man I thought he was.

Worth pulls my hand in his onto his lap and takes a deep breath, like he's about to belt out an eighties rock ballad, then stops. "Not going to do that to you." He brings our hands to his mouth and presses a kiss on the back of my hand.

"We're going to have a great weekend," he says simply.

The road bends again and we're faced with a fresh landscape, even more beautiful than the one before.

TWENTY-FOUR

Sophia

When Worth said *cabin in the woods*, I was expecting something rustic.

"You lied," I say, gazing up at the impressive home in front of us. It's huge and has a wraparound porch, complete with Adirondacks pointing out at the surrounding trees. The structure might have been made of logs, but that's the only rustic thing about it. I can see through the window to a modern kitchen that would look right at home in some Scandi billionaire retreat.

"Lied because?"

"You said log cabin. Not log palace."

He chuckles as he pulls our bags from the trunk. I follow him up the wooden steps to the porch.

"We need to get stuff for s'mores," I say. "Where's the nearest store?"

"We have everything we need inside. The place is stocked."

"How? And wow!" I say as I step inside and look up at the eighteen-foot ceilings. The inside walls look like actual logs. It's like where you imagine Santa would live, if Santa was a billionaire and not an oversized elf.

"This is the actual best," I say. "It's so peaceful."

"It really is."

"Do you come up here a lot?"

"Not a lot, but I get my use out of it."

"And there are always s'mores packed, just in case?" How is it possible that I can feel jealous right now? Somehow I do. I feel regretful of the time Worth and I haven't had together, jealous of the people who've gotten to have time with him other than me. "Do you come here with your sisters?" It's not really what I want to know, but it's what I ask.

He drops our bags on the floor and heads to the refrigerator. He pulls out two beers, takes the caps off of both and hands one to me. "Absolutely not. This is a place to escape." He grins and takes a swig.

I watch his Adam's apple bob. Everything this man does is sexy. I can't even watch him drink a beer without wanting to mount him. What's the matter with me? I wonder how many other women have felt the same way.

"You don't talk about your exes," I say, leaning against the counter and taking a swig of my beer.

His gaze dances between my lips and my eyes. "What do you want to know?"

"How many have you brought here?"

Confusion ripples across his face and he frowns. "None. I've never brought anyone here. Not even the guys. Bennett and Efa borrowed it once, but I only ever come here alone."

"Until me?"

"Right," he replies. "Until you. There are lots of things I've never done before you."

A smile tugs at my mouth. I step forward and hook my fingers into his belt. "Oh yeah? Like what else?"

His chest expands as he takes a breath in. He slides his bottle onto the counter and takes my face in his hands, sweeping his thumbs over my cheeks. He drops his hands and slides his palms up my arms. "Well, I've never had a wife before."

I laugh. "I'm not sure I count. We don't even live together. And we haven't known each other very long."

"Legally, it counts. And if you want to move in, let's talk about it. Your commute would be easier."

I fix him with a look that says, *You can't be serious.*

"We'd spend more time together that way," he says.

"I'm not sure that would work," I say, honestly. "I'd feel like a roommate. That's your place, Worth. It's always going to be your place."

"You're probably right." He pulls me toward him and I wrap my arms around his waist, my cheek nuzzling against the soft flannel of his shirt. "Have I mentioned I've been thinking of moving?" His voice reverberates in his chest.

"I'm not saying you should move," I say.

"But if we're going to live together—"

"Worth, we've known each other five minutes."

"It's been weeks. And I'm not sure how you're feeling, but I'm not feeling like this is going to end... anytime soon."

I smooth my hand up his back. "Same. But I'm in the middle of stuff with my family right now. I don't want to make life-changing decisions just yet."

He growls and I look up, trying to take in his expression. Is he pissed? He looks frustrated.

"I'm sorry," I say.

"Don't," he says. "You have nothing to be sorry about. I'm annoyed with myself. I never should have let you marry me. I knew you were vulnerable and I went along with it anyway."

"Worth," I say, taking a step back. "You didn't make that decision. I did."

"But I knew you were going through something."

"We were basically strangers. You can't take on everything everyone else is going through and be responsible for it. I'm an adult woman, and I married you because I wanted to do something wild. I wanted not to care for a night, to make a mockery of the institution that my parents had before me." I shake my head. "I don't know if I was even thinking much at all. But I do know it was *my* decision to marry you."

He takes me in, listening. "It's hard," he says. "I often feel... responsible for..."

"Everyone?" I suggest. "Like you're everyone's caretaker, father, benefactor, protector."

"Maybe," he says, and I link my fingers through his.

"But who's looking after you?" I ask. "You're busy running around, making sure everyone else is taken care of. Who's taking care of you? Who's meeting your needs?"

"I do okay," he says.

I raise my eyebrows. Doing okay isn't enough.

"Marrying you is one of the first times I felt like I wanted something for me," he says. "I knew it could potentially cause problems with the guys. I knew I might piss off Efa and Jules, and I might even permanently damage my relationship with Fisher or Leo. And I knew when my sisters found out, they'd be pissed. But I did it anyway. You had your reasons for marrying me—but I wasn't trying to make a mockery of the institution of marriage. Not at all."

I swallow. "I've hurt your feelings," I say. "I don't want to lie to you. And I didn't know you then. I felt something between us. But honestly, I wasn't thinking about being with you forever. I wasn't thinking past the next hour. Things are... different now."

He nods, and I slide my hand up his chest, but I don't say more. I want to hear what he's thinking.

"I understand. My feelings aren't hurt. But it was different for me. The moment I saw you, it was like a beacon went off in me. I wanted more immediately. If I'm honest, it frightened me a little. I've never felt that way. And then when I saw you in Vegas again, I longed for something to bind us together. The shots. The conversation. The ceremony."

His eyes flit across my face, one way, then the other. "I still feel like that. Like you're *it* for me. Like I want to dive in deeper every time I see you. I know we're not going at the same pace. I know you're going through things, so I'm hanging back, happy to be ready when *you're* ready. But, Sophia, I need you to know that I'm ready whenever you are. I'm here. Waiting. If you don't want to move into the brownstone because of what you've got going on with your dad, that's fine. If you don't want to move into the brownstone because it's my place and you'd feel like a roommate, then let's find somewhere else together, because I'm right there next to you, ready. Not because I want to be your benefactor or caretaker. But because I want to be your husband. I want you."

I don't know what to say. I've never felt so adored by a guy. And it's not that I don't feel the same, but I'm holding back. I can't help it. When I'm with Worth, I want to stay exactly like this, with him. I can't imagine my life any other way. It's only when I take a step back, when I see the other parts of my life moving in different directions, that I doubt what we have. I'd like to fast-forward to the future to see how things shift. Will I catch up to Worth? Will I be able to set aside everything other than him, for him? I don't have the answers to those questions. But I owe it to him to be honest.

"I'm not ready to move in with you because of what I've got going on back in Cincinnati." I can't even bring myself to say the word "dad" or "father" right now. "And honestly, I don't know when I'm going to be ready."

"That's okay," he says. "I'm a patient man."

Something in my stomach stirs like the silt at the bottom of a clear river, making everything murky. I don't know if I'm *ever* going to be ready. Worth's standing in front of me, offering me everything I could ever want in a man. And I'm still not ready. What's it going to take?

"Promise me one thing, Worth?" I ask.

"Anything," he replies.

"That if waiting becomes too much, you walk away. You don't stay to help me or support me. You go."

He closes his eyes in a long blink. "I don't know if I can make that promise."

And that's the thing with Worth: he's honest to his core. I know I'll have to be the one who walks away if the time comes.

But that time isn't here yet. And I hope it never arrives.

My phone interrupts the conversation, which is probably for the best. It's Noah.

"Hey," I say as I answer. Worth kisses me on the head and heads to collect the bags from where he dumped them.

"What are you doing next weekend?" Noah asks.

I watch Worth as he takes the bags through to the back. I know my suitcase is heavy, but he makes it look effortless. He makes everything look effortless.

"Um, I'm not sure. Why?"

"Oliver and I might come and stay," he says, like he just told me the sky is blue.

"What do you mean, you and Oliver might come and stay? You've never stayed with me before."

"There's a first time for everything."

"Noah," I say. "Just come out with it. What are you planning? There's no way you and Oliver have decided to just come and stay. There's more to it than that."

I can practically hear him shaking his head. "We just thought, with everything going on, it would be good for the three of us—"

"Did Mom put you up to this?" I ask.

"No. Well, not really."

"So you mean yes. Mom wants you to come and check on me?"

"No, she didn't suggest visiting, but she suggested we stay in touch with you. And honestly, Sophia, I think it would be nice for the three of us to see each other, given what's been going on." I don't know if Noah is trying to keep our family together or emotionally blackmailing me into seeing our dad. At the moment, I just want to block it all out.

Worth emerges from the back, his eyes searching mine. I just want to hang out with my husband. Escape the city and everything it brings with it.

"You can come," I say. "But don't think you can convince me to talk to Dad. I'm not ready."

"Not on the agenda. I promise."

"Okay, gotta go," I say, locking eyes with Worth. "I've got some escaping to do."

"What?" he asks.

"Never mind," I say and hang up the phone. "Hey," I say, cocking my head to the side. "You wanna show me around?"

Worth nods, and I can tell by his expression something's shifted. "Yes," he says. "I want to show you around." He stalks over to me and, instead of taking my hand or putting his arm around me, reaches for the hem of my shirt and lifts it over my head.

"You want to do a naked tour?" I ask, grinning at him.

He nods again. "I want to do everything naked this weekend."

"A nudist weekend? Is that your jam?"

"I don't want to see people nude generally, but I absolutely want you naked specifically."

I strip off my jeans. "I can make that happen."

He reaches for my lace-covered breasts, kneading them together, his thumbs circling my nipples. I groan. He's so possessive during sex, so dominant and commanding. I'm under his spell completely.

He reaches around me, lifts me up onto the kitchen island, and strips off my panties, my bare ass cheeks on the cool marble counter.

"You're beautiful," he says as he kneels before me, opening my knees wide. He presses his tongue against my folds and I whimper. His breath is hot on my sex, his fingers digging into the flesh of my thighs. He dips and licks, circles and flicks his tongue like it's his job. He's CEO of whatever he's doing, that's for sure.

I can barely keep myself upright. I put one arm back, laying my palm behind me to stop myself from falling. I use my other hand to thread my fingers through his hair. Feeling his head move as he feasts on me is too much. He knows exactly my weak spots. He understands how to make me moan, how to make me want more, how to undo me.

The scrub of his beard grazes my skin, adding a slice of sour to the sweet of his tongue. I jolt, forcing myself forward, pressing myself against him.

More. More. More.

It's the call of my body and mind. I just can't get enough of him. It shouldn't be possible to feel this connected to another person. To feel so worshipped. Savored. Loved.

My body starts to shake and he slides his fingers into me. My head falls back, and I resign myself to the way my orgasm is creeping over me. I have no control. My body is completely his. My back arches and I call out. My arm gives out and I collapse backwards onto the counter.

He stands, wiping his mouth with the back of his hand. "You're fucking delicious," he growls. "So fucking wet for me. But now I want to feel you around my cock."

His voice has a ragged tone to it, like he's only inches away from losing control. I'm grateful that it's not just me who feels so helpless when we're together like this.

I slide off the counter, turn, spread my legs and lay my torso onto the cool marble.

I want him to feel me. I want him to take me. I want him to have all of me.

"Fuuuck," he growls. I hear the clinking of his belt buckle and the tear of the condom wrapper. He presses his hand on the small of my back, holding me in place.

This time, he doesn't inch in slowly, but I know it's not because he's being inconsiderate. He knows how ready for him I am. I don't want to wait a second longer.

TWENTY-FIVE

Sophia

The smell of something butter and vanilla wafts into my bedroom as I pull on my jeans. If Oliver's trying to cook, he's going to burn down the entire building. I grab a sweater and head out.

I poke my head into the kitchen and find Noah over the stove.

"I'm making pancakes," he says.

"You are?" I ask. "I don't have ingredients for pancakes."

"But you have a store on the corner that does."

"I do?" I start to laugh, and Noah grins.

"I'm not sure I've ever been to your apartment before," he says.

"You live in Cincinnati," I say.

"It's nice," he adds.

I can't remember the last time I spent time with Noah without Mom around. She was always the central point that we'd all circle.

"Thanks. It's a rental. And Jules is still paying rent. At some point, I guess I'll have to find something else." Then I think about Worth. He'd have us living together. It's weird, because if I'd just started dating someone and we liked each other a whole lot, I might consider moving in together if my lease was up or something. But with Worth it feels different somehow. Like it would be a lifetime commitment instead of it being about sharing utilities.

"Maybe you could get another roommate," he says. "What about that guy you came to Cincinnati with on Thanksgiving?"

"Not sure he'd want to room with me here." But if I asked him to, he probably would. "Where's Oliver?" I ask, keen to change the subject from Worth.

"Running. He'll be back in a minute."

"So what are we going to do today? Go to a museum or something?"

Noah shrugs. "Hang out. Watch a movie. Take a walk."

"And, just so I can brace myself, when am I getting The Talk?"

"The Talk?" he asks.

"The one where you tell me Dad's still our dad and I should make an effort because he's sorry or whatever."

Noah slides a pancake onto the plate resting on the side of the stove. "Oliver might have that planned—it was his idea to come and visit—but that kind of talk isn't on my agenda."

"So, out of the blue, the two of you just came to hang out?"

Noah flips two pancakes in the pan and I watch, willing him to do it without breaking them. "It's not out of the blue," he says. "Dad's second family bombshell has... well, it's been a lot."

I grab plates from the cupboard and flatware from the drawer.

"Understatement of the year, but yeah," I say.

"To say that I'm pissed off with Dad doesn't even come close," he says. "But you know, I'm also pissed with Mom."

My heart lifts and squeezes in my chest. I thought he and Oliver were so blasé about the situation. It's comforting to know Noah isn't just taking it all in stride, although I wish he wasn't hurting. "I know what you mean," I reply.

"Mom was trying to protect us, and she didn't want to have three kids on her own—I get it. But it feels like our entire childhood was a lie."

"Exactly," I say, relieved he *gets it.*

Oliver comes in from his run and his gaze volleys between us. "What happened?"

"We were just talking about Mom and Dad," Noah says.

Oliver scrapes his hand through his hair. "I don't know how to feel," he says. "I'm mad at them but I love them. I want things to go back to normal but that can't ever happen."

"Right," Noah says. "I can't imagine not having Dad in my life, but I can barely look at him at the moment. I used to think he was the kind of man I wanted to be. But now... he's exactly the opposite of the man I want to be. I'd never want to hurt my family, my kids, the way he's hurt us."

I don't think I've ever felt so connected to my brothers than I do in this moment. The three of us are all going through the exact same thing—and no one else in the world can relate in precisely the same way. It's just the three of us on this island.

"I've been selfish," I say. "I thought you two were happy to go along with things. I had no idea you felt this way."

"It's been hard," Oliver says. "On all of us."

"Normally I'd talk to Mom if something massive happened in my life, but I can't talk to her about this," Noah says. "Because she's part of the problem. If I criticize Dad, she's so unfazed by it, because she's had twenty-five years to get used to it, that it just makes me feel angrier. It doesn't help at all."

"Yeah, I think Mom just wants us to be over it already," Oliver says.

"She's ready to live her life—and that's the other thing. I feel intense guilt that I was the reason Mom *hasn't* lived the life she's wanted to all these years," Noah says, pressing his fingers into his eyebrows. I've never heard him sound so bereft before. Noah's always so measured and even. It's hard seeing him so upset.

I slide my arm around his waist. "We've got each other," I say, trying to be reassuring. I'm so pleased they're here. I should have invited them sooner.

"Let's agree that we always tell each other the truth," Noah says, slipping two more pancakes onto the plate and turning to face us. "The three of us can be a family within a family. Nothing should come between us."

Oliver agrees, but I can't do anything but wince. I haven't told them I'm married.

"There's something you should know," I say.

"Fucking hell," Noah says. "You don't have a secret family, do you?"

"No," I say, but then I stop. Do I? "Not really," I amend.

Two bulbous pairs of eyes stare at me.

"Let's eat," I say, pulling the stack of pancakes from the counter and slipping out of the kitchen. "Bring the plates and silverware and whatever toppings you bought, because I know I didn't have anything in my pantry."

"What pantry?" Noah asks.

"Exactly."

I sit and serve up two pancakes on each plate. I'm going to need the carbs to energize me through this conversation.

"Spit it out, Sophia," Oliver says.

"You know that guy that you met at the hospital?" I ask.

They both stare silently at me.

"Well, funny story, but he's Jules' husband's bestie. We were all in Vegas for their wedding a few weeks ago. It was only the second time I'd met him and we just kinda ended up... sorta getting married."

Noah drops his flatware and sits back in his chair. Oliver goes completely still.

"It's not like we got married to be together or anything. It was kind of a joke and... now we're dating because it turns out we like each other."

"Jesus Christ," Oliver says. "Can I just say for the record that my life is an open book? No wife stashed in a closet in my bedroom. No children, at least none that I know about. I'm not even really dating since Debbie moved to Florida. There's nothing big in my life that you don't know."

Noah sighs and shakes his head. "Fuck, Sophia. Is he a good guy?"

"He's talking to his lawyers about an annulment or divorce or something. It's not like we're going to be hosting Thanksgiving next year. But we're dating, so conversations about getting divorced are weird... but yeah, he's a good guy."

"Can we meet him? Like properly?" Noah asks. "I don't want to feel like I don't know what's going on in your life."

I squeezed his arm. "You know what's going on. I just think I was pissed at the institution of marriage and wanted to do something wild."

"But you're still seeing him," Oliver says. "So can we meet him?"

My skin feels awkwardly tight and my head begins to hurt. "Maybe," I say. "I just don't want to give him the wrong signal by introducing him to my family."

"He likes you more than you like him?"

I shake my head, because that's not it. "No, more like... he's in a place where he's ready for his future. I just don't think I am. I'm trying to come to terms with all these big feelings about my past, about our parents. And that's where my energy is. It's not at all that I don't like him. I absolutely do. More than I've liked anyone. Ever. I like him so much that I can't tell him anything but the truth. I can't pretend I'm ready to move forward with him when I'm not."

Oliver rubs my back, trying to comfort me. It's the first time I've fully realized that Worth and I might not work out. It hurts.

"If he likes you, he'll wait," Oliver says. "Things will even out with Mom and Dad. We'll come to a new normal at some point."

"You think?" I say. "I don't know anything anymore."

"Did you ever know anything?" Noah asks with a wink.

"Only just slightly more than you." I elbow him in the side.

"We'll figure it out," Oliver says, stuffing half a pancake in his mouth.

I'm glad he thinks so. The problem is, the foundation of our lives has been upturned. I'm not sure that's something we can "figure out." Any new normal that comes after what's happened is going to be full of suspicion and bitterness. That's what I'm most afraid of—that I'll be suspicious of everyone, think everyone is lying, believe every man in my life is concocting a series of fairy tales for me to believe in, so they can manipulate situations to their benefit.

I'm done being lied to.

I'm done being manipulated.

I didn't grow up the way I thought I did, and I'm just not sure how to deal with that.

"I know I'm not the guy who should be giving relationship advice," Oliver says.

"That's for sure," Noah says. "You are horrible with women."

"He's horrible *to* women," I correct him. "There's a difference."

"I'm not horrible to women," Oliver says. "They just think I'm a liar. So when I tell them I only want something casual, they think I actually mean I want to get married and have babies."

I laugh. "Words are one thing. Actions are entirely another. You act like husband material—that's your problem." In contrast, Worth's words and actions are completely aligned.

"Yes," Noah says. "You need to act like a dick. Then you'll be fine."

I smile, gaze roving from Noah inhaling pancakes to Oliver, who's sweaty and eye-rolling Noah.

I'm really pleased they came to visit.

TWENTY-SIX

Worth

I finger the pages from my lawyer as I pull them out of the envelope. I didn't exactly ask him to draw up the papers, but I told him what happened and inquired about the easiest way to exit a spur-of-the-moment marriage. He's taken the initiative to draw up divorce papers for us to sign. I knew what they were when they arrived at my office, which is why I brought them home. I didn't want to look at them earlier, and I don't want to look at them now. The last thing I want is to divorce Sophia.

The doorbell rings and I put the papers down on the console table before opening the door. Sophia is on the front stoop, looking beautiful. Her cheeks are pink from the cold and her hair peeks out from under her hat, making her look younger than usual.

"Hey," she says with an adorable little wave.

"Thanks for coming." I kiss her on the cheek and take the duffel she has by her side. I usually stay at her place. Tonight is the first time we'll be staying together at the brownstone.

"This feels weird," she says. "And you look so formal."

She looks nervous, and I can't help but smile at her. She's so beautiful. It's good to have her here. "I just stepped through the door. You must have followed me up the street."

"Did you walk?" she asks, as I help her out of her coat.

I laugh. "No. My driver dropped me."

"So here we are," she says. "I'm officially staying over at the brownstone."

I want her to feel comfortable here, like she's at home. I know she doesn't want to move in, but I want her to see that living together would be something positive. Nights spent at her apartment are just that: nights. We go there after dinner or a movie. But I want to hang out here. I want this to be *ours*.

I put down her bag and pull her into my arms. "I'm happy to have you here."

Her smile falters. I don't know why.

She glances sideways, and I follow her gaze. She's staring at the papers from my lawyer.

"I got them today from my lawyer. I've not had a chance to look at them."

"Divorce papers?" she asks.

"I think so."

"Let's look," she says, nodding at the table.

My body sags. This is not what I had planned for our first evening here. I want to cook together, slow dance in the kitchen to some Luther Vandross, eat dinner, then take a bath together. I want us to talk. I want to hold her. I really don't want to talk about divorce.

"You can read it," I say. I'm not hiding anything from her.

She picks up the papers, follows me into the kitchen, and slides them onto the kitchen table.

"Would you like some wine?" I ask.

She nods, and I show where the glasses are while I get a bottle of red from the wine fridge. "This Argentinian malbec is gorgeous," I say. "Efa says her brother-in-law owns the vineyard."

"Really?"

"Efa has a brother-in-law for every occasion."

"I like her," Sophia says.

"I do too. She's good for Bennett."

"You're lucky to have such wonderful people around you, Worth."

I pour the wine. "I know. I'm a very lucky man." My eyes slice to hers and she offers me a half-smile.

"How's Avril?" she asks. "Have you decided on the hotel yet?"

I pull out a chair and take a seat. "Not yet. I think Avril's committed and it would really give her a focus. A challenge. Apparently Poppy is interested in getting involved, too."

"Wow. A family affair." Sophia takes a seat at the end of the table and our legs intertwine.

"She's got it in her head that the hotel would be a family legacy. Something positive to work on together, rather than something negative binding us together."

Sophia nods but doesn't offer an opinion.

"I think it's a good idea," I say.

"For them," Sophia says. "Or for you? Is it what you want?"

"I want Avril and Poppy to be happy."

"But beyond that, what do you want? You're so good at caring for everyone else, it worries me that you don't take time to figure out what you want."

"Well, I'd like to beat Bennett in Hotel Games."

"Hotel Games?" Sophia asks, frowning.

Have I never explained to her that the six of us all have hotels, which we use to compete against each other? "It's like the Hunger Games, but nobody dies and all the competitors own luxury hotels."

"So not at all like the Hunger Games," Sophia says. "Whatever keeps a billionaire feeling alive, I guess."

I chuckle. "That's why we all have hotels. We compete against each other for whose property is the most successful. It was a way of keeping a connection between us after business school. The criteria gets more and more complicated, but somehow Bennett seems to win more often than not. Having a hotel in New York City rather than Boston would mean I could pay it more attention. It would give me a better chance at winning."

Sophia's gaze falls to my mouth, then the wineglass I'm holding, then back up to my eyes. "So your goals in life are to keep everyone else happy and beat Bennett at the Hotel Games?"

"That's not all," I say. "I've been thinking about this a lot. You're right that I tend to prioritize the needs of the people I love before my own. When I was a kid, I did it because I knew it would keep my family together, and that's what I wanted more than anything. Not to lose anything or anyone else after my dad died. Since then, I've built a successful career by helping other people achieve their dreams. And while you're right—those dreams aren't mine—my work isn't just for them. It's also for me. Say, for example, I'm a math teacher, or a dance teacher at a high school for the arts."

She raises her eyebrows with a smile.

"It could happen."

"If anyone could make it happen, it's you," she says. She's being funny, but she wouldn't say it if she didn't believe it.

"Isn't that the same thing? If I'm a teacher, aren't I helping kids achieve their dreams and their potential? If I'm a nurse or a doctor, aren't my achievements linked to positive outcomes for my patients?"

"Yeah," she replies. "It's a good point. But are you getting what *you* need by turning the Ninth Street building into a hotel?"

"Maybe," I say. "Maybe like Avril said, I need a family legacy that isn't about grief. Something positive to keep me close with my sisters."

"If that's really how you feel, Worth, that's wonderful. You should do something to make yourself happy."

Heat starts to bubble inside me. I'm on the verge of telling her everything I've been trying to hold back. Here she is, sitting in my home. My wife. I should tell her what I want. Because I've been pretending to myself that I don't know but I do. "I can tell you what I want, beyond the hotel, beyond rewiring our family history."

"I'd love to hear."

I sit forward in my chair and take her hand. "I want you," I say simply. "I want us to tear up those papers and never think about divorce. I want us to move in together. Happy to move wherever you want, because my priority is being with you, wherever that is. That doesn't mean I'm sacrificing what I want to make you happy, it just means I want you and nothing else matters. I want to build a family together. A future. I'm all in. You're what I want."

She stills, but there's no stopping me now.

"I think I *have* been going through life prioritizing other people. But I don't think that was selfless. Stepping up after my dad died got me what I wanted—I kept my family together. Helping entrepreneurs and businesses made me a wealthy man. Money gives control and choices, and for a boy who had neither growing up, it's really important to me.

"But you? I want you because I feel like you've awoken parts of me I didn't know were asleep. I feel we're each other's destiny. Thinking about you makes me happy. Seeing you makes me fucking joyful. Being with you makes me truly happy. I'm in love with you, Sophia Jones, and I want you to stay my wife."

What I want to happen next is for Sophia to slide into my lap, put her arms around my neck, and tell me she loves me too.

But that isn't what happens next.

Her gaze drops from mine and hits the table. "That's…" She pulls in a breath. "That's not what I was expecting you to say."

Silence stretches out between us, but I don't let go of her hand.

"I mean it, Sophia. You said I should focus on what I want, and what I want is you. I want to share my life with you."

Sophia pulls her hand from mine and rubs her face. "Worth," she says. Seconds tick by like minutes. I feel paralyzed, rooted to the spot. "A huge part of me wants that too. In fact, sometimes that's all I want."

I want to feel hopeful as she speaks, but I don't let myself, because I can hear the *but* echoing in her words.

"But I don't trust that feeling," she says eventually. "I don't trust anything at the moment."

I sigh. I can't blame her. What she's discovered about her dad would cause anyone to have massive trust issues.

"You're such a good man," she says. "You deserve a woman who can give you what you want."

I feel the vibrations from the beat of kettle drums in my chest, like a warning of impending danger. I don't care what I deserve—I know what I *want*.

"I told you I'll wait, and I'm happy to. But you asked me what I wanted."

She looks over my shoulder at god-knows-what. Why doesn't she just look at me?

Because she can't.

Fuck.

"I don't know how long I'll feel like this, or if I'll ever *not* feel like this," she says, her gaze finally meeting mine.

"And I've said I'll wait."

"But you deserve your future, Worth. You deserve certainty."

"We've been together weeks, Sophia. I'm not trying to force your hand. I'm not issuing any ultimatums. I'm doing the exact opposite. I'm telling you I'll wait for as long as you need."

She shakes her head. "That's not fair. I want more for you."

"More than you? You're all I want."

She presses the heels of her hands over her eyes. "This is going to get worse rather than better. I don't know who I am if I'm not the daughter of a perfect couple from Cincinnati. I don't know what that means for me. I have a nonexistent relationship with my father at the moment, and a tenuous one with my mother. I have shit to deal with. It's shit that stinks. And stains."

Before I can tell her that I can put up with it all, that I want to hold her hand through the whole thing, she continues.

"I have to do this myself. I know you're going to say you'll wait or help me through it..." She shakes her head. "But honestly, Worth, we've been together weeks, like you said, and if I'm going to commit the rest of my life to someone, I want to know that I'm with them because I want to build a life and a future. I want to feel sure that I want to create a family with them—all the things you said. And if I'm being honest with myself, at the moment, I'm worried I'd be with you because I was afraid to do this by myself."

I sigh. She doesn't have to do it by herself, doesn't she see? Accepting support doesn't make you weak—just gives you a soft place to land if you fall.

"I don't want to be with you just because you're great at helping people through difficult times."

"That's what partnership is," I mutter. But it's futile to argue—I can't force her to stay when what she wants to do is leave.

"In the long run, you're right. Partnership should mean helping each other through the lows and celebrating the highs. But we're just starting out. I can't offer you what you need at the moment."

"So, that's it?" I ask.

She stands. My legs are so weak, I'm not sure I'll be able to get to my feet.

She eyes the papers on the table next to me. It's like someone has stuck a knife into me and I'm waiting for my brain to receive the pain signals. My entire body goes numb. She pulls a pen from her purse and turns to the final page, where the signature blocks are located. "I can't be with you when things are so undone. When my life is so... when I don't know who I am. I'm sorry."

She signs next to her name and pushes the pen back into her purse.

It feels like someone has ripped out my guts. I've lost any ability to move or speak.

I keep my gaze forward, not able to look her in the eye, concerned I'll disintegrate if I do. What if I find indifference there? What if I find pity? I don't think I'd recover.

"I'm going to go," she whispers. "I'm really sorry, Worth."

I don't know if she says anything else, because I can't hear it. Something inside me blocks the rest of the world out, Sophia included. Maybe it's a survival instinct, or maybe this is what happens when you have your heart broken for the first time.

TWENTY-SEVEN

Worth

Thank god Monday night drinks have been switched to Friday. I need my friends. I'm not sure I've ever felt the need so acutely, but Sophia, and now the lack of her, has changed everything.

We're all meeting at a private members' club on East Sixtieth. It attracts the oldest of old money, which is why Jack is the only one of us who has a membership. This is the club we've all been coming to longest. The familiar wood-paneled walls are like a balm to my soul tonight. I need to be reassured that my foundations are still solid. For now.

I walk into the bar and see Bennett right away. To my surprise, Byron is sitting right next to him. I wasn't expecting to see him tonight.

We greet each other, and I order a drink before taking a seat around the low polished table.

Bennett looks at me, then back at Byron, then does a double take and stares at me. "Everything okay?"

I nod and take a sip of my drink.

His gaze doesn't leave me. I look at Byron, pretending I don't notice.

"Wasn't expecting to see you, Byron," I say, trying to redirect Bennett's attention. I don't need to spend the evening talking about myself. I just want to be around people I can count on.

"Flew in this morning," he replies.

"From Acapulco?" Bennett makes air quotes, like he doesn't believe for a second that Byron's been in Mexico.

"Colorado actually," Byron says.

I'm surprised he's actually told Bennett the truth. I don't know why, but Byron has been keeping this latest project close to the chest. He was raised in Colorado, which I suspect has something to do with how mysterious this project has been, though I can't figure out why.

"Really?" Bennett asks. "Everything okay with your parents?"

"Yeah, they're fine. I actually have some business there."

"What kind of business?"

Byron nods as if he's considering Bennett's question and whether to answer it. "I've invested in a resort." He glances around the room. I'm not sure if he's hoping the ceiling will collapse to stop Bennett's questions or whether he's trying to gauge the ceiling height. He's acting... off. "I want to tell you about it. It's going to be announced this week."

"So tell us," Bennett says.

"Later," Byron says.

Bennett sighs and turns his attention to me. "You want to share what's got your face looking like that?"

"Genetics?" I offer. "I don't have a beauty regime I can let you in on if that's what you're hoping."

He ignores me. "How's it going with Sophia?"

My heart clunks in my chest, like it's an engine trying to start but failing miserably.

"I thought that was a Vegas thing. You still seeing her?" Byron asks.

I shake my head and gaze into my drink. *Seeing her.* Is that what was happening with us? It felt like more than that. I felt like we were together. No, we weren't living together, but that was just logistics. We were *married*. With every passing hour, that felt more and more important.

Bennett calls the waiter over. "We'll take a bottle of the Macallan 1990."

The three of us settle into silence.

"Did you end things?" Bennett asks eventually.

I shake my head. "Let's not talk about it." I don't know what I'd say. I don't have any answers.

Leo arrives, along with Jack and Fisher. I relax a little. There are too many people here for Bennett to press the issue with Sophia. I can just be.

Byron gets the most effusive welcome. He hasn't been around much, and it's good to have him here.

"What's the latest with everyone?" Leo asks, taking a low stool between Bennett and me. The bartender brings over the Macallan and Leo looks to me and then Bennett. "We're either celebrating or commiserating. Which is it?"

I glance between Byron and Bennett. Are they going to say anything?

"You want to take that question, Worth?" Byron asks.

Leo waits. Maybe I'm being paranoid, but it feels like he knows something. It would make sense. Sophia is bound to speak to Jules.

"Is it a binary choice? Can't we just be having a drink?" I ask. Okay, so I'm more tetchy that usual, but can't they talk amongst themselves and let me brood in peace?

"Things okay with Sophia?" Leo asks. Bennett can't hide the way his eyebrows disappear into his hairline.

I sigh, exasperated. I feel like I'm a plate of seeds being pecked at by a houseful of hens.

"We're not together anymore," I say.

"Wait, *what*?" Fisher interrupts whatever it was he was talking about with Jack. "What happened?"

Now five pairs of eyes are on me and everyone knows about my breakup with Sophia. This was exactly what I didn't want.

"She's going through some personal stuff and needs the time and space to do that on her own."

It's an obtuse answer, but I'm not going to give them personal, private details about Sophia's family. Anyway, the why doesn't really matter. Only the what: she doesn't want to be married to me anymore.

"Man, I'm sorry," Fisher says. "I had a good feeling about you two."

"Doesn't sound like it's over though," Bennett says. "It sounds like things might... resolve."

I huff out a laugh. "I don't think so. Not for me anyway." I raise my glass, a signal that I want to be done with this conversation. There's no point in keeping the wounds fresh. I want to forget about them for a while. Hope they heal while I'm not looking.

I've never felt the way I feel about Sophia. I opened up to her completely and allowed myself to want something—someone—just for me. Not because it was a necessity, not because it was a requirement for survival, but because I loved her. *Love* her.

And so I have my answer. She doesn't want me. Or doesn't want me enough. There's no coming back from that. I just have to move forward.

I slide my empty glass on the table and excuse myself to the restrooms. I need to splash some water on my face. Regroup.

When I emerge, I'm feeling no better. Maybe I'll just head home. Thank god Sophia never stayed at the brownstone. I don't think I'd be able to go back there if the ghost of her was waiting for me in every corner.

I head back to find Byron on his feet, making his way toward me. He nods to the bar and we both take seats at the mahogany counter, leaving the other four sitting at the table.

"I've been really cagey about Colorado," he says.

"Can I get a drink?" I ask the bartender. "A glass of malbec." No more whisky for me. It's going down too quickly. I turn back to Byron. "You ready to share now?"

"It's weird, because you five are the best friends I ever had. You're more than friends, you're my brothers. But you're also rich as fuck and move in certain circles…"

"You didn't trust us not to share your secrets?" I ask, irritated by the implication. Why the fuck am I the guy who can't be trusted these days? What the fuck did I do?

"It's not that," he says. "Of course I trust you. All of you. It's more that you're all wealthy and clever and so, sometimes, that becomes an echo chamber when it comes to business."

"Right," I say, feeling better.

"What I'm doing in Colorado is a risk. A huge risk. Part of me thinks I'm nuts. And then the bigger part of me thinks I don't care if I'm nuts, this is what I want to do."

I chuckle and realize I haven't done that in a while. I'm so fucking miserable without Sophia. "Are you going to actually tell us what this resort is about?"

"Yeah, I am. I can't turn back now. Too much time and money are committed, so none of you can talk me out of skirting the edge of bankruptcy to get this off the ground. I'm risking everything with this thing."

It's the exact opposite of the way I run my business. I have so many investments in so many businesses that it doesn't matter if any of them don't work because I'm so well hedged. I'm not the risk-taker Byron is. Or Leo or Bennett. Probably because I know it's not just my future at stake, it's my sisters' too. Or it used to be.

"Byron, do me a favor and just tell me. I need something to take my mind off…" I can't even say her name out loud.

"It's a billionaire playground," he says. "Combined with a wilderness reserve."

"Okay," I say cautiously. "What does that mean?"

He glances up and around the bar. This place is so opulent, it's a place where I'd expect people with the names Vanderbilt or Rockefeller to feel at home. He can't be thinking of creating a club like this in Colorado? He's not certifiably insane.

"A private members' club that guarantees anonymity, exclusivity, and complete luxury," he says. "And the experiences of a lifetime. The Colorado Club costs a million dollars to join and fifty thousand dollars a month in membership fees."

"Are you serious?" I ask. "How many people in the world can afford that? How many people in *Colorado* can afford that?"

"In Colorado? Fifteen. In the world? Not many? Thirty thousand max."

"So it's a club for the fifteen centimillionaires who live in Colorado?"

He shakes his head. "It's a destination resort. People will come from all over the world for the incredible skiing with world-class instructors on empty slopes and virgin snow. Restaurants and bars that stock the best food and beverages with unbeatable service and discreet staff. In the summer, we'll have hiking trails where you are as removed from the industrial world as you can get. We'll have pools and wellness offerings. We'll have cutting-edge sport scientists perfecting your workout in state-of-the-art gyms, Olympic athletes coaching your crawl. This is..."

"A retreat for the very wealthy."

"Exactly. The world keeps wanting more and more from all of us. And most of the time, we keep giving it. This is the ultimate place to escape and live in the now."

I pause, thinking about what Byron's saying. It's not adding up. I'm missing a piece of the puzzle.

"Why?" I ask.

"You should see the profit projections."

I don't buy it. I shake my head. "There's always a why. With all of us. It's never just about the money."

He shrugs, and I can tell I'm not going to get him to admit his motivations for creating this billionaire resort. "Enough about me."

"Then what are we going to talk about?" I ask. "Because I don't want to talk about me."

He nods. "You know what the best thing about you is?"

I groan. I really don't want to think about me or look inwards or celebrate my finer qualities. I just want to keep drinking to the point where I can't feel anything anymore.

"The best thing about you is how selfless you are," he says.

I fight the urge to roll my eyes. I'm sick of hearing what a great guy I am.

"But that's also the worst thing about you."

I choke out a laugh. "Wow, thanks, friend."

"I mean it. Sometimes you're so worried about everyone else's feelings, you don't ask for what you want."

I tip back another gulp of wine. "Well, this isn't one of those times. I told her what I wanted. And you're right, it's one of the few times I've ever asked for something entirely for myself. And here I am. Alone. About to file divorce papers from the only woman I ever loved. The woman I still love."

"Fuck," he spits out. "That fucking sucks."

"Too fucking true that fucking sucks."

"She doesn't feel the same?"

I nod to the bartender, asking him to top up my glass. Of course he pours me a fresh glass. At this point, I wouldn't care if he gave me a straw and the bottle.

"I think she does, but she doesn't trust herself. Doesn't think she should fully trust me."

"Can you prove to her you're trustworthy?"

I tell him what her father did to her and her brothers and mom. How the truth has rocked her world, undermining her trust in her father and also her mother.

"She says she needs to work through it, but there's no endpoint to that. It's not that I wouldn't wait—of course I would, I'm in love with the woman. But I think the wait might kill me. The next phase of my life is going to be about what I don't have and can't do a damn thing about it. When I was a kid and my dad died, I cooked my sisters dinner or cleaned the house—anything to keep our family together. Yes, I missed my dad, but his death gave me purpose. I channeled my grief into something positive. But with this? What the fuck do I do, Byron? I've never felt so fucking helpless in my life."

"I feel like I've got to have an answer for this." He presses his fingers on his temple, like he's channeling the spirit world. As much as I know it's futile, I will him to come up with an answer. "I'm trying to think. Bennett did that interview in *Forbes*, but something like that's not going to work."

"That's the fucking problem! It's not like there's something lacking between us that's driven her away. Efa knew she couldn't live the life Bennett was living, so he changed. For her."

"Right," Byron says. "And Jules needed Leo to fight for her. To show her that he wouldn't abandon her, even when she pushed him away."

"Exactly. But how do I prove to Sophia she can trust me? I've never done anything to make her think I can't be trusted."

"But her dad hid things her entire life."

That's the problem. Her father's lie was so deeply buried, so completely a part of her reality, that its roots are part of who Sophia is. "There's no solution," I say, and take another swig of wine.

Byron takes the glass from my hand. "Drinking won't help. It will just make you depressed. I'm going to stop by the brownstone tomorrow morning at six. We're going for a run."

"Fuck I am."

"Worth, this isn't going to take you down. I won't allow it. I'm going to see you at six."

"Make it eight," I mumble.

That's why I'm here tonight. Because I know my five best friends won't let me go under. Whether or not I knew it before I got here, that's my biggest fear—that after everything I've survived in this world, losing Sophia will finally break me.

TWENTY-EIGHT

Sophia

Normally after a breakup, I curl up on the couch with Jules and lick my wounds for a weekend before getting up on Monday morning and moving on. Or I'd go back to Cincinnati and hang out for a few days, and find my heart had totally healed by the time I got back to New York.

But Jules is living with Leo, I'm not sure I ever want to go back to Cincinnati, and this isn't any ordinary breakup.

This time the person I've broken up with doesn't live a thousand miles away and isn't emotionally unavailable. This time, I'm married and in love.

When Worth told me he loved me, I wanted to say it back, but I knew it would only make things worse.

The buzzer to the apartment makes me jump and I drop the pile of clothes I was carrying to the open suitcase in my living room. Leaving the clothes where they fall, I head to the door. When I open it and see Jules' expression, I know she knows. The sadness and disappointment in her eyes is a final blow.

"What happened?" she asks. I cover my face with my hands and slump against the wall. "Leo told me last night that you guys split."

I try and even out my breathing. I have so little energy, I'm not sure how I'll get to the couch, let alone finish packing. I check my watch. I have to leave in an hour if I'm going to make my flight. "Yeah," I say. "I wasn't planning to end things. It just... happened."

Jules puts her arm around me and leads me into the living room. "I thought you really liked him."

"I did. I *do*."

"Then isn't there a way to work through things?"

I sigh and collapse on the sofa. "It's not a question of working through issues between us. There *are* no issues between us." I feel horrible for leaving Worth the way I did, but it will be better for him in the long run.

Her brows knit together. "Then why?"

"Because I have stuff I need to work through."

"And you had to end things with Worth to do that?"

"I kind of did, yeah." I tell her about my trust issues and the way I feel like my past was a lie. How I'm not sure who I am when my foundations aren't just rocked but smashed to smithereens. "I need to figure it out," I say. "And I don't want to lean on Worth because he would take the weight—that's the man he is. I'd never really know if I was with Worth because I needed the support or because I wanted to be with him. I don't want to spend my life with someone who I feel I owe a debt to. If I'm going to sink, I need to do that on my own. If I swim, I want to know I did that on my own, too. That's the only way I can be the kind of woman who deserves a man like Worth. Does that make sense?"

"Okay," she says, tilting her head to one side. "But say I got some devastating news about my past that rocks me to my core. I wouldn't just walk away from my marriage to deal with it on my own."

"Right," I say. "But I married Worth *because* of what happened with my parents. The whole wedding was a reaction. I don't want to stay married to him as a reaction, too. It would be like I was using him. I want to be with him because I love him. Because I want to build a future with him."

"So that's it?" she asks.

"I don't know," I say. I feel like I love the man, but I don't trust anything anymore. "He says he'll wait, but I can't expect him to wait forever."

Her eyes widen at the possibility that it's not the end between us, but I can't think too much about what might happen.

"I don't know how long it will take to sort my shit out."

She glances down at my suitcase. "So for now, you're running away?"

I shake my head. "The exact opposite. If I was running away, I wouldn't be going to Cincinnati. I'm facing shit straight-on. No more avoiding my problems or pretending they're not happening. I'm going to speak to my mom, tell her I feel betrayed by her as well as Dad, and I'm... I'm going to consider seeing my father."

I want to be the kind of wife Worth deserves. If I figure stuff out and he's still there, I'll be in a position to tell him I love him. And if he moves on? It will break my heart, but I will wish with everything I have that he's happy. Because he deserves it.

TWENTY-NINE

Worth

I wake with a start and wonder where I am. I can't remember getting into bed last night. Probably something to do with all the whisky I drank. At least I slept. It's the first time since Sophia ended things between us. I still haven't looked at the divorce papers she signed. As soon as she left, I folded them up and stuffed them in my coat pocket, trying to get them out of sight even if there was no hope of putting them out of mind. I didn't even want to think about what to do with them next. Drunk me was holding out hope that Sophia would have a change of heart. In the sober light of day, I know that's not going to happen.

Banging from downstairs makes the floorboards vibrate. After a second of confusion, I realize someone's at my front door. I scrub my hands over my face and sit up in bed.

More banging.

I pull on joggers and a tee shirt and go and see who the hell is trying to break down my front door.

I pull the door open to find Leo and Byron on my stoop, Leo

holding a cardboard cup carrier with three cups in it and Byron holding a bottle of whisky.

"We're covering all bases." Byron lifts his other hand to reveal a full-sized chess set. "And whether it's coffee or whisky, I'm going to beat you at chess."

I glance at my watch. Eight sharp. I'd forgotten Byron said he was coming over. At least he's not insisting we go running.

I groan and turn, padding down the hallway, Byron and Leo following me. I just need some solitude this weekend. Some time to myself so I can be miserable. "I have things to do."

"Like what?" Leo asks.

"Like… work," I reply.

"You weren't going to work," Byron says. "And now we're here, so you can't. Do you want to go through the schedule now or after you've put your ass in the shower?"

"Schedule?" I ask.

"The schedule of events," Byron says. "We start the day with whisky and chess—"

"Coffee and chess," Leo corrects.

"Both? Maybe a dash of whisky in my coffee will help my head," I say, slumping down on the sofa by the fireplace. I barely drink. I *never* day drink, but here I am thinking about starting the day with whisky. "Scratch that," I say. "Coffee and chess."

"Then in about two hours, Bennett and Fisher are coming by with games," Byron says as he settles into the chair opposite me, Leo in the chair next to him. "We will all be equally shit at them as none of us have ever played video games—"

"Sorry, but tell me again why my house has become a hangout for grown men trying to relive the teenage years they never had?"

"Because we're keeping you company," Leo says. "Then this afternoon, we're going out."

"Guys, I'm fine," I say. "You can stay for coffee, but then…"

"Then what?" Byron asks.

"Then I'll get on with the day," I say. "I can handle anything life throws at me. I've got a track record."

"We know," Leo says. "But the fact is, you don't *have* to do it alone. We're here. And it's not like we can solve the problem, but we can talk, not talk, offer perspective, keep quiet, come up with a plan to win her back, or talk shit about her. Whatever you want to do, we're here, right by your side. Just like you're right by our sides whenever the shit hits the fan for any of us. Believe it or not, it's a two-way street, Worth. You've just had a road closure up for a long time. We're here with bulldozers, and we're completely ignoring the No Entry signs."

"What Leo's trying to say," Byron says. "With more metaphors than is good for anyone at this time in the morning, is that we know you're not good at receiving help. We're here to make it easy for you."

"That," Leo says.

I sigh in resignation. "Give me a coffee." I lean forward and pull a cup from the holder. Byron slides the chessboard onto the coffee table between us.

NEW YORK IS COLDER than usual. I pull the collar up on my coat and push my hands into the pockets.

"I don't understand why you won't tell me where we're going," I say to the five men flanking me. This is starting to feel like an extremely low-key kidnapping. "I also don't understand why we're walking."

"The sun is shining. The sky is blue. It's good for your mental health to be outside. I read it somewhere," Bennett says.

"We're here," Byron says, looking up at a storefront. In gold lettering against a black background reads *House of Flowers*.

My heart drops to the sidewalk. They can't be thinking I should order flowers for Sophia. I know that's not what she'd want. She didn't walk away with a skip in her step. Sending her flowers would just be tortuous for both of us.

"I'm not doing that," I say. "I'm not sending her flowers."

Fisher pats me on the back. "We're not sending flowers." He nods toward the shop. "Let's go in."

The shop has that very distinct smell all florists have—pleasant dampness. It's fresh and there's color everywhere.

"Is someone buying *me* flowers?"

Jack goes up to the counter and speaks to the assistant. We're escorted to the back, where there's a small room with a heavy table filled with foliage and stools either side of it.

What the fuck are we doing here?

"Take a seat, gentlemen." A woman about the same age as my mom, with tight red curls and a round, smiling face, greets us. "My name is Rose. We'll come around and get your coffee orders when you're seated, then we can get started."

I glance between my friends, but all of them avoid my gaze.

"Can't wait," Leo says, as if trying to match the smiling woman's energy.

Bennett is the first to sit and I take the stool next to him.

"We've put some materials on the counter in front of you, but there's plenty more around the room. Use what you like." Rose points to the worktables set up against the walls, piled with green blocks of stuff florists use to stick flowers into, vases, wreaths, and greenery. "While we're taking your coffee orders, pick out a wreath size you think you'll want to work with." Rose smooths her green apron before leaving us.

"What do you call five billionaires attending a Christmas-wreath-making class?" Byron asks.

"Unusual," Bennett replies, and I can't hold back my chuckle.

"Anyone want to tell me why we're doing this? Of all things?" I ask.

Leo shrugs. "It's a chance to hang out. Chew the fat."

I know that's not the only reason. These guys are trying to keep my mind off Sophia. It won't work—it's impossible. But I really appreciate that they're trying.

I glance around the room at these four super-successful guys who I get to call my best friends. "Thanks," I say. "This is unbelievably weird, but... yeah, thanks."

I don't know if I've ever felt like I can lean on people. I've just always let people lean on me, because I'm strong enough to carry them. This is the first time I feel like I'm not shouldering everything alone.

I pick out a large rattan wreath big enough to fill the door of the brownstone. I give my coffee order to Rose, the woman with the rosy cheeks. Her name suits her personality and her job. Floristry was clearly her destiny.

My phone buzzes. It's Avril asking me to meet her at Ninth Street tomorrow afternoon. I have a feeling that's less about trying to keep me occupied and more about trying to get me to change my plans for the building.

"Tomorrow we thought bowling rather than the usual brunch," Fisher says.

"Bowling?" I ask in case I misheard him. "I'm meeting my sister in the afternoon."

"She still want to make Ninth Street a hotel?" Bennett asks.

I nod, turning my wreath in my hands, trying to figure out if I should find one that's less haphazard or if they'll all look like this.

"You want my advice?" Bennett asks.

I set my wreath on the bench in front of me. "Sure."

"Take out all the arguments she's making about family legacy and ask yourself if buying the hotel will make you happy."

It's not the advice I expected from Bennett. I thought he'd talk about break-even points or projected inflation over the next five years. "Happy?"

"Yeah, with something like that, you've got to put business aside. Do you want to work with your sisters? If so, is it the hotel business you want to get into? Not for profitability reasons, but because that's what you'll enjoy doing."

"I don't think I'll be involved on a day-to-day basis," I say.

"But you'll still be the owner," Bennett says. "Only say yes if you think you'll enjoy it."

I've never made business decisions based on personal enjoyment. "Really?" I ask, and even I can hear the skepticism in my voice.

"We've all got more than we could possibly ever want. You've secured your family's future, Worth. No matter what happens, you and your sisters and your mom—you're all okay. Do what makes you happy, not what you think you should do, or what will make someone else's life better. Forget about the money and whether you *should* do it. Just ask yourself if you *want* to do it."

I don't get a chance to let his question marinate before Fisher pulls out a wreath from the center of the counter. "We can do bowling early," he says, almost out of nowhere. "If you have to go to Ninth Street in the afternoon, I mean."

"I think I'll take this one," Bennett says, choosing a wreath even bigger than mine. "It will take a big bow."

I might have unwittingly slipped into the twilight zone. We're not a natural fit for a crafting workshop.

"It's safe to leave me on my own, you know. Monday is just around the corner, and I'm not taking any of you to work."

"I could meet you for lunch," Leo says.

"I have a lunch," I lie. "But thanks."

"Then Monday night is our normal get-together," Fisher says.

"But we swapped Friday out instead of Mon—" I realize they weren't swapping Monday out; they *added* Friday to be with me.

I have the best friends.

"Then Tuesday, you want to go for a run in the park?" Byron asks.

"And if you feel like ditching the day job, I could do a gym session, maybe pitch some business ideas at you and you can tell me

I'm crazy." Fisher pulls out a length of ivy from a pile of greenery, then thinks better of it, abandoning it in a verdant pile.

"Thanks, but I'm going to be busy at work this week."

"Good," Fisher says. "Not good that you can't come to the gym with me, but good that you're going to be busy at work. That will be... good."

Bennett rolls his eyes at Fisher's awkwardness, then thanks the person delivering our coffees.

I don't want to tell them they're being overbearing mother hens—even if they are. I appreciate them more than they can ever know.

"Okay, guys," says Rose, clapping her hands together. "Is everyone ready to create their own festive wreath?"

Never in my entire life have I been as ready as I am right now, on a December afternoon, surrounded by my best friends, drinking coffee—like this is just another normal day.

THIRTY

Sophia

Costco with my mom makes me feel twelve years old again.

"You want some gummy bears?" she asks as we pass a display of a million boxes of multicolored chewy candy.

"Urm, no, thanks."

"Is there anything you do want?"

An honest conversation. Some kind of certainty you haven't lied about other fundamental aspects of my childhood. The voice inside my head sounds bratty, but somewhere in the airspace over Ohio, I reverted to the kid I used to be, ready to arrive at around fourteen as soon as the airplane wheels hit the tarmac.

"Nothing I can think of," I say. I know at some point I need to speak to my mom about how I'm feeling, but right here in the middle of Costco isn't the time or the place.

"Well, let's go right to the middle aisles, then."

We're here because Mom wants to buy holiday decorations. Because she definitely needs more of them. Our house was always decorated for the holidays, no surface or wall escaping ornaments and fake snow. We're only a couple of weeks out, and her house looks like a winter wonderland.

I wonder if Worth decorates the brownstone. I didn't see much of it, but the bits I saw were so pretty—so quintessentially New York—it definitely deserves a real fir, strung with multicolored lights and candy canes. Worth deserves that too, along with a magical Christmas where all his festive wishes come true. My teeth saw over my bottom lip. I know he's hurting, and I know I've caused it. I just hope he doesn't do what he promised to and wait—because I don't know if I'll ever be the woman he deserves. He needs a woman who can love him with her whole heart. One who trusts him. I don't know if I'll ever be that woman, given what my dad did.

"You take the cart," Mom says, pushing the empty buggy toward me as she heads over to a Christmas display. "Isn't this darling?"

I pull the cart over to where she's standing. It's a miniature Christmas town made up of various models with moving parts. There's a station on one side, and a train pulling up to the station with passengers waiting on the platforms. The windows of stores either side of a snowy, old-fashioned main street are filled with Christmas presents and toys. Little figurines are scattered across the scene, some throwing snowballs, others singing carols. A pond on the other side of the railway station is full of ice-skaters moving in circles. A boy lugs a cart full of presents across a patch of grass.

It looks idyllic. If you're an inch tall.

"I can't wait for you to have kids. You would have loved this as a child. All three of you would."

I snort out a laugh. "Kids? There's no hint of that on the horizon."

Mom pulls her attention from the Christmas scene and regards me. "What happened to that nice man who brought you to the hospital on Thanksgiving?"

It feels like someone wrapped a cloak around my heart, but instead of providing warmth, it's tightening around it, threatening to stop its beating. "He deserves better than me," I mumble.

"What on earth can you mean?" she asks. "You are a wonderful woman who would make an excellent wife and mother. You're kind and loyal and clever. A little stubborn at times, but that's not the worst trait to have. Means you don't give up on the good stuff."

"The good stuff?"

"You know, all your exams and stuff. You were a great student exactly because you were a little pigheaded. You never let anything beat you."

I used to think I knew my mom almost as well as I knew myself. Now, I'm not sure if I know her at all. First putting up with my dad having another family in the next city over, and then calling me pigheaded?

"So what happened. Did you two get in a fight?"

I can't imagine Worth ever being in a fight with anyone. Not physical or mental. He's far too... stable. "No, but..."

"Then what? I thought he was very handsome. You two would have the prettiest babies."

"Mom," I groan.

"And it was so kind of him to come with you—traveling from New York to Cincinnati on Thanksgiving? I don't know how one of you got a plane ticket, let alone two of you."

If she thought Worth was nice before, the fact that he chartered a private plane to get me to my father's hospital bedside would no doubt push her over the edge. She'd march me back to New York to marry him.

"He's very kind."

"Then what's the problem? Why have you got it into your head that he deserves better? Who on this earth could be better than my daughter?"

I start to push the cart away and she grabs it and holds it in place, trying to catch my eye, while I look everywhere but at her.

"Sophia Amelia! Answer your mother."

"I don't know, Mom. How about he deserves someone who trusts that he's the good man he seems to be? The kind of man who wouldn't betray his wife and kids for over twenty years. How about a woman who doesn't have a cheating father and a mother who put up with it for decades?"

As soon as the words are out, I regret them. I know my mom was just trying to do the right thing. But knowing she lied to me all these years doesn't feel right. "I'm sorry—"

My mom puts up a finger to stop me from finishing a sentence. "Don't apologize for having your feelings about this whole situation. I get it. I've had plenty of feelings over the years, believe me. And I'm sorry for lying to you." She sighs and shakes her head. "When your kids are little, you're telling them so many lies, another one doesn't seem so bad."

"What other lies?" I shriek.

"Like Santa and the Tooth Fairy. And that's just the start. All those toys that suddenly went missing and I blamed the Borrowers. When I said you were the best volleyball player on the team and Noah was an excellent violinist. We all lie to our kids, Sophia. We lie to save their feelings and to preserve their innocence as long as humanly possible."

"But lies always get found out," I say.

"Exactly, but the stakes are usually a lot lower, and as long as y'all are getting presents in your stockings, parents get forgiven."

"It's not the same," I say. "You can't equate lying about Santa with lying to your kids about who their father is."

"Really?" She turns and pulls a box from the shelf underneath the setup of the model town. "I wanted you to believe in magic for as long as possible, Sophia. I wanted you to think your father hung the moon, because I wish he did. I wanted that for all of you. For all of me. Maybe I didn't get it right. Your father *definitely* didn't get it right. But don't give away a good man because you've seen the failings of another."

She tips the box she's holding into the cart.

"You're going to buy the ice rink?" I ask.

She moves down the aisle slightly and pulls out another box. "I'm buying the whole darn town. I want a reason for my grandchildren to visit Cincinnati in the middle of winter."

"Mom! You can't buy this for nonexistent grandchildren."

"I can do anything I want. I'm grown. My kids have flown the nest, my husband is shacked up with another woman, and *finally* I can do what I please. And I *please* to prepare for my future grandchildren."

She makes a compelling point. I might feel betrayed by my mom, but she did what she did for the right reasons. She was trying to protect me—to do her job as a mother. I scan the shelves for the train station and pull it out of the rack. "You want this?"

"Who wouldn't want a Christmas train station, Sophia?"

I grin twitches at the corner of my mouth and I pile the box on top of the other two.

"We're going to need another cart," she says. "And while we're doing this, you're going to tell me about Worth. That's his name, right?"

I nod and swallow. "I get that you were trying to protect us," I say, snaking an arm around my mom's waist. She pulls me in for a hug.

"I just did the best I could at the time." Her voice wobbles at the end of the sentence and I squeeze her tighter.

"Worth thinks it's his job to protect everyone. Especially the people he loves. I don't know if the man would be capable of telling me the truth if it meant he hurt me."

"Have you tried talking to him? If he wants to avoid hurting you, and he knows lying to you would hurt you worst of all, then wouldn't he tell the truth at all costs?"

I'd never thought about it like that. I can't imagine asking anything of Worth that he wasn't prepared to give me if he were able.

"How do I trust that he's as good a man as I think he is?"

"Well," she says, "you bring him around your family. You meet his family and friends. You see what they say about him, what his quirks are. And you see if it all aligns with what your heart is telling you. After that, it's a leap of faith, Sophia. Just like most of life is."

She makes it sound so simple, so obvious. But if I've learned anything over these last few weeks, it's that nothing is simple.

We fill another cart with the rest of the model village. Mom circles back to the display to make sure we've got everything.

"Do we have it all?" she asks. "I'm going to be disappointed if I've missed something, because I'll come back next week and this will be a fly-fishing display. Christmas Town will be sold out."

"Let's check." I methodically scan the shelves to ensure we have one of everything. "Oh, there's the tree. But that's not on the display."

"Let me see."

I pull the box out and she gets her readers on to check the picture.

"This is beautiful," she says. "And they didn't put it out."

I look back at the shelf. "Looks like it's the only one left," I say. "Maybe they didn't see it."

There's genuine excitement in her eyes. "It will be the center of the entire town. Oh, sweetheart, I'm so glad you came today. It's been a while since we went shopping together."

"You're right, Mom. It has been a while. And hopefully we won't come Christmas Town shopping again anytime soon."

"Who knows? This time next year, I might want to expand." She's grinning ear to ear. I don't know if it's because she's decided to spend way too much money on a Christmas village, or if it's because she's happy to have me home.

We wheel the carts over to the cash registers. As we wait in line, Mom scoops up my hand. "Worth isn't your father, Sophia. Don't let the actions of one man taint your view of the world. You'll rob yourself of the joy of living. I'm not proud of much in my life, but I have three healthy, funny kids. Now I get to find out what's in store for me in the next chapter of my life. I'm determined to make the most of it. I want to ride a horse—I've never done that. I want to learn how to surf. And I'm going to date."

I almost choke on my own tongue. Date?

"I deserve a good life, Sophia. And so do you."

"And the cherry on the sundae is your Costco Christmas Town."

"That too," she says, bumping me with her hip.

"You really think you could trust a man again?"

"I think I'm not going to give up before I've even tried. Sounds like you didn't give Worth a shot. Life never turns out quite how you expect, but we have to make sure we revel in the good parts."

It's absolutely bizarre to me that after twenty-five years of betrayal by her husband, my mom could even think about dating. She's had a long time to process things, but she's also never given up. Is that what I did? Gave up on Worth and me without ever giving us a chance? I let what happened with my dad erase the possibility for a future *not* built on lies and disaster. I never believed an alternative could be possible. But if Mom can still believe in love after all this time...

Shouldn't I?

THIRTY-ONE

As I round the corner on Ninth Street, I take a sip from the unexpectedly excellent coffee I got on the way out of the bowling alley. Before today, I hadn't bowled in over a decade. I'd forgotten how much fun it could be. Obviously we all wanted to win, but that's not why I had fun. It was probably something to do with Bennett's hyper-competitiveness or how entirely terrible Jack had been. We teased him relentlessly, but he took it in stride. I guess if you're hanging out on Martha's Vineyard every summer, there aren't many opportunities to practice bowling.

Bowling, of all things. My friends' support means the world, especially when my heart is breaking.

Avril's half running, half walking up the street. I check my watch. She's not even late. She must really want me to go the hotel route on this place if she's prepared to be on time not once, but twice.

"Hey," she says, beaming. She envelops me in a hug. "Thanks for coming."

"Not a problem."

"I just want you to keep an open mind. I had some plans drawn up."

It's only then I realize she's got a cardboard tube in her hand.

"I thought it would be good to see the plans in situ."

I've got to hand it to her, she's determined. On any other day, I would have said yes just because she's on time and clearly committed to the project, but today I'm going to figure out if I genuinely want to be involved with this hotel redevelopment. If I do, the decision's easy. If I don't, I'm not sure how to proceed. I might say yes because I can see how badly Avril wants this.

"Lead the way," I say, holding out the keys for the place.

"Oh, I have my own set. How do you think I got architects in here?" She opens the doors and I resist the urge to ask how she managed to get a set of keys cut. I'd rather not know.

Inside there's a folding table where Avril spreads out the plans she's had drawn up. "You've seen the financials, so you know it works from a business perspective."

"I've seen *some* financials. But I haven't stress-tested them. There's no such thing as a cut-and-dried, guaranteed win in business."

She groans. "Let me show you the plans. We'll start with floor two, which is a standard bedroom floor. Because of the shape of the building, the architect says it will be easy to maximize the space. We've ended up getting five more rooms than we projected in the financials, so it's an even better proposition." She keeps talking about square footage and the average hotel room size in New York City. She seems to have every fact and figure memorized.

I'm only half listening, busy imagining the space and how it would look. I'm trying to picture myself in here. How would I feel being part of the renovation, the owner of a hotel? Would it make me happy?

"And what are the plans for down here?" I ask.

Avril pulls out one of the huge sheets of paper and smooths her hands over it. "Here," she says. "The main entrance would stay in the same place. This would be the lobby."

I vaguely remember some of the things she said in her presentation. If I'd said yes to the hotel then, it wouldn't have had anything to do with Avril's vision for the space or the financials. I would have done it to make her happy.

"When you presented the financials, I wasn't really thinking about whether I wanted to take on the project to make me happy." I'm thinking aloud.

Avril stares at me as if I've just started reciting limericks.

"That's not normally a consideration when I make a decision. About anything really." I shove my hands into my pockets as I realize it's true in other aspects of my life, too. "Even the brownstone. I bought it because it was close to my office and had enough space if you and Poppy wanted to live with me at any point."

"I'm lost. Are you saying you don't like your house?"

I pull in a breath as I think. "I'm saying I've never really thought about it. It fulfilled the criteria I set out, so I moved forward."

"Worth, you have money. Why don't you live somewhere you like?"

"I'm not saying I don't like living at the brownstone. But if I had to start from scratch, would I pick that place?" I shrug. "Maybe." It's like I've unlocked a part of my brain I've only just discovered. I'm always so focused on whether something makes practical sense and whether it benefits the people I'm trying to make happy. I don't think further than that.

"If there was something wrong, you'd tell me, right?" Avril says, her eyebrows drawing together. "Like if you were sick or something, you wouldn't try to hide it from us, just to keep us from worrying?"

"I'm not sick," I say with a smile. "I'm just... rearranging things."

"But if anything was wrong, would you tell us?"

If she'd asked me a week ago, I wouldn't have been able to answer the same way. "Yes," I say.

"Because I know what you're like. You're a great big brother, but me and Poppy are adults now. You can't shield us from everything that goes wrong in life."

"You're right. If I'm ever terminally ill, I'll tell you." I start to chuckle. "You can stop mentally making funeral arrangements. There's nothing wrong with me."

That's not true. There's plenty wrong with me. I miss Sophia like we've been together a decade and known each other our entire lives. Emptiness has burrowed into my chest, cold and vast, and I'm sure now that she's gone, it will be there forever. I'll have to live with this chasm inside me—an empty space where Sophia should be.

But I have to keep putting one foot in front of the other, because too many people count on me for me to just give up. What I didn't realize before now is that I can count on them too.

"I want to have the final say on major decisions if we go ahead and do this."

Avril's eyes grow wide and then she squeals. "You're considering it? For real?"

"Of course I'm considering it, otherwise I wouldn't be here. But I'm not just doing it for you," I say.

She nods. "Worth, it's going to be a great investment *and* a family legacy."

"I get that, but I want to make sure that overall, doing this is going to make me happy."

She pauses. "So, will it?"

"I'm not sure." Sophia made me happy, I know that much. Whatever she thought, my feelings for her weren't about saving her. She was *lovely*. Being with her made me happy. "I'm going to have to sit with it for a while. But if you and Poppy are involved—"

"We're going to be involved. That's the entire point of this place."

"I'm going to be involved," I say, finishing my sentence. "Maybe we could set up a way for you to earn shares in the hotel, up to a maximum."

"So we'd all be part owners?" She lets go of the plans she's holding so fast, they roll up and slide off the table.

"Maybe," I say.

"Worth, that would be amazing."

"But I'd have to have fifty-one percent," I say. "Because I'm not having you two join forces against me."

She laughs. "Well, that's inevitable no matter how the shareholding's arranged."

I regard her for a second. She's smart, determined, fun. "I like you," I say.

"Of course you like me. I'm your sister."

"I don't think the two always go together. Anyway, I never realized until now."

"You thought you hated me?" She puts her hand on her hip and lifts her chin, like she might be trying to start a fight.

"No, I just didn't think about our relationship like that before. You were young and needed me. I loved you, obviously. I just never realized I liked hanging out with you."

She shakes her head and turns back to the plans. "Don't tell Poppy you only just realized you liked her. Her therapy bill is big enough as it is."

I laugh. "You're right there. I promise not to tell if you don't."

Refurbishing this hotel will be good in a lot of ways. Financially, it makes sense. It creates something good out of a lot of years of pain. And it might just rebalance the relationship among me and my sisters, so instead of me just being their safety net, I get to be their brother—plain and simple.

Yes, I think I'll enjoy having a family legacy on Ninth Street.

THIRTY-TWO

Sophia

He looks older than I remember him, even though it's only been a few weeks since I last saw my dad. The revelation of his secrets has aged him, and the heart attack probably didn't help. Or maybe I just see him differently now.

I've been putting off this day for as long as possible, but I know if I'm going to get through this, I need answers from Dad. I need to look him in the eye when I ask him my questions.

"Hey, Sophia," he says, his arms open like he expects me to run into them. I wanted to meet him in the park he'd always take us to the day after he got home from a "work trip." It's twenty-five degrees and I'm wrapped up in my down coat, hat, and gloves. I can barely move I have so many clothes on.

"Hey, Dad," I say, staying seated.

"You don't want to go inside? We could go to that coffee shop on the corner?" His words come out in puffy clouds of breath and hang there before slowly dissolving into the air.

I stand, but don't move toward him. There's no point in niceties when I'm feeling anything but nice. "Nope. We can walk." I push my gloved hands into my pockets.

We walk in silence for a while, toward the fenced-off playground.

"Remember when I used to bring you here?" he asks.

"Yeah. There was always a trip to the park after you'd been on one of your long work trips."

A white ribbon of breath pushes out of him, like he's being exorcised. But we stand in silence.

"I don't know what you want me to say, Sophia." His tone is harder than I expected. I'm not sure *what* I expected, exactly. That he'd pretend everything was fine and we wouldn't talk about his betrayal? Or that he'd beg my forgiveness?

Yes, the second one. I expected him to be contrite. Or that he'd feel some kind of shame. From his tone, it's like I'm holding on to some unjustifiable grudge.

"Is there anything you *want* to say?"

"Not really," he says.

I turn to him. "Really? I just found out you've been living a double life my entire existence and you have nothing to say?"

"Sophia," he says exasperatedly, "you had a good upbringing. You never wanted for anything. It was adult business. I don't know what you're so upset about."

"Oh, I don't know, the fact that my father lied to me every day of my life? The fact that I can't trust another living soul because of the decisions you made to lie and cheat on your family?"

"Your mother knew everything."

"We didn't."

"You were children."

"You don't think we deserved an honest man for a father? One who modeled how to tell the truth? How to be a faithful husband? You don't think this has anything to do with us?"

"You're being oversimplistic about the entire thing. You weren't an adult at the time, so you can't understand why I made the decisions I made."

"So explain it to me," I say. "I'm here, standing in front of you as an adult, asking you why?"

He shakes his head, sighing, like I'm exasperating. Me. When all I've done is worship the man in front of me. And all along, patterns have been set in my head, pushing me toward men just like him—men who didn't live in the same city as me. Men who weren't as into me as I was into them. Men who wanted the best of both worlds—being single and being in a relationship.

"It wasn't planned, Sophia. Rita was never *supposed* to get pregnant." He pushes a hand through his thinning hair as my blood turns ever icier at the mention of her name.

I know it wasn't just her—my dad was the cheater. He had the family and children. But did she know he was married when they started their affair? Did she not care?

"That's what happens when you fuck women who aren't your wife."

"Oh god, Sophia. I hope one day someone can sit in judgement of the life you've lived. This wasn't some plan to annoy you. Life happens."

"Annoy me? Is that what you think I am? Annoyed?"

"Well, aren't you?"

"It's not the adjective I would have started with. I probably would have started with *heartbroken*. Then I might have moved on to *devastated*. *Cheated* that my father wasn't actually the wonderful, loving father I thought he was—the hardworking man who sacrificed time with the family he loved in order to provide us with a better life. That was the way you and Mom always framed it. You traveled because you loved us so much. But the opposite was actually true, wasn't it? You traveled so much, because you didn't love us enough to stay faithful to your wife and family."

The betrayal hits me again, like a knife to the chest. It's so hard and sharp that my breath catches, and I cough into the frigid air.

"It's worse that you don't see it," I say in a whisper. "That you're trying to justify what you did." I sigh as I talk into the silence. "But then, why wouldn't you? If you had to confront the man you truly are, you'd be as horrified as I am."

I've never spoken so directly to my father. It never occurred to me that I ever would. This isn't the man I kept on a pedestal my whole life. This man is weak. Pathetic. Someone who tricked me into loving him.

"I don't want to fight with you," he says. "I just want you to see my side."

"What side is that, Dad?"

Silence tightens between us and I've never felt so… untethered as I do right now. He was always my port in the storm. Even though I was closer to Mom in lots of ways, Dad was the one who'd come back and blanket us in a feeling that everything was always going to be okay, so long as he was there.

He was never the man I thought he was.

"I was young," he says.

I can't decide if he's trying a different tack, now that he knows I'm not going to be brought down by the "you were fine" argument, or the "you don't know what you're talking about" strategy.

"I found out about this less than a month ago. You haven't been young for a while."

I think back to Worth at fourteen, making dinner for his sisters, doing the laundry, signing permission slips. Worth was more of a man at fourteen than my dad is at sixty.

"The die has been cast for a long time," he says. "I was doing the best I could with the cards I was dealt."

"Was *dealt*?" I say, frustrated that he's not taking any responsibility whatsoever. "I think you dealt those cards to yourself."

"You're trying to trip me up with semantics."

It's my turn to be exasperated. "It's my fault, all this, is it?"

"I'm saying I was young when things happened and Rita got pregnant. I've been dealing with the consequences the best way I can. None of you have ever wanted for anything."

"Don't say that," I say through gritted teeth. "You have no idea how much I've lost. Noah and Oliver too. Finding out this kind of thing about our father? Do you have any idea how this rocks all our foundations? And your other kids—our half-siblings. You've taken something from all of us."

He puts his gloved hands up in surrender. "Look, I'm not saying I got everything right. I didn't. But don't make me out to be a monster. I didn't do a bad job, considering the circumstances."

I feel like I'm talking to the sidewalk. He doesn't seem to be seeing this from our perspective at all. He just has his guard up, trying to defend himself—like anything he's done is defensible.

"I think Mom did the best *she* could, considering the circumstances," I say, but not to him. I'm rehashing things in my mind.

"Well, that's something we can agree on," he says. "She's a good woman. Has been a very good mother."

She sacrificed everything for Oliver, Noah, and me. I respect that and I'm thankful. I just wish she hadn't had to do it.

"I'm going to go now, Dad," I say.

I glance across at him as he slides his palm over his hair.

"I do love you, you know. That's why—"

"Don't do that. Don't dress up your betrayal in love. You had a whole other family. You didn't do that because you loved us."

"But I didn't walk out," he says.

Is that how he justifies it to himself? Is that how he shuns responsibility? By saying it could have been worse.

"No, you didn't walk out."

I need to leave. The man I thought my father was has disappeared. It's like I'm talking to a stranger. I no longer think he hung the moon, although I think he might take credit for it, if anyone let him.

"I love you," Dad says again. "And I know I got things wrong—I'm still getting things wrong. I don't want to... lose you." His eyes are tired and sad. I don't know what to say to him. "I never wanted to lose any of you." What he's saying is selfish, but I know now that's who he is. At least it feels more authentic than anything he's said so far today.

It's like he's lowered his shield, just a little bit. It brings a sliver of hope that there might be some possibility of a relationship going forward.

"You need to stop saying your actions didn't affect us. What happened was your fault. Until you accept that..." I leave the rest unspoken, but I hope he hears the truth in my silence: Until he takes accountability for his actions, I won't be able to forgive him.

He swallows and chews the side of his cheek, a habit he's always had. But maybe it's a tell. Evidence of vulnerability.

"It was my fault." He doesn't look at me as he speaks. Instead he stares at the climbing frame my brothers and I spent hours hanging from, trying to best each other's times. "I should never have taken up with Rita in the first place."

It's a start, even if my father will never again be the man I thought he was.

Then it hits me like a freight train: Worth is the man who steps up and shoulders responsibilities that aren't his to keep his family together. The one who worries about his sister dropping out of college. The one who flies me across the country to visit my sick father.

He'd *never* betray me like this.

Why am I concerned that I won't be able to trust Worth when he's so clearly ten times the man my father is? Why do I think I don't know him or can't trust my judgment of him?

My stomach begins to churn and my cheeks burn hot, despite the cold. What was I thinking, letting Worth go? I was right that he deserves more than someone who doesn't trust him, but I can. It's taken this conversation for me to see it clearly. I don't just want him to lean on—though his strength makes my heart soar.

I want him because he's the best man I've ever known, and I love him.

I just hope I can convince him to trust *me* after I ran away.

THIRTY-THREE

Worth

Christmas Eve

I've been descended on. The brownstone has been taken over.

It's Efa's doing, but she's surrounded by enablers. "Worth, is that the door?" she bellows from the far side of the kitchen.

"Nope." I shake my head. It's the first time today I've been able to say there aren't people on my doorstep, trying to get in.

When I woke up this morning, there was not a single pinecone or ornament in my house. Now it feels like the brownstone is a pinecone and ornament superstore. Christmas music starts to play all around us. Did Efa have a sound system installed? At least it's Frank Sinatra and not Mariah Carey.

"Efa thinks you won't go for artificial snow," Eira, Efa's sister, says expectantly as she holds up a can of spray. "It's just that I know a guy who owes me a favor. And he can do amazing artwork on the windows over there." She nods toward the pocket doors that stretch all along the back wall of the first floor. "Let me show you his Instagram."

I don't know why she's asking me, to be honest. I've learned with Efa and Eira, it's just easier to let them do whatever they want.

"Just say yes, mate," Dax, Eira's husband, calls from the other side of the kitchen island. "I know she's not your wife, but believe me when I say you shouldn't argue."

Eira blows him a kiss.

I shrug. "As long as it comes off."

Eira holds up her phone. "You see that?" She shows me a guy working with a spray can of snow and what looks like a credit card to produce a Christmas scene that looks like it's from a Dickens novel. "He's a snow graffiti artist."

"How long will it take?" I ask.

"Just an hour or two. I'll clean it off myself if necessary."

"Let's do it." I check my watch. It's not even 1 p.m., and everyone's working like we're hosting a Christmas Eve ball at the Met rather than having our close circle of friends, plus Eira and Dax, over for dinner and drinks. Efa said she wanted to make it special. I don't hate the idea. Not that my heart isn't broken in two because Sophia isn't here—it is—but my friends are keeping my head above water, and I appreciate it. Embracing it, even. It's why I've allowed them to turn my perfectly respectable home into a winter wonderland. If nothing else, the chaos is distracting.

"How are you?" Jules comes over with two red mugs of hot chocolate and hands one to me. A candy cane pokes out from the top of a whipped swirl, and gingerbread sprinkles finish it off.

"Thanks." I raise my cup to her. "It feels like I'm... in the eye of a storm."

Jules laughs. "I thought I was fierce and well organized, but I look like an amateur compared to these two."

Jules and I haven't exactly been ignoring each other, but we haven't been seeking each other out either. She needs to support her friend, and I absolutely get that. I haven't asked her questions about

Sophia, and she hasn't offered any information. What would be the point?

"I just wanted to let you know I haven't heard from her other than a text saying she was back in Cincinnati for the holidays."

I nod my head. It's good to know Sophia is with her family. "Thanks for telling me."

"I think it was just a lot for her. But I'm hopeful she'll— Things will change and—"

I wince at her words and interrupt before she can say anything more. "Do you mind if we don't do that?" I ask. "I don't want false hope. I just want to keep moving forward." I pat Jules on the shoulder. "I appreciate you're trying to make me feel better and you're in a difficult position. You don't need to say anything."

She pulls her mouth into a sad smile. "I wish I could help."

"Did I tell you my sisters and I are refurbishing a hotel?" I ask. "On Forty-Sixth and Ninth Street."

"Really?" she asks, her eyes brightening at the change of subject.

"We're going to need some advice. In fact, I was wondering if Avril could come and get some work experience at The Mayfair. She could go to the Boston hotel, but she's going to supervise the build at the same time."

"That's going to be amazing." Her smile turns to a frown. "But it means you're upping the ante for the annual competition."

I laugh. "It's not going to be ready for a while yet." Then I narrow my eyes. "But then get ready."

It's her turn to laugh.

The door buzzer sounds and I take my hot chocolate and go answer it. I can see the wreath I made through the frosted glass on the other side of the door. I'm weirdly proud of it. Who knows? I might take a flower-arranging course. I'm getting better at recognizing what I like and what I'm only drawn to because it helps others. I can say with confidence that flower arrangement would be for my own happiness.

Just like marrying Sophia.

I pull open the door and it's like my thoughts have come alive. Sophia is standing in front of me in a huge quilted coat, with a cream hat and gloves that seem to make her blue eyes sparkle.

It's like my body has stopped functioning. I can't breathe. I can't speak. I'm not sure my heart's still beating.

She looks beautiful. Beyond beautiful. Her long blonde hair is splayed over the dark navy of her coat like shards of ice, and her cheeks are reddened by the cold. She's breathtaking.

She offers an awkward smile. "Hi," she says.

Someone shouting my name from inside the brownstone distracts me for a moment. I'm not sure if I've hit my head and am passed out, imagining all of this, or whether Sophia is really standing on my stoop.

"Hi," I say. I want to ask her why she's not in Cincinnati, but before I can say anything, Eira pushes past me.

"Are you the snow graffiti artist? I was expecting a man."

"No, Eira," I interrupt, and she rolls her eyes and disappears.

"You're busy," Sophia says, glancing past me to where Eira is running down the hall.

"We're just having dinner and drinks..." I see she has a gift bag in her hand. When she follows my gaze, she holds it up.

"I brought you a gift," she says.

"Do you want to come in?" I'm confused. Why is she here? Does she want to talk? My heart pulls in my chest. Has she changed her mind?

Laughter echoes from inside the house, pulling her attention. At the same time, a truck pulls up on the street, and in seconds, people are ascending the stairs carrying covered platters of god-knows-what, as if the brownstone is a public building.

"You've got a lot of people in there already. Another time, maybe," she says, offering an uncertain smile.

I want to scream for everyone to get out of the house so I can talk to Sophia and understand what brought her to my door.

She loops the gift bag she's brought onto the door handle and turns to leave. "Merry Christmas Eve, Worth."

My body is frozen as I watch her descend the steps. She looks back at me as she takes a right and heads west.

I don't seem to be able to react.

I don't know what to do or say. Do I ask her to stay? I don't want her to do anything she doesn't want to do.

But what do *I* want?

THIRTY-FOUR

I'm not sure how to land on someone's doorstep on Christmas Eve and tell them you want to be their wife. Or girlfriend. Honestly, if Worth said he'd moved on or didn't want to be with me in that way, I'd take his friendship instead. I just miss him.

I miss the way he loves me.

I miss the way I trust him.

I miss the way I love him.

I could have called Jules to see if he was busy or had moved on or hated me, but I didn't want to put her in an awkward position. I'm an adult, ready to face the consequences of my decisions. It's what I wanted from my dad, so how could I be a hypocrite when it comes to Worth? I want to put it all out there for him, even if it's not enough. He deserves that from me.

My hands are shaking as I walk up the stoop to his front door. The last time I was here, I signed divorce papers. I'm not sure if he had them filed. Maybe we're divorced already.

I answer the door, hoping he's in. I'm sure I can hear movement and music inside. It's nearly two in the afternoon on Christmas Eve.

I should have texted.

Before I can spiral further, the door yanks open and Worth appears.

My heart strains in my chest and I exhale. This is where I'm meant to be.

Seeing him here, his hair rumpled, glasses on, wearing a sweater with a hole in the elbow, makes everything slot into place. This man is my home.

After we exchange hellos, a beautiful woman appears from inside the house and looks me up and down. My entire body tightens

"Are you the snow graffiti artist?" she asks. "I was expecting a man."

The bubble pops.

I look between them, unable to figure out who she is and whether there's something between them. But if not, who is she and what's she doing in his home?

He doesn't offer an explanation.

"No, Eira," he says, and she disappears.

Eira. Eira. That name is familiar, but I can't place it.

"You're busy," I say, watching the woman run down the hall.

"We're just having dinner and drinks..." His gaze shifts to the gift bag I'm carrying.

I hold it up. "I brought you a gift."

"Do you want to come in?" he asks.

Yes, I think. Yes, I want to come in and take off my coat and drink tea and talk and sink into your body while we promise never to leave each other.

I want it all from him.

A burst of laughter echoes from inside the house. It's not just Eira inside. All his friends are probably in there, too. Squealing brakes sound behind me and a white truck parks at the curb. Three people in smart gray uniforms carry covered platters up the steps.

He's having a party. Or maybe he's hosting Christmas lunch tomorrow. Whatever he's doing, his plans don't include me. "You've got a lot of people in there already. Another time, maybe," I suggest. I want him to offer a specific date. Maybe the day after tomorrow. Or he could call me? But I don't want to push, because I don't need Worth to save me. I just want him to love me.

I hang the gift on the door handle and turn to leave. "Merry Christmas Eve, Worth."

I practically run down the stairs.

I hadn't dared to hope what might happen when I turned up on his doorstep, but I can't help feeling the weight of disappointment in every atom of my body.

Being so close to him and not being able to touch him was like torture. It would have been better not to come, because watching the way he moves, seeing his face, almost being able to take in his scent— it's just made me realize what a complete fool I was for ever thinking I wanted to walk away from him.

I pick up my speed, desperate to get to the corner of his street so I can let go and... miss him.

I scrub my hands over my face and start to run toward the park. I need space. The tears are threatening to fall, and I just need to be far enough away so I don't crumble where he might see me.

"Sophia!"

I stop and swallow, not daring to turn around.

"Sophia," Worth says, quieter now that he's only a few feet away.

I press my gloved hands over my face, willing myself not to cry. *Deep breath in, deep breath out.* I lower my arms and turn to face him. "Hi." I'm trying to sound breezy, but I know my voice sounds like splintered glass. I'm about to fall apart and I don't want him to witness it because I know he'll feel bad. That's the last thing I want.

He looks panicked. "Sophia," he says again. His voice is ragged and desperate. "Why did you come?"

"I... I... I... To wish you merry Christmas Eve."

He shakes his head. "No, you didn't." His gaze locks on to mine and I'm helpless. I can't run from him anymore. I don't want to.

"I wanted to see you," I confess.

He nods, encouraging me to say more.

"Who was the woman at the door?" I ask. I have no right to expect Worth to be alone, but that doesn't stop me hoping.

He frowns and I hold my breath, steeling myself for his reply. "Who? Eira?"

Something in my expression—maybe the jealousy oozing out of my pores—must give me away, because he continues, "The one asking whether you were a graffiti artist was Efa's sister. She's over for the holidays. With her husband, Dax. They're both here. Efa wanted to throw a Christmas Eve dinner at the brownstone." He takes a step toward me. "Of course there's no other woman, Sophia."

Relief washes over me.

"There'll never be anyone but you for me."

My eyes flutter shut as I take in his words.

"You never have to concern yourself with that. I'm yours. Forever."

I swallow past the lump of hope and exhaustion gathered in my throat. "Worth," I say. I try and blink away the tears in my eyes. "I know you're not my father. I know I can trust you."

He groans out a sigh. "Yes," he says. "Always."

I nod and take a step toward him. "I shouldn't have walked out on you."

"I understand why you did. I get it, Sophia."

I shake my head. "You can understand—because that's the man you are—but it's still not okay. I can't run when things get scary. That's not what trust is. That's not what love is."

"Love?" he asks.

"I love you," I whisper. He closes his eyes for one second, then two, like he's feeling the words trail over his body. "I won't do it again."

He fixes me with his gaze. "I won't survive if you do."

My chest tightens. I can see the hurt in his eyes, the pain in his expression.

"I'm sorry." I step forward and press my palm to his chest. He feels solid, like one of the trees standing tall and steady in the Catskills. He feels like shelter. Like home. "I'm truly sorry."

He circles me with his strong arms and pulls me closer. I sink into his warm body and let myself go. Being here with him, anywhere with him, feels like exactly where I should be. Cincinnati isn't home —not anymore. It's only a place I used to live. It's my history. My present and future are with Worth, wherever that might be.

"So you're back for good," he says, like he's turning the words over on his tongue to see how they taste.

I tilt my chin up to look at him. "If you'll have me," I say. "For as long as you'll be my husband and my hero."

"That's forever, then." A smile curls at the edge of his mouth.

"I want it to be forever with you, Worth. You're an incredible man and I'm lucky just to know you. I'm the luckiest person alive to be married to you." I gasp. "I signed those papers." I look up, searching his face.

"I sent them to my lawyer," he says. "We'll figure it out."

"But what if we're not married?" I ask.

"Then we'll do it all over again. I'd marry you every day for the rest of my life if I could."

I pull off my gloves, lift up on tiptoes and cup his face in my hands, pulling him down to meet me in a kiss. It's like the Fourth of July inside my body as his touch lights up every part of me.

His hands hold the back of my neck and he deepens the kiss. My knees weaken and my heart lifts in my chest like it might float away at any moment. It feels as if we're in a bubble, just the two of us. It doesn't matter where we are; if I'm with Worth, I'm where I'm meant to be.

His cheek scrapes mine, and goose bumps scatter across my skin. He's cold.

"Shit." I pull away. "You're out here without a coat. It's twenty degrees." I take his hand in mine and kiss it. "You need to get inside."

He doesn't say anything, he just smiles at me. "I haven't noticed the cold."

"I mean it, Worth. You'll get sick. Let's get you inside."

He sighs. "The house is full of people. I just want to have you to myself for a little while."

I can't help but smile at his wish. "They're holding it at your house to make you feel better," I say.

He nods. "I know. They've been amazing. I was... in a bad place there for a bit."

I tilt my head. "If I could take it back, I would."

"Don't," he says. "Don't say that. We've been tested and survived. You left and you came back. We're stronger because of that. It doesn't mean it wasn't hard, but look—it's all worked out in the end."

I tug on his hand a little, leading us back to the brownstone. "Let's go see your friends."

"They're your friends too."

"Maybe not anymore."

He stops, turns to face me, and holds my shoulders. "Yes. They're your friends too. They want us both to be happy."

I nod. That's true. Worth's friends adore him. They would only want what's good for him. I just might have to convince them that's me. But I'll prove myself. I know where my heart is. With time, they'll see it too.

"I'm not going back without you," he says. "You want to celebrate Christmas Eve at the brownstone or do you want to go somewhere else?"

There he goes again, ignoring his own wants for mine.

"Before you ask," he says, before I can push the decision back on him, "I'd like us to spend the rest of the day with our friends, and then I want to take you to bed and keep you awake all night." Worth's always been able to read my mind. I shouldn't be surprised he's doing it now. "It doesn't come naturally to me, but I've been working on figuring out what *I* want. So... that's what I want."

"I see that," I say. "And I love that." I reach up and press my fingers along his jaw. "And your suggestion sounds better than perfect."

"*You're* better than perfect," he says. "Because you're you."

I have a feeling this man is going to continue to make me melt every day for the rest of my life. But first, I have to make sure he doesn't freeze to death. "Let's go home," I say, and slide my hand into his.

THIRTY-FIVE

Worth

I thought it was going to be the worst Christmas ever. Turns out, I couldn't have imagined one this good. We come up the stoop and the gift bag Sophia brought is still hanging on the doorknob.

"Should I open it?" I ask her.

"You can." She sounds uncertain. "It's not anything really. Just a reason to drop by."

I press a kiss to the top of her head. "You didn't need a reason."

Inside the gift bag, I find a fridge magnet. But not any old fridge magnet. It's the New York Loves Vegas Chapel logo, with a heart replacing the "o" in "love." A print of our selfie in front of the Vegas sign is framed inside.

It's perfect. "You're an excellent gift giver," I say. "Thank you."

"I think it will look fabulous on your refrigerator."

"I've always thought that room was missing something." I smile. "I just realized, I haven't bought you anything."

Her eyes soften and she smiles. "I have everything I need, now that I'm with you."

There's nothing more to resolve between us. I've never felt so certain about anyone in my life, and I know she feels the same. There may be hurdles ahead of us—although I can't think of any specifics at the moment. Whatever they are, we'll face them as a couple. We're together, now and forever. I see it in her eyes. I feel it in her heart.

As we step into the front hallway, the mixture of voices and clatter of dishes fills the air. For a moment, I want to turn right around and escape, so it can be just the two of us a little longer.

"Are they here yet?" A voice draws closer and Jules appears at the kitchen door. "Worth, have you seen—" She sees Sophia and looks back at me, then down to our joined hands. A moment later, she throws herself at Sophia. "You've come back!"

The two of them almost fall to the floor.

"You think you can rustle up another table setting?" Sophia asks.

"Absolutely! How are you? I've been so worried. Did you see your dad? What happened? How's your mom? Are your brothers okay? You're all set?" She lifts her chin in my direction, letting me know the last question was fired at me.

"I came to my senses. Spoke to my mom and my dad. Both helped me see Worth more clearly." She glances over at me, and I can't help but stare back and think about all the ways I'm going to claim her body when everyone has left.

But I can't. Not yet. Before that, we have to celebrate Christmas Eve with our chosen family.

"So you two are back together now?" Jules asks.

Sophia nods effusively. "Forever," she and I chorus.

Jules shakes her head with a smile and pulls us both in for a three-way hug. "You two are perfect for each other. I've never met two kinder souls."

"Jules?" Leo fills the kitchen doorway and he takes in the three of us.

"Sophia's back," Jules says, releasing us from the hug and stating the obvious.

Leo's eyes bulge. I know he'll be concerned. "Oh wow. I wasn't expecting to see you."

"I didn't want to miss the first Christmas with my husband," she says.

It takes everything I have not to drag her upstairs. I'm never going to get tired of hearing her call me her husband.

He nods, glancing from Sophia to me, gauging my reaction.

"I'm really sorry," she says. "For upsetting Worth. He's a wonderful, kind, trusting man and I questioned that for a second. Not because of anything he ever did. I just had my own side of the street to clean up."

I pull Sophia closer. She doesn't need to do an apology tour. That's not what my friends expect. But it's nice that she's prepared to. It means we're both at the same starting point—the point where we'll do whatever it takes to be together and make each other happy.

"We've all been there," Leo says, visibly relaxing. "I just want Worth happy."

"I know," she says. "So do I. I just wasn't sure I was the person to make that happen. But now I'm going to work really hard to make sure I am."

"I'm not sure you'll have to do much," Leo says, patting me on the arm. "The way he looks at you? I think just being his wife does the job."

"Leo speaks the truth," I say, trying to reassure Sophia. "It's understandable that you were frightened to trust people, given everything you've had going on."

She glances up at me from under her lashes. "How could I ever have thought walking away from you was a good idea?"

I don't care that she walked away. I only care that she came back.

"Are things okay with your dad now?" Jules asks.

"No," she says. "But we had a conversation. I'm seeing things a little differently now."

"So... you forgave him?"

She shakes her head. "No. But I'm starting to accept him for who he is. He's not the hero I thought he was. The pedestal I've had him on for so long has crashed to the ground. I can see him more clearly now, and that lets me see everything else more clearly, too." I squeeze her hand. "But Mom and I are working on things. I honestly believe she did the best she could in the circumstances. She was acting in our best interest—me and my brothers'. Things among the four of us are different, but good."

"That's great," I say, pressing a kiss to the top of her head. I want to hear the entire story, in detail, when she's ready to tell me.

The doorbell interrupts our reunion. Leo skirts past us to answer it. "That will be the entertainment."

"Entertainment?" I ask.

He opens the door and is handed a huge cardboard box.

"Pass the parcel," he says, as if that explains everything.

The door goes again. This time, I'm closest. When I open it, Jack and Fisher are standing there with Byron behind them. "Worth's wreath was definitely the best," Byron says as all three of them stare at my homemade creation hanging on the front door.

"What can I say?" I reply. "I'm a master at whatever I turn my hand to."

"You made that?" Sophia says, her tone impressed. "I didn't take you for a crafter."

"Sophia!" Jack says when he sees who's talking. We go into brief explanations about how she's back for good. They all look to me to check everything's okay. But it's more than okay. I'm better than I've ever been.

"Anyone else missing?" I ask as everyone starts taking off coats and boots. The scent of cinnamon and gingerbread waft from the kitchen. I'm not sure the brownstone has ever been so festive.

"That's all of us," Byron says, taking stock of everyone scattered throughout the first floor.

Our tight group of six has expanded a lot this year. Love has hit three of us hard—so hard, we won't ever be the same. We'll just keep getting better.

THIRTY-SIX

It's nearly midnight. Dinner ended so long ago, I just snuck some cheese and crackers from the board still sitting out on the counter. Frank Sinatra's crooning about it being a white Christmas, Eira's simmer pot is still making the house smell of oranges and cinnamon and nutmeg, and cozy, tipsy chatter fills the room.

It's the best Christmas Eve I've ever had.

Worth slides his hand over my thigh from where he sits next to me at the head of the table. "What are you thinking about?" he asks.

"How lucky we are to know such great people, and what a lovely evening I've had." I turn my face to his and steal a kiss.

"It's like you never left," he says. "And it's better than before at the same time."

I nod. "I feel it too."

"What are we doing tomorrow?" he asks. "We could fly back to Cincinnati if you'd like?"

I shake my head. "No, I want to stay here in New York. Maybe we can go house hunting."

"You don't want to stay here?" he asks.

I don't, but I will if it's important to him. "It might be nice to have a fresh start. A place that's not yours, but ours."

"That makes sense. Though I want a house," he says. "I'm going to get you pregnant and we're going to need the space."

I press my lips tight together to stop myself from smiling. "You planning on enacting that plan tonight?"

"I'm going to do my best." His eyes grow hooded and he looks at me like he wants to fuck me right here, right now.

I saw my teeth against my bottom lip and tilt my head. "Maybe we should aim for a year from now. I think I want you to myself for a little while."

"I might be able to live with that idea," he says.

Under the table, he links his fingers through mine. The heat of his skin sets something off in me—a timer racing toward zero. I'm done with having a houseful of people. It's time for Worth and me to be alone.

"It's officially Christmas," Efa says. "Happy Christmas!" she raises her glass and everyone joins in the toast.

"It's time for everyone to be going," Worth says, and I can't help but laugh. It's such an un-Worth-like thing to say. He's usually so focused on everyone else's happiness, he doesn't think about what he wants. But right now, the smolder in his eyes says he wants *me*. I like it. It's hot.

"You're right, bud," Fisher says, pushing out his chair and standing.

"I have dinner with the fam at the Peninsula tomorrow," Jack says. "I need some sleep to be able to endure it."

"Say hi to Pat for me," Fisher says.

I'm not sure who Pat is, or why Jack is so bummed about spending Christmas with his family, but I'm going to be around this group for the rest of my life, so there's plenty of time to find out.

Everyone starts to leave and heads into the hallway to retrieve coats and boots.

"What about you, Byron?" Leo asks. "What are you doing tomorrow?"

"I'm headed to Colorado," he says "Change is afoot."

"What does that mean?" Leo asks.

Byron shrugs. "Just that I'm going to be spending a lot more time there from now on. I'm not sure how much I'm going to be in New York over the next couple of years."

"What?" everyone choruses at once.

"You'll have to come out and visit," he says. Everyone starts asking him questions, but he keeps quiet, wrapping his scarf around his neck with a flourish. As he opens the door, a whoosh of cold air comes in and he announces, "Everything will be revealed. Good night and merry Christmas, my friends."

With that, he disappears into the dark.

After hugs and promises of texts, calls, and visits over the next few days, Worth finally closes the door.

We're alone.

At last.

I'm shaking, I want Worth so much. Heat radiates from between my thighs and I transfer my weight from foot to foot as I squirm under his stare.

"Come here," he says.

I exhale a sharp breath.

"You seem a little wound up."

"I want you," I say, my voice breathy.

"Say it again."

"I want you, Worth. Please."

He closes his eyes in a long blink, like he's savoring my words. Like he's been waiting to hear them and now that he has, he can relax.

He cups my face in his hands and places a kiss on my lips. "Good girl."

My nipples pebble against the lace of my bra and my breathing is labored. Everything he does makes me feel worshipped and desired and cherished. I smooth my hands up his chest and start to undo the buttons on his shirt. He pulls my hand into his and leads me upstairs. When we get to his bedroom, I realize I've never seen it before. It's dark and grand and somehow doesn't feel like him. There are dark gray velvet drapes at the windows and a brown leather couch at the end of the biggest bed I've ever seen. The sheets are a crisp white, with a velvet comforter folded at the bottom.

I glance at Worth, who's watching me.

"What are you thinking?" he asks.

"This room doesn't feel like you," I say. "Or maybe it's a part of you I don't know."

"You know all of me," he says. "You don't need to worry about that."

"I'm not worried," I say, as he stalks over to me and slips his hands around my waist. "I know who you are in your heart, but we're still getting to know each other."

"In all the ways that don't count," he says. "I know you to your core, in all the ways that do."

I smile and press my palm against his cheek. He always knows what to say to make me feel better.

He gathers my top and pulls it over my head. I shiver.

"You won't be cold for long," he says.

He releases the clasp of my bra and lets it drop to the floor. Worth catches my breasts in his hands, kneads them together and kisses me once quickly before flicking my nipples, making me gasp.

A small grin teases at his lips. "I know what you like," he says, his words melting me like butter in a hot pan. He knows better than I do.

He kneels, undoes my jeans, and takes them off. I'm entirely naked standing in front of Worth, who's fully clothed.

"Put your sweater back on."

I frown, not knowing if I understand what he's saying at first.

He just nods, as if to say, *Yes, you heard me right.*

I turn and find my discarded lilac sweater on the bed behind me. I slip it over my head and push my arms through the sleeves.

"Lie on the bed," he says. "Face up. For now."

I do what he asks, pushing myself up on the high mattress and shifting so I'm lying in the middle of the bed in nothing but my sweater. Is he worried about me getting cold?

I don't have time to think any further when he crawls over me, lifting my sweater. I shift to try and help make it easier. Why have I just put this on if he's just going to take it right off?

"Don't move," he says. "Let me."

He shifts the sweater up, up, up, gently lifting my arms overhead as he goes. But when the sweater is halfway over my head, he stops. My eyes are covered, my upper arms held in place over my head.

"You can't see. And you can't touch me," he says. "Just feel."

I gasp. He planned this.

Suddenly a little self-conscious, I cross my ankles.

"No," he snaps and uncrosses them. Then he pushes my legs as far apart as possible. I can't see if he's looking at me. I don't know if he's checking to see if I'm wet. I don't know what he's doing.

I hear a rustle of clothes. Is he undressing? I imagine his hard body, the hair that covers his pecs and trails down to his cock.

I let out a gasp at the thought of his cock and how big it is. How it seems to vibrate when it's inside me. I can't stay still. I shift my hips, thinking of how he'll be touching me soon. How he'll be inside me— his tongue, his fingers, his hard dick, shoving into me, plowing deeper and deeper.

I let out another gasp.

"Oh, you're so ready for this, aren't you?" he asks.

"Yes," I call out. "Please."

"I can see it. I can see how wet you are. I can smell it." He groans and the bed dips beside me.

Is he going to touch me?

Where?

How?

When?

"Please, Worth."

He growls, and I feel him hover over me, his body caging mine.

"God, Sophia. All the things I want to do to you."

"Yes," I gasp. I want all of them. Right now.

"And you want that too. That's the best part. You and I want exactly the same things." I feel his breath on my neck, followed by his tongue. He lowers his body to mine and I feel his erection on my thigh. I shift, trying to get closer, to urge him inside me.

"Not yet, baby," he says. "Not yet. First I've got to get myself reacquainted with this body." He trails kisses down my throat and sets to work, squeezing and pinching one nipple while biting, grazing, and sucking the other. My breaths grow shorter. Everything feels even more intense than it usually does. I don't know if it's because I can't see, or because it's been so long, but pleasure bursts through me harder and harder with every touch.

"Worth," I moan. "I'm so close."

He chuckles and releases me. "Oh no. Not yet, princess."

I whimper at the lost contact and the subsequent ebb of my orgasm.

"Soon," he whispers, and I feel his breath against my pussy. His attention has shifted but I don't know if I can take his tongue without coming immediately.

He works his tongue against my clit and I arch up from the bed. I've waited too long for this. I've wanted it too much.

He grasps my hips, holding me in place. "Don't come, Sophia. Not until I tell you."

I whimper. I have no idea how I'm supposed to stop myself.

He delves between my folds and I try and block out the sensation of the slip of his tongue, the press of it against my clit, the way I feel him right at the center of my being. My breathing comes heavier now. Sharper. Faster.

It's as if he doesn't notice. He doesn't alter his plan. He just holds me still, pressing, licking, tasting, and growling against me like I'm a feast for him alone.

Then all of a sudden his tongue is gone, and all I can feel is the throb of my pussy in the comparatively cool air.

"Good girl, Sophia. Now you can come."

I feel a breeze against my sex. It's Worth. He's blowing against my clitoris.

A thousand butterfly wings beat against my chest. My insides turn inside out as I dissolve into an orgasm without Worth laying a finger—or his tongue—on me.

All I see is a cluster of stars exploding against my eyelids. My entire body begins to shake.

I hear the rip of a condom packet from somewhere. I can't feel Worth anywhere. I don't know if he's on the bed. I'm so disorientated—high from my climax.

And then I feel him *everywhere*.

His body slots against mine and his mouth is on my neck, then my lips. His kisses are teasing, wet, and possessive.

"You're such a good girl, Sophia," he growls against my skin. He pulls my sweater off my eyes, off my arms, and suddenly I'm free. The desire I see in his expression is a relief. I know he wants me, but seeing confirmation feels good. It seems almost impossible that he could want me as much as I want him, but seeing him, I believe it.

We lock eyes and he pushes into me. I cry out—it's not painful, I'm so wet it couldn't be. But it's a shock. I forgot how big he is, how full I feel with him inside me. How connected I feel to him when he's fucking me.

When he's as deep as he can go, he stops, as if he knows he needs to let me get used to him. I spread my legs wider.

"This," I breathe out, holding his gaze. "Forever."

He nods. "That's right." He starts to move, drawing out slowly and pushing in, more quickly this time.

I cry out again, because it's almost as much of a shock as it was a moment ago.

"That's right, Sophia. I get to fuck you forever."

Finally, I can move my hands and touch him. I smooth my fingers over his shoulders, pressing into his hard skin, the muscles bunched and tight with effort.

He reaches down and presses my thigh wider, trying to go deeper, like he wants to own me. But he already does. Everything I have, everything I am, is his.

I slide my hand down his chest. He glances down at where my palm presses over his heart. Then I go lower, circling my fingers around the base of his cock. He alternates between looking me in the eye and where we're joined—right where he's fucking me.

"You feel so good," he says. "Like you were designed just for me."

I let out a squeal as he shifts us around and lifts my leg over his shoulder.

When he pushes in again, it's deeper this time—the edge of too much.

"No," I let out, barely able to catch my breath. "*You* were designed for *me*."

His skin begins to glisten with sweat as he moves over me. His jaw tightens and he clenches his teeth.

I reach for him. I want his body pressed to mine. I want to feel his weight—his solidity. I want us joined. He shifts and lies over me, my palms coming to rest on his back.

"Don't leave me again," he whispers into my ear.

"Never," I say. "Never, Worth. I promise."

I don't know if it's the promise I make to him or the fact that this is the first time we've had sex since our breakup. But it's as if the physical binds with the mental and emotional, my connection to this man ballooning suddenly and all at once. I have an overwhelming sensation of *giving* myself to Worth, physically and emotionally, and him doing the same in return. I don't think I could feel more need for a person than I do for Worth, but right now, I don't need anything *but* him. Sex has transformed into a reaffirmation of our love for each other—our commitment to forever. It's a wedding, but better.

I don't know if it's possible for our love to keep growing, or for our connection to be any deeper. It already feels like the roots of our union go to the core of the earth. I don't know how and I don't know why, but I know that it will always be this way between us. We were made for each other.

EPILOGUE

Two months later

Sophia

Whenever I've been back to Cincinnati before, I've felt like a version of the child I was when I lived here—but not this trip. I don't know if it's because I'm with Worth, or if it's because I feel distance between me and Cincinnati since all the drama with my dad. Whatever it is, I'm back and I feel like a woman. Lots has changed, but for the first time in a long time, I'm not coming back to Ohio with dread in my heart.

Worth and I are staying at the hotel we stayed at last time. Mom tried to persuade us to stay with her, but Worth was clear that staying in the hotel was what *he* wanted. I was happy to go along with it.

I wouldn't normally make the trip for Oliver's birthday, but I want to make sure Mom's doing as well as she says she is. I also want to see my brothers. The three of us have made an unspoken pact to be more connected, without relying on Mom to be the glue binding us together. I'm not seeing Dad on this trip. We've exchanged a few messages and maybe I'll see him later in the year. Everything's still raw. No one is pushing me or Oliver or Noah into seeing him. We need time. And maybe we don't want anything to do with him, but if we do, it won't be out of a sense of obligation. It will be out of any love that still exists between us.

"Worth!" Oliver almost squeals as he opens my mom's front door. It's like he hasn't even seen me. Maybe I should find it irritating how much Oliver and Noah like Worth, but I can't. It's beyond cute to watch the three of them bond.

In the kitchen, Worth hands my mom a huge bouquet of flowers and kisses her on the cheek. We all take a seat around the kitchen table. Oliver takes the stool without a fight. We must be maturing.

"Any news on this second wedding you've been promising me?" Mom says as she slides a tray of freshly baked cookies onto the counter. "Or are you here to tell me it's not going to happen?"

I glance at Worth. We've talked about this a lot. A big wedding doesn't suit either of us. But our families want to celebrate, which is lovely and uplifting and truly heartwarming. We're here for the love. "We thought we'd do something in May," I say.

"And what exactly is *something*?" Mom asks.

"A party," Worth says.

Mom will be disappointed. She wants to go dress shopping with me and see me hold a bouquet and walk down an aisle, but it's not what I want. And it's not what Worth wants. Our ceremony was strange and unplanned, but it's going to be the only one we need. We got married that day and I don't want to dilute it by doing it again. It was special and private, and the fact that it was only the two of us makes it feel more *about* us than a big wedding could. Plus, the sheer luck of our divorce papers never getting filed feels like a good omen.

Mom tries to mask her disappointment with a forced smile. "And where will this party be?" she asks.

"New York," I say. Cincinnati isn't my home. There's no reason to have it here.

"I suppose that makes sense," she says. "But remember, I have my Christmas Town, so your kids are going to make you come back once a year at least."

"Are you pregnant?" Oliver asks.

"No, not yet," I say. "But we hope to be one day."

"So New York in May." She sniffs and unties her apron before coming to sit. Noah pours us all drinks. Somehow, Worth gets served first.

"You'd better give me the dates sooner rather than later," she says. "I have a vacation scheduled around that time."

Noah, Oliver, and I exchange glances. Mom doesn't go on vacation. Not ever.

"Oh?" I ask, without trying to sound like I'm *what the fuck*-ing her. "Where are you going?"

"Vancouver. A hiking vacation," she announces.

None of Mom's friends hike. Like, *none* of them.

"Who are you going with?" Oliver asks.

"Well..." Mom stands and transfers the cookies to a cooling rack, then brings them to the table. "I'm going with my new friend, Liam."

Oliver's eye bulge out of his head and Noah nods slightly manically.

"Vancouver's beautiful," Worth says. "And spring is the perfect time to go. The hiking is incredible."

Mom and Worth chat for a few minutes about Vancouver, which gives the three of us a moment to collect ourselves. Worth is more aware of his needs now, but that doesn't stop him being acutely cognizant of other people's. I'm not sure he's ever been to Vancouver. I'll have to ask him later.

"I think that's great, Mom," Noah says, his nodding having subsided a little.

"Yeah," Oliver says. "Great."

"Will we meet him anytime soon?" I ask.

"Sure," she says. "He's on standby to come to dinner tonight." A smile curls around my mom's lips.

I rest a hand on top of hers. "I can't wait," I say. "How did you two meet?"

"He's a regular at the library." She starts to laugh. "Turns out he's never been the greatest reader, but came to return some books for his neighbor, who was sick. I checked them in for him. And he came back after that every week for fifteen years."

"Oh, Mom," I say. "That's so romantic."

"We used to chat about the books he took out and brought back. But he never asked me out until the day he saw me without a wedding ring."

"And he's not married?" Oliver asks.

"His wife passed away about seventeen years ago."

"And he's been in love with you for how many years?" I ask.

"We hardly knew each other," she scoffs.

"I didn't believe in love at first sight before I met your daughter," Worth says. "But now I do. Sounds like Liam had the same kind of experience when he met you fifteen years ago." Worth turns to me. "Thank god it didn't take fifteen years for you to be mine. Although I would have waited twice as long."

Mom deserves the kind of man who waits fifteen years for her. A man who fell in love with her the moment he saw her. The kind of man who went into the library every week, just to catch a glimpse of her or exchange a few words.

Liam sounds perfect. She deserves her happily ever after.

A MONTH *Later*

Worth

Having lunch with my wife never gets old.

"You look beautiful," I say as I take in Sophia. It's not the first time I've told her today. And it won't be the last. I can't help myself. It's the truth.

She smiles, and it warms me like palms raised up against an open fire. "It's our last lunch for two days."

I groan. I head to Colorado tomorrow, which means we'll spend two nights away from each other. These will be the first nights we've spent apart since she came back to me on Christmas Eve. "I wish you could come with me." I open the door to the car I have waiting for us. Lunch today isn't about eating. I need to visit Hotel on Ninth Street and it's the only time I have before heading off tomorrow.

"Next time," she says. I slide in next to her and pull the door shut. It should only take us a few minutes to get across town to the hotel. But they're precious minutes I get to speak to my wife.

"Will Avril be there?" Sophia asks.

"I doubt it. She's juggling a lot at the moment. I didn't tell her I was coming."

"I can't believe she's trying to finish her degree and oversee the refurbishment at the same time."

When Avril came to me and said that because the hotel refurbishment was going to take nearly eighteen months, she'd like to try to finish her degree, I thought she was kidding. It was all the proof I needed that I'd done something right as her brother—that she was taking responsibility for her own life and making the most out of the opportunities she'd been given. "We have a great project manager. She's going to learn what it is to hustle, and this is her first lesson."

"Oh, I think she had a pretty good teacher." She squeezes my hand.

"Not many people would describe me as a hustler." To most people, I'm the ultimate cool head—the planner and provider.

She laughs. "Yeah, but not many people know your story. Your sisters know what you did to get through the tough times. The apple doesn't fall far from the tree." Her eyes are bright, pride shining in them like she's lucky to know me. Doesn't she know it's the other way around?

I bend and press a kiss to her neck. Her fingers thread through my hair just as we come to a stop. I glance out the window at the boarded-up exterior to the hotel. I sigh. The one time I needed a little New York City traffic.

She laughs like she knows exactly what I was thinking. "I'm excited to see the progress."

I like to check on things down here at least once a week. It's not because I don't trust my sister—I completely do. Truth is, I'm excited. This hotel is one of the first things I've ever worked on that feels personal.

We punch the key code into the panel on the doorway and make our way inside. I stalk out in front and Sophia pulls me to the panel of hard hats and high-vis vests on the other side of the entryway.

"Did I ever tell you how hot you look in luminous yellow?" she asks, placing a hard hat on my head.

"Liar."

Her eyes flash. "I dare you to steal your hat and vest and bring them home, and you can judge for yourself."

I growl and grab her ass, pressing a kiss to her lips.

"Hey, you guys!" Avril interrupts us.

Sophia bats my hand away from her ass. "Avril! We didn't know if you'd be here."

"Yeah, Worth didn't say he'd be down."

"I thought you'd be on campus."

"I don't have any classes until three today. One of the lecture theaters had a flood. So I thought I'd come down and do a walk-through."

"That makes three of us," I say.

Avril grins and it feels like she's really pleased to have me here. She doesn't get pissed when I ask her questions about the site and progress—even though part of me is testing her, making sure she's on top of everything. She seems to relish it. Like she enjoys my involvement in the project and isn't trying to shoo me away.

"Where should we start?" she asks.

"How's the top floor coming along?" Sophia asks. Last time we were here, they'd started on the interior walls and electrical on the top floor, and were working their way down.

"It's actually pretty cool," Avril says. "They're working on the top three floors now."

That seems fast. I was only here a week ago and they were slightly behind schedule.

"It's going exactly per the project plan," Avril says. "Pete is doing an incredible job keeping everyone on track. You were right—I couldn't have project-managed this place."

Avril had listened to me when I said she wasn't qualified to manage a build like this. Luckily for me, Pete agreed to step in and guide Avril through the process while he acts as PM. I have the best of both worlds.

"Hello!" someone calls after us as we head to the only working elevator in the place.

"Is that Poppy?" I ask, just as my sister appears.

"Worth?" She pulls Sophia into a hug. "I wasn't expecting to see you."

"What are you doing here?" I ask.

She grins like she just won the lottery. "I just handed in my notice."

Before we had an honest conversation about it, I hadn't realized Poppy wasn't enjoying her work at the bank. Or as Avril put it, "Hated the bank with every molecule of her being."

"You did it," I say. She's been threatening to quit for months now.

"I did. It feels great."

"Okay, good. You can start at my office tomorrow. I'm in Colorado for two nights. Veronica can find you a desk there."

"And I found you a desk here," Avril says.

"Here?" we all chorus, looking around at the bare floorboards and listening to the sound of shouts and drilling coming from above our heads.

"You need to be onsite," Avril says to Poppy.

"I can come to site. I don't need to work here all the time. The dust alone will drive me crazy."

"Okay, but I picked us out an office to share."

Poppy groans. "I didn't agree to share a room with you. We haven't done that since we were kids."

"Are we all going up or not?" I snap. I can only listen to Poppy and Avril bicker for so long.

Sophia's hand shifts in mine and she finds my pulse point on my wrist. This simple movement calms me. Her touch makes me aware of her—makes me remember what's important. "I'm going to miss you," she whispers as we step into the elevator.

I tune out Avril and Poppy and start to think about the journey tomorrow. None of our friend group knows I'm headed out to Colorado. It's not a secret exactly, we're just not telling anyone.

"I'm going to miss you too. You could come with me."

"I have a job," Sophia says, her tone teasing.

"A job you don't like."

"Right. But until I figure out what I'm going to do, it's a job I'm keeping."

"If you quit, you'd have time to think about what you want to do."

"Maybe you're right. Or maybe I'd just follow you to Colorado and wherever else you're traveling to, and then I'll start getting up later and going to the gym at noon, and then five years would have passed by."

"You could find us somewhere to live."

"Oh, I did that already," she says as we exit the elevator. "Your kiss scrambled my brain and I forgot to tell you."

"You found a place?" We've looked at a couple of places in the last month or so.

"Well, only on Zillow, because surfing Zillow's my side hustle now. It's on the next street over from ours, just a block away."

"Sounds good. Can we go have a look at it?" Sophia's gone back and forth on moving out of the brownstone now that she's settled in. But even though it was she who first suggested a move, it's me who's pushing for it now. I want a fresh start. Marrying Sophia was the beginning of so much, and I want to honor that by living somewhere I bought because I want to live there with my wife—not because it was convenient and big enough for my sisters to move in if the need arose.

"Sure—oh wow, progress," she says as she looks around. I follow her gaze.

"Walls," I say.

"And electrical and plumbing and HVAC. We're completely back on schedule."

I'm impressed. They've achieved a lot this week.

We step off the corridor and into one of the newly constructed rooms. The drywall hasn't had a plaster veneer yet, and the floors are covered, so it's difficult to get a sense of proportion. "Is this a bedroom?"

"Yes," Avril says. "It's a standard bedroom. Most of them will be this size. Bathroom is in there. Or will be." She lifts her chin at a doorway to the right of the entry.

"It doesn't seem especially big," I say.

"A typical New York hotel room is three hundred square feet. This will be four-ten. It's very generous. We're going to be able to bring in rollaway beds for families."

"It's great," Sophia says. "You're going to be opening the doors in no time."

"You mean, *we're* going to be opening the doors," Avril corrects her. "We're family now."

Sophia's mouth curves into a shy smile and I pull her closer. I've been hers since the moment I laid eyes on her. And now she's mine. My lover, my best friend, my wife—my family.

"What hotel are you staying at in Colorado?" Sophia asks.

"I'm staying with Byron. He has a place there. Why?"

She shrugs. "I don't know. I was just thinking maybe... you know, I'm owed some PTO. But if you're staying with Byron, that might not be a good idea."

It's the last thing I expected her to say. "I'll buy a hotel out there if it means you'll come with me."

She laughs. "I'm going to put you on a budget. No more hotel purchases. But the thought of you being away for two nights—" She shivers, and I kiss the top of her head.

"Get a room," Avril calls as she brushes past us.

"If I can figure things out with work, I'd like to come with you if you think Byron won't mind."

"I know he won't." I cup her face in my hands. If she'd waved a magic wand and finished this place, I couldn't be happier.

"And while you have all that free time up on your trip," Avril says, appearing at the doorway, "please arrange for your brothers to come to New York. I've seen Noah on Insta and I'm all in."

Sophia groans. "This could go badly wrong."

"Very badly wrong," Worth says. "Let's escape to Colorado. Quick."

TO READ BYRON'S STORY, *read Love Fast*

If you enjoy instant chemistry, slightly forbidden romance read **Dr. Off Limits** (Read on for a sneak peek)

For exclusive excerpts, new release news and additional content sign up for the Louise Bay Newsletter www.louisebay.com/newsletter

DR. OFF LIMITS

Sutton

In just five days' time, I'd be working at one of the most prestigious hospitals in London, answering to the name I'd worked hard to make mine: Doctor Scott. The thought was very likely to hospitalize me with a panic attack between now and then.

"How are the odds looking?" Parker asked me.

"Not good." I winced at the tightness of the strap around my chin. I fiddled with the fastenings of my helmet and instantly the harness that I'd just been strapped into started to bite into my thighs. Normally being in the outdoors, in the midst of trees the height of skyscrapers, breathing in air as fresh as it got in London would be a welcome change from studying at my desk. Not today. As I took in the crisscross of wires between the trees and the so-called bridges between them that I was expected to walk along, I decided this kind of change, I could live without. "The likelihood of me having a panic attack just went to ninety-two percent."

"But we got down to forty yesterday," Parker said, her tone a teenager who'd been told her curfew was 9pm.

"*Yesterday* involved an open-top bus, an uber-enthusiastic tour guide with a passion for the fire of London, and mimosas. Today is different territory. In every sense."

My best friend was well aware of my anxiety when it came to starting at the hospital. She'd witnessed the years I'd spent studying. The long days that ran into longer nights. The nonexistent social life, sacrificed to the study gods. The way I used to send up a tiny prayer that my clients would cancel their haircuts so I could cram in an extra forty-five minutes of study. Over the years, enough of my prayers were answered that I passed each stage of my journey on the way to being a doctor. My new job had been a long time coming, the culmination of every second of hard work I'd put in over the last seven years.

"I thought a ropes course would be the *height* of distracting," Parker argued. "Pun intended."

"Not from my imminent death, it's not."

"I suppose I didn't think about that. You want me to go first?"

I shook my head. I always found it was better not to know how difficult things were about to get or you risked chickening out before even trying. If I'd known what I was going to face studying to become a doctor back when I was cutting hair and discussing people's holidays six days a week, I would have never filled out that first application form. For many of the years since, it had been beyond hard, but if I'd known how hard it was about to get, there were a thousand times I would have given up. Naivety and blind ambition were a powerful combination.

One of the instructors clipped my harness onto the twisted metal rope and ushered me forward. "Keep moving. There are arrows showing you the direction you're heading and instructors placed regularly along the route."

"You all dressed in black in case we fall from fifty meters, die, and you don't want to look like you're ready to break out the party tunes?" I asked.

He squinted. "Wow, quite the optimist, aren't you?"

"Just asking," I replied.

"We dress in black so we don't distract anyone with bright colors."

"Sure," I said noncommittally.

"And no one has died on this ropes course," he added.

The elephant on my chest decided to stand and take a stroll. "No deaths" might seem like a low bar for a safety record, but I'd take what I could get.

"Not today anyway." He gave me a little shove off the platform where we were standing, onto the first "bridge" to the next tree. The so-called bridge was a series of wooden slats spaced about fifty centimeters apart and connected by chains that tinkled in the wind. A more fanciful person might say it sounded like we were in the home of the fairies. I knew it was probably a fake soundtrack played to drown out the sound of screams.

I took a step forward onto the first plank and grabbed the horizontal wires placed either side of my head.

"All those years ago when you first considered training to be a doctor, did you always know you'd get to this point?" Parker asked.

"What, staring into the jaws of death?"

As I took the next step, I realized I was only about a meter above the ground—for now. A broken toe was the most likely scenario if I fell and the safety harness didn't do its job. I took the next few steps more confidently, and found it wasn't as bad as I thought it would be. The slats were a comfortable distance apart. We weren't too high up and things felt pretty sturdy—the same way I might have described my life after getting on my feet again following a rough few years. I had a job, a roof over my head, cereal in the cupboard, and milk in the fridge.

I stepped up onto the next platform and turned as Parker started on the other end of the bridge.

"You okay?" I asked her as she reached me.

"I will be when we're done here." She grinned up at me. "But at least you're thinking about your imminent death rather than starting work."

"Every cloud has a silver lining," I said. She knew that I hated that phrase because it was total rubbish. Every cloud didn't have a silver lining. When a door closed another one didn't magically open, and I wanted nothing to do with any ill winds. I hated those kinds of platitudes. I liked reality. And reality was that life was hard. And to get anything in this life took hard work, dedication, and sacrifice.

"Okay, onto the next," I said, following the arrows. "This one looks a little higher but not too bad." The slats on the next bridge were arranged in a more haphazard way—some crossed, some small, some big. With a little more confidence, I stepped across the bridge and my threatening panic attack receded slightly. That was until I was just about to step up to the platform and the entire bridge started to shake.

I screamed.

Had the metal ropes holding my harness clip fallen down? I turned my head—it was just Parker stepping onto the bridge before I'd finished.

"Is that safe? Us both being on the bridge at one time?" I asked the instructor right in front of me.

He offered his hand and I took it, letting him hoist me up onto the platform. "It's perfectly safe. A hundred people on this bridge at the same time would be perfectly safe."

I wasn't sure a hundred people would fit, but I wasn't going to be one of a hundred that went on that bridge to find out.

"Next, you need to use that climbing wall to reach the platform above and commando crawl across the net to the next platform."

I bent my head so I could see where he was pointing. About five meters above us, the next section was not only higher, but you weren't upright. People were crawling over a rope net, forced to look down. "Who designed this thing? Sadists?"

"Some people like to push themselves," Parker said, coming up behind me. "Like you. You're always pushing yourself to do better."

"The difference is I like to push myself at a desk in front of a computer. There's no mortality risk involved." I grabbed onto the pebble-shaped blue plastic holds on the climbing wall and started my ascent.

"Then dinner on Saturday night should be right up your street."

I groaned. "Noooo."

"It's dinner. And it will be hellishly distracting. I've seen a photo. You're not going to be able to look at anything else or think about anything else while you're sitting opposite this guy. Also, your arse looks fantastic from down here. You need to show it off more."

I reached the top of the climbing wall and inelegantly pulled myself up onto the platform. I rolled to safety and just lay there on my back, wondering if there was an easy exit and whether Parker would forgive me if I abandoned her. "This, for the record, is a terrible place for a date."

"Saturday night is in a restaurant. With chairs and everything. And although there's a lovely view, there's a lift. No harnesses required."

"Sounds like all my dreams come true. But no. I'm not going on a date. The last thing I want to do is get involved with anyone at the moment. I'm about to start as a foundation doctor at one of the best hospitals in the country. I don't want to be distracted from Monday. I want to be completely and utterly focused on my job. It's going to be difficult enough to just survive the next two years without trying to keep a relationship alive."

"You're going to be just fine."

"I need to prove myself. I can guarantee you there will be plenty of doctors there waiting for me to fail. Getting into medical school the way I did is already controversial. I don't need to be proving anyone right."

"I don't see how working your arse off can be controversial. I know loads of them are from Oxford and Cambridge and all that, but you all had to sit the same exams."

I didn't say anything. There was no point. Parker was right—the snobbery that existed in medical circles about where you went to school and university and who your parents were didn't make sense and wasn't fair. I'd learned a long time ago that life wasn't fair. Complaining about it didn't help.

"Anyway, your job starts on Monday," Parker continued. "The date is Saturday night. I'm not introducing you to your future husband or even boyfriend. He's a hot way to spend an evening, that's all. And he's leaving for Medecins Sans Frontieres the week after next, so even if you wanted to be distracted by him again, it won't be an option."

I sighed. Parker was right—I should enjoy my last weekend of freedom before exhaustion and shift patterns meant that weekends didn't exist for me anymore. "I'm going to have to crawl across this net backwards, I think. You've seen enough of my arse today." I crouched down and dangled my legs over the edge of the platform, trying to find a foothold on the net.

"Fantastic technique," the instructor called over at me. He was kidding, right?

"You see? You get it right without trying," Parker said.

"I'm trying to spare you the sight of my bottom, not be a ropes-course whiz."

"You surprise yourself. It will be the same on Saturday night when you come to the end of the dinner and realize you've had a wonderful evening and haven't thought about Monday at all."

I groaned. "Stop trying to convince me." She knew better than to take any notice of what I was saying. I wanted to be convinced. The problem was, when I wasn't working or studying, I felt guilty. Like downtime, fun, or relaxation wasn't something I deserved. Parker was the person in my life who reminded me that I was allowed to be human sometimes.

"It might be the last time you have sex for two years if you're so intent on being relationship-free while you're at the hospital."

Maybe I should reach out to a guy in another hospital who was also just starting out and we could have an arrangement of no-strings hook-ups for the next two years. At least that would be entirely consistent with my dating history so far. I'd never found time to indulge in relationships when I was trying to keep a roof over my head. I had to keep focused on my future.

"I thought you said Saturday night was dinner. Not sex."

"It might turn into sex. I mean, this guy is seriously hot."

"If you showed me his picture, maybe I'd change my mind."

"No," she called after me. I could tell by the strain in her voice that she was lowering herself onto the net. "It's a blind date. That way it takes up more of your headspace as you think about what he might be like. It's more distracting. What have you got to lose? It's one night of your life."

"I'll tell you what I've got to lose—a night in with Nick and Vanessa Lachey and a bunch of Instagram-influencer wannabes. God I'm going to miss Netflix."

"Exactly. You'll have much more fun with a hot doctor you never have to see again."

I had to admire her persistence. She was genuinely trying to do what she thought was best for me. As always. Now she was so happy with her fiancé, Tristan, she felt my life needed a little man-injection. I couldn't blame her for that. It was just delightful to see her so in love. And she'd put so much effort into this week of distraction, I felt bad saying no to her.

"Tell you what, if we get to the end of the day without ending up in hospital and we can work in a mimosa at some point, I'll go on the date with your mystery man." Truth be told, I was a little curious to meet someone who was going to do Doctors Without Borders. Though I couldn't imagine doing it myself, I liked the idea of spending time with someone who hadn't taken the traditional route. Maybe this ex-hairdresser would find something in common with another doctor. For a change.

Jacob

If an hour went by without one of my four little brothers calling or texting, it was a good day. Anyone would think I sat in a darkened room, just waiting for one of them to need me, rather than held down a demanding job at the Royal Free, one of the best hospitals in the country. I ignored the call from Beau and stuffed my phone back into my pocket.

"Good evening, Dr. Cove," Dina, one of the receptionists from A&E, said as I passed her in the corridor. I smiled, nodded, and then thanked heaven that when she'd told me she'd like to suck my cock at last year's Christmas party, I'd politely declined. Not because she wasn't gorgeous. And not because I hated blow jobs—was that even a thing? No, it was because I didn't want to pass a line of women who'd had my dick in their mouth in the hospital corridors, sober and under the glare of the fluorescent hospital lights as my shoes squeaked on the freshly-mopped linoleum floor.

Call me old fashioned.

"Keep your private life private." It was almost a mantra in our house growing up. My father wasn't around much when I was a kid, but he was quick to bark out pieces of advice here and there. I could always count on him for a *could be better* or *why wasn't it one hundred percent*, whenever I presented him with an imperfect test score. He didn't seem to be so easy with the advice with my other brothers, but the one thing he'd said to all of us was, "Keep your private life private." He'd said it when each of us had gotten into med school, every time any of us got a job, and if any of us got into trouble —no matter whether it was relevant.

There was a lot of my father's advice I didn't agree with, but I'd always lived by his private life mantra. A friend I'd gone to school with ended up leaving the Royal Free last year because he'd fucked too many nurses and junior doctors. He'd gone for a promotion and was told he had *too much baggage*.

There was no rule about fraternization in the hospital. Or maybe there was and everyone ignored it. The medical staff spent far too much of their lives in the place for sex and even romance not to happen. Hooking up with someone at work was easy. And when you were exhausted from the long hours and demanding work, and wanted to blow off some steam or have some human contact with a person who wasn't sick or dying, it made sense that you'd reach for someone close.

But not me.

Partly because of my dad's advice and partly because . . . well, because of my last name. I was a Cove. First-born son of doctors Carole and John Cove. That last name brought a profile. I was never just "Jacob" or "Dr. Cove." I was always "Jacob Cove, yes that Cove," or "Dr. Cove's son" or "Cove—was your mother Carole Cove?" It was a label I was used to and not one I wanted to swap for Jacob Cove, the guy who'd dated everyone in pediatric medicine. Or Jacob Cove, the disappointing son of the Coves. I didn't want people I had to see every day and give instructions to and take instructions from, to know intimate details about me and my sex life. I didn't want the Cove name associated with anything other than being game-changing doctors. I was ambitious and I wanted to be a groundbreaking doctor in pediatric cardiology or even the advisor to the government on child health. I never wanted to be denied a promotion because I'd slept with the wrong person or too many people. It wasn't worth it. When people heard my name, the association should be with excellence. Not sex.

My phone buzzed in my pocket and I pulled it out. A message from Beau.

Pick up. I need a favor.

Nothing new about that. Before I had the chance to reply, his name flashed up on my screen.

I answered as I strode through the exit doors to the stairs and started to head down. Beau was the most tenacious of us all and that was saying something. "The answer's no," I barked into the phone.

"You haven't even heard me out. It's not even that bad."

"I beg to differ. If I'm helping you, it's bound to be bad." Beau was mischievous. A stint doing Medecins Sans Frontieres would do him good.

"I'm serious. All I need you to do is eat some mouth-watering food and drink some wine that might even be good enough for your sophisticated palate." He must really need my help if he was dishing out compliments.

"Out with it. What do you need?"

"I need you to go on a date for me. It's just dinner and drinks. No big thing."

"A date? Are you my pimp now?"

"I'm not setting you up. A friend set *me* up—gorgeous girl apparently. I'm totally pissed off I'm missing it. I don't want to let anyone down at the last minute."

I paused at the door to the ground floor so I could finish our call in privacy. "This sounds suspiciously like a pity date. Why—"

"No, seriously, it's not at all. She's really pretty by all accounts. And she's a doctor. You can talk shop. She's at Tommy's, I think. New to London or something. Her friend said something about it. I can't quite remember. I can't go because . . ." He started to laugh. "You're not going to believe it, but I'm in hospital. I think I've broken my nose."

"What?" Why was he laughing?

"Had rugby practice this afternoon. Took an elbow to the face."

Only Beau could laugh about getting his nose broken.

"Is it going to affect your trip?" He was due to fly out in a week.

"No idea," he said. "I guess we'll have to see if it's broken first. But no way I'm going to be out of hospital in time to make the date."

"The date is tonight?"

"Yes, why do you think I've been calling you non-stop for an hour?"

Shit, I had just finished my shift. I was exhausted. I just wanted to check in on one patient then head home and go to bed. "Can't you ask Zach?"

"He's in Norfolk."

I'd forgotten he was spending the weekend with our parents.

"One of your mates then?"

"Like I'd trust any of them."

It was a good point. I sighed, finally accepting I wasn't going to get the early night I'd been hoping for. "You're going to owe me big for this."

"You're the best big brother I could wish for. You're meeting her at the top of the NatWest Tower. Her name's Sutton. Eight forty-five. Anyway, it's all on me. I've given the restaurant my credit card. If it were any other brother, I'd tell them not to do anything I wouldn't do, but for you that's a given. Go wild."

Before I had a chance to ask for Sutton's last name, he hung up. I'd kill him when I next saw him.

"You heading home?" a woman asked from behind me.

Dina appeared from nowhere and I pulled my mouth into a smile. "No such luck."

She tilted her head. "Shame. I need a lift."

"Good luck. I have to see a patient."

I hated being late but there was no way I wasn't going to stop to see Barnaby. He'd been an inpatient for nearly two months now and was the oldest of five children. His parents didn't have time for daily visits.

I turned into ward six and saw Barnaby staring out the window. I leaned across the nurses' desk. "Anyone been in to see Barnaby today?"

Annette, the nurse in charge, shook her head and scrunched up her nose. No one liked it when the kids didn't have visitors.

He wasn't my patient, but Barnaby had been on the ward for so long that it was impossible not to notice him as I came in to check on my own patients.

From my back pocket, I pulled out a credit token for the vending machine. I'd put twenty quid on it before I'd picked up the call from Beau.

"Barnaby, mate," I said, striding over to the end bed. "I found something with your name on it." I wafted the credit token in his direction.

Barnaby scowled back at me. "What is it?"

I shrugged my shoulders. "Try it in the vending machine."

"It can't be mine. I didn't have one." I was pretty sure Barnaby's parents didn't have much money.

"You're right. It's mine, but I need to give up junk food—you know how it is, old man that I am. So . . . have it."

He glanced at me and then the card. I tossed it on his table.

He nodded. "Thanks."

"What have you been watching?" I nodded toward the TV.

"Nothing," he said.

I glanced at the clock over the nurses' station. It would probably take me over half an hour to get to Tower 42 and it was nearly ten past eight now. Why did Beau have to choose a restaurant in the City to take his date when the West End was so much closer?

"Don't tell anyone I told you, but Peaky Blinders is on BBC iPlayer and it's good. Trust me."

"I don't have any headphones," he said. "I couldn't watch it if I wanted to."

Poor kid.

"Oh, let me get you some. We have plenty of spares." I turned. I wasn't sure where I'd find any headphones at all, especially not in the forty seconds I had before I needed to leave. I sped down the corridor toward the supplies cupboard. Maybe there'd be some lost property. Angie, a healthcare assistant coming off shift overtook me. She smiled and waved her hand, the tinny tick, tick, tick from the earbud waving loosely by her waist catching my attention.

"Hey, Angie?" She stopped and turned around. "Can I buy your headphones?"

She pulled out the ear bud that was in her ear. "What?"

"Your headphones. How much?" I grabbed my wallet from my back pocket.

Angie frowned at me. "They're not special. They cost me about five pounds. Why do you want them?"

I didn't have time to explain. Pulling out a twenty-pound note, I said. "Would you give them up for twenty pounds?"

She shrugged, handed them over but didn't take the money. "Just give them back to me tomorrow." Angie earned minimum wage.

"Please let me buy them from you."

"You can have them," she said.

I stuffed the purple note into her hand and she handed them over.

"You're strange, Dr. Cove," she said in a tone that told me she didn't really care—she was just going with it.

"Thanks so much," I said and raced back to Barnaby.

Maybe I'd make it to the restaurant on time after all.

Read more in Dr. Off Limits

All Louise Bay Books are available for free in Kindle Unlimited or on Amazon to buy.

Each book is a stand alone

The Colorado Club Billionaires

Love Fast

Love Deep

Love More

The New York City Billionaires

The Boss + The Maid = Chemistry

The Play + The Pact = I Do

The Hero + Vegas = No Regrets

The Doctors Series

Dr. Off Limits

Dr. Perfect

Dr. CEO

Dr. Fake Fiancé

Dr. Single Dad

The Mister Series

Mr. Mayfair

Mr. Knightsbridge

Mr. Smithfield

Mr. Park Lane

Mr. Bloomsbury

Mr. Notting Hill

The Player Series

International Player

Private Player

The Gentleman Series

The Ruthless Gentleman

The Wrong Gentleman

The Royals Series

King of Wall Street

Park Avenue Prince

Duke of Manhattan

The British Knight

The Earl of London

The Nights Series

Indigo Nights

Promised Nights

Parisian Nights

Standalones

An American in London

14 Days of Christmas

Hollywood Scandal

Love Unexpected

Hopeful

The Empire State Series

What kind of books do you like?

Friends to lovers

Mr. Mayfair

Promised Nights

International Player

Fake relationship (marriage of convenience)

Duke of Manhattan

Mr. Mayfair

Mr. Notting Hill

Dr. Fake Fiancé

Dr. Single Dad

The Play + The Pact = I Do

An American in London

Enemies to Lovers

King of Wall Street

The British Knight

The Earl of London

Hollywood Scandal

Parisian Nights

14 Days of Christmas

Mr. Bloomsbury

The Play + The Pact = I Do

Office Romance/ Workplace romance

Mr. Knightsbridge

King of Wall Street

The British Knight

The Ruthless Gentleman

Mr. Bloomsbury

Dr. Off Limits

The Boss + The Maid = Chemistry

The Play + The Pact = I Do

Second Chance

International Player

Hopeful

Best Friend's Brother

Promised Nights

Vacation/Holiday Romance

The Empire State Series

Indigo Nights

The Ruthless Gentleman

The Wrong Gentleman

Love Unexpected

14 Days of Christmas

The Hero + Vegas = No Regrets

An American in London

Holiday/Christmas Romance

14 Days of Christmas

British Hero

Promised Nights (British heroine)

Indigo Nights (American heroine)

Hopeful (British heroine)

Duke of Manhattan (American heroine)

The British Knight (American heroine)

The Earl of London (British heroine)

The Wrong Gentleman (American heroine)

The Ruthless Gentleman (American heroine)

International Player (British heroine)

Mr. Mayfair (British heroine)

Mr. Knightsbridge (American heroine)

Mr. Smithfield (American heroine)

Private Player (British heroine)

Mr. Bloomsbury (American heroine)

14 Days of Christmas (British heroine)

Mr. Notting Hill (British heroine)

Dr. Off Limits

Dr. Perfect

Dr. Fake Fiancé (American heroine)

Dr. Single Dad

The Play + The Pact = I Do (American heroine)

An American in London (American heroine)

Sign up to the Louise Bay mailing list on my website www.louisebay.com

www.ingramcontent.com/pod-product-compliance
Lightning Source LLC
Chambersburg PA
CBHW051141190726
48290CB00006B/1941